BLACK WREATH

THE STOLEN LIFE OF JAMES LOVETT

Peter Sirr lives in Dublin. He is a prize-winning poet as well as a critic, essayist and translator.

He has published eight collection of poetry with The Gallery Press, including *The Thing Is* (2009), winner of the Michael Hartnett Award, and *Selected Poems* (2004).

For many years he was Director of the Irish Writers' Centre and was also editor of the national poetry magazine, *Poetry Ireland Review*. He is a member of Aosdána. He is married to the poet and children's writer Enda Wyley.

Black Wreath is his first novel.

BLACK WREATH

THE STOLEN LIFE OF JAMES LOVETT

PETER SIRR

THE O'BRIEN PRESS
DUBLIN

First published 2014 by The O'Brien Press Ltd,
12 Terenure Road East, Rathgar, Dublin 6, Ireland.
Tel: +353 1 4923333; Fax: +353 1 4922777
E-mail: books@obrien.ie
Website: www.obrien.ie

ISBN: 978-1-84717-560-1

10 9 8 7 6 5 4 3 2 1
19 18 17 16 15 14

Cover image: iStockphoto
Printed and bound by CPI Group (UK) Ltd, Croydon, CR0 4YY
The paper in this book is produced using pulp from managed forests.

The O'Brien Press receives financial assistance from

For Enda and Freya

CONTENTS

• •

ONE

A Ghost in the Cellar

James crouched in the darkest part of the cellar, behind two old wine barrels the house had forgotten. Everything in this corner of the cellar was discarded or forgotten: old bits of tackle, broken cups, a goblet, the rotting shafts from an old sedan chair. The cellar was damp and smelly, the smell not just of old things, but of evil, of rats and kidnappers and old blood. The smell of ghosts with ragged hair and claws for hands.

James was afraid. He was afraid of the evil-smelling cellar and its ghosts. On the shelf above his head he spotted the largest spider he had ever seen scuttling towards him. He wanted to shout out, but he couldn't say a word. For if he was afraid of everything here in this horrible place, he was even more afraid of his father, whose heavy footsteps he could hear clumping around the house. Lord Dunmain was on the rampage again. He had been drinking and playing cards with his friends and as always happened as the drinking and the card playing went on, Lord Dunmain became louder and angrier. Eventually he would send all the card players out of the house with a curse, and on particularly bad days he would shout at Smeadie to bring his son to him. The elderly servant would shuffle around the house calling the boy's name in his squeaky voice, and if James wasn't quick enough he would find himself standing meekly in front of the red-faced Lord Dunmain as he spat and spluttered and looked at his son as if he were a rat or an insect he couldn't wait to crush with his heavy boots.

'Where the devil were you, boy?' his father would roar. 'You will answer to me as long as you are in this house. Do you understand?'

'Yes, Father,' James would answer, his voice small.

'Speak up, can't you? How can I hear that miserable snivelling?'

And on it would go, the name-calling, and sometimes a kick or a blow to accompany it.

Today would be worse; he could tell from the weight of the boots on the floor above. His anger always made Lord Dunmain heavier, as if a dark creature had crept inside him and weighed him down.

James stayed where he was and didn't make a sound. He could hear the old servant shuffling about upstairs, but he would never find him here. Suddenly his heart froze – he heard his father's feet on the stone steps and then the sound of the door being kicked open as his father came crashing into the cellar. Lord Dunmain straightened up in the room and looked around him. James kept as still as he could, hardly daring to breathe. He mustn't let his teeth chatter or any part of his body betray his presence there. He could hear his father's loud breathing. Nothing Lord Dunmain did was quiet.

'Claret!' his father roared in the darkness, almost as if he expected the room to hand him out his wine.

Lord of the Dark, James thought; he thinks even the dark and its creatures should obey him.

Nothing answered Dunmain's call, and he clattered around in the cellar until he found the wine he wanted. 'Where are you, boy?' he roared, his thunderous voice filling the small space.

Don't move, James told himself. Don't give him any sign that there is anything in here besides the cobwebs and the spiders, and the ghosts who don't talk but watch and wait in the dark.

Dunmain reached out and fetched a bottle from the shelf in front of him. He looked as if he were about to leave when James heard a second, lighter set of steps descend the stairs to the cellar. Miss Deakin entered the room. James shrank back even further into his hiding place. He did not want to be seen by the woman who was now his father's wife.

'This will do you no good,' her high, complaining voice was saying. 'You need to act, not to drink.'

'What would you have me do?' his father said crankily.

'We must have money!' Miss Deakin said. James was supposed to call her Lady Dunmain, but to him she would always be Miss Deakin. 'We can't live like paupers. We have our positions to think of!'

His father grunted. 'We're hardly paupers yet,' he answered. 'And I have expectations. Lord Allen's estate will pass to me in time ...'

'He may yet live fifty years!' came the high voice again, impatient now.

'But I can sell the leases on the land now. There are plenty of buyers. As soon as he dies the land will pass to whoever has the leases. They can make plenty of money out of it. I'll get money now; they'll get their reward later. Everybody will be happy. There's only one problem.'

'And what's that?'

'After my death the land would go back to James as my heir, and then the buyers would be stuck. Unless the heir had agreed to the sale.'

'Well that's the answer, isn't it? Get the boy to sign an agreement.'

James felt his hands turn clammy. Something was going on here that was not good for him. The coldness of the woman's voice told him as much.

'That's just it,' James heard his father say. 'He's too young. The law wouldn't recognise his agreement unless he was a legal adult.'

A brief silence followed that information. Although he did not understand the detail, James knew that his own future was being weighed in that silence. Then he heard Miss Deakin's voice again, and something new in it, an eagerness. 'There may be opportunity in that.'

'How so?'

'The boy was always a hindrance to our plans.'

'Meaning?'

'Things would be much simpler if he were not here, if he were not ...'

James suddenly felt sick. He wanted to run upstairs to his room, but he forced himself to stay where he was.

'If he were not what?'

'Just that' came her voice, lower this time, as if she could hardly believe what she was saying. 'If he were not ...'

'Do you propose to do away with him then?' His father's voice was indignant.

'Boys die all the time, they sicken, they ... fall, they are attacked. The city is a dangerous place, gangs everywhere, Bloods and Bucks and Pinkinindies. Anything can happen to a boy.'

'Not to my boy,' Lord Dunmain determined. 'Not to my own flesh and blood.'

'That's just the point, isn't it? It's the flesh and blood that causes the problem.'

'There are other ways it may be resolved.'

'What do you intend then?'

'He may be concealed. He can live out of sight in the city.'

This idea did not seem to please Miss Deakin.

'He may be found.'

'He's a boy, like any boy. He will be a boy in the city.'

Suddenly Miss Deakin was animated again. 'Well, if that's the way, I think I know someone who would be discreet.'

'Who?'

'My uncle, the dancing master. Mr Kavanagh. Of course

he'd need payment. He is not rich, but he is discreet.'

'We will talk of it again.' Lord Dunmain was suddenly weary. The storming fury had died down in him: there was no energy in his voice now. They left the cellar and climbed up the steps.

When he was sure they were gone, James climbed out of his hiding place and stood in the middle of the cellar. He rested his forehead against a wooden beam, as if the touch of the wood might help him make sense of what he had just heard. What did it all mean? They wanted money, and he was somehow in the way of their getting it. He remembered the cold excitement in Miss Deakin's voice as she talked about the things that could happen to boys in the city. He had always disliked Miss Deakin, but in his dislike he had failed to understand the extent of her hatred for him. She wasn't his mother, and therefore he was just an obstacle to her, somebody to be turned out onto the streets. He replayed the conversation over and over in his mind, the silences and hesitations of his father, the definiteness of Miss Deakin.

Maybe his father wasn't as indifferent to him as it seemed. And yet he seemed quite prepared to let him go. It wouldn't be the first time. When he was born he had been given to a nursemaid from the village. For years he had thought she was his mother, and not the thin lady in elegant clothes who drove up the driveway to the estate cottage to visit. They had widened that driveway especially for his mother's carriage, but he didn't know that.

Later, he had come back to live with the people he finally

came to realise were his real parents, and he saw his mother several times in the same week. That was before the trouble started and his father would come home roaring with drink and badness. A black night came when he had cursed his wife and ordered her out of the house, but James closed his mind to it now and tried to think only of the present, and what might happen next.

If he could get his father on his own, surely he would change his mind? He wasn't so bad, was he? I'm his own flesh and blood, James said to himself. I just needed to talk to him when Miss Deakin isn't there, and things will be alright again, won't they?

People don't harm their own children, after all – no one is that cruel. He remembered the time his father helped him onto the little pony and led him round the paddock. Lord Dunmain had gathered all the servants to watch, he was so proud. 'Easy, James, and let him know who's master. That's my boy.' James closed his eyes and let his mind drift back to the pony and the paddock and his father's gentle, encouraging voice. Later, he would talk to his father. Later, everything would be alright again.

Right now, though, he needed to escape. He needed to get out of this house and breathe the air of the city. He needed to see Harry. He picked his way as gently as he could across the floor, careful not to tread on anything that might rattle or clatter. It took an age to get to the door, and then another age to climb the steps without making a sound. The cellar stairs led up to the back kitchen and from there a door led to the stables at the back and out into the lane.

James moved quickly and quietly until he was well down the lane that ran along the back of the houses. The day was drizzly, and the city smelled of damp horses and horse dung. A rat the size of a small dog ran brazenly up the centre of the road as if he had every right to be there, and look out any who denied it. A recently dead cat lay in front of a doorway, its entrails hanging out. A woman stood in front of the door and swore at a young child, and if she saw or smelled the cat she gave no sign of it. She looked up at James as he passed and half-smiled, half-scowled at him.

'Your lordship,' she said elaborately, and James didn't know whether she was being polite or mocking. Sometimes it was hard to tell the difference. Everyone here knew who his father was, but they did not seem to admire him much. They admired Miss Deakin even less, especially since she was now calling herself Lady Dunmain.

That couldn't be right, James thought. His mother was still alive, even if he didn't know where she was. It was two years since he'd seen her. Shortly after she left, Lord Dunmain had taken him to Dublin in a coach. His father had claimed that his mother had died of an illness after she left, but James didn't believe him; he had heard it said she was still alive, and was now in London. That meant his father must have two wives, and there must be two Lady Dunmains walking the earth.

James kicked a stone so hard it nearly hit the window of a house at the corner, and he ran off before anyone came to investigate. Then he walked quickly towards the river.

TWO

A Decision

J ames crossed the bridge and made for the archway that gave onto the quay where the ships docked. This was his favourite spot in the city, the place where he felt happiest on his escapes from the gloomy house across the river that he could never think of as home. He dodged a cart bearing a cask of wine and watched as Harry the shoeboy finished polishing a customer's boots.

'You here again?' Harry laughed. 'Yer shoes need shinin' again?'

'Alright then,' James said, though his boots were still gleaming from the last time Harry did them. The two talked and swapped gossip as the carts trundled around them and loud men went in and out of the taverns and coffee houses. He gave Harry a coin but neither of them looked at it; they just kept up their talk as Harry slipped the invisible coin into his coat.

'How's your new mother?' he asked with a grin. Everybody in the city seemed to know about Miss Deakin. 'Or should I say Lady Dunmain?'

James flushed hotly. 'She's not my mother, and she's not Lady Dunmain! And well you know it, Harry Taaffe!'

He almost felt like fighting his friend, he was so angry, but James knew Harry meant only to tease him and he let it go. His father might well have married her, even if James didn't know how this was possible, but to James she would always be a stranger.

'Something's going on, Harry,' he said to his friend. 'I don't know what, exactly, but I think they mean me harm.'

Harry looked up sharply. 'Who means you harm?'

'My father and that woman, Miss Deakin. It's something to do with money. I heard them speak about it. They want to get rid of me.'

Harry whistled softly. 'They can't do that,' he said. 'You can't just go round getting rid of people. Not even them. I know the rich can do pretty much what they like, but they can't kill their own. Maybe you heard wrong.'

'It might not be killing,' James said. 'There are other ways to get rid of someone. I think they mean to give me away.'

Harry looked worried, then touched James's sleeve. 'I can't see anyone wanting to give you away. Just let them try. They'll have Harry Taaffe to worry about.'

James smiled. He always felt better after talking to Harry, even if he didn't think Harry really understood how serious this was. He went back in his mind to the scene in the cellar.

Had he really understood it properly? The woman's cold voice still chilled him.

A drunk came crashing out of the Elephant and filled the street with a stream of oaths. James bade his friend farewell and slipped away down the covered arcade they called the piazzas. He wasn't ready to go home yet. He went into a bookseller's and browsed the shelves for as long as he could; when he came out, the evening had begun to darken. It was time to go home but he was in no hurry to return, so he took a winding route towards the river again. Boats and water were what he needed. If only he could be on one of those boats on its way back to the sea and off to some great land far from here.

It was late when James entered the house by means of the back lane. Smeadie was sitting at the kitchen table while Mrs Rudge was ladling some mutton stew into a bowl for him. She took another bowl when she saw James and poured some for him too. James ate hungrily.

'Is my father at home?'

'Aye,' Smeadie said. 'He's in the drawing room with Miss Deakin ...'

'Lady Dunmain, you mean,' Mrs Rudge chipped in, a faint smile playing about her lips.

'Miss Deakin,' James insisted. He would never grant her that title as long as he lived.

'How and ever,' Smeadie said. 'They're upstairs.'

James was only half interested. He was tired after his trip around the city and as soon as he had finished eating he went upstairs to his room. He tried to sleep, but sleep wouldn't come. He went back to the scene in the paddock, riding the little pony under his father's proud eyes. It was a long time ago. He wasn't even sure what age he was then. But it was real, and even now it gave him hope. He would talk to his father tomorrow ...

The next morning Smeadie brought in a bowl of warm water.

'You're late this morning, master,' Smeadie said. 'It's almost breakfast time.'

James leapt from the bed, furious that he had overslept. It had taken him so long to get to sleep, he hadn't been able to wake up early and carry out his plan of getting his father alone. He washed and dressed hastily.

Down on the street the Drogheda coach was setting off on its journey. All the coaches to the north started out from this street, and James often liked to sit and watch the preparations: the luggage being loaded onto the roof of the coach, the people alighting, the horses stamping their feet, and finally the coachman cracking his whip and the horses snorting as the coach clattered over the cobbles and went echoing off towards Drumcondra. He didn't have much interest in the scene this morning, but as his eyes travelled back towards his own house he saw a knot of people on the pavement outside. Although he couldn't hear them this high up, they were gesticulating and talking animatedly. They looked angry. James recognised one as his father's linen merchant; he had seen him in the house before, speaking anxiously to his father. The other men had been in the house before too. James wasn't sure who they were, but he could imagine why they were here. Lord Dunmain owed money to half the city, and James had often come home to angry scenes in the hall as his father roared and, by sheer force of character, drove his creditors from the house, oaths raining down on their heads.

Yesterday's overheard conversation kept flooding into his mind. He thought about leaving the house immediately and not returning until night-time. They might have forgotten their conversation by then, and life would go as before. He could run down to the ships, maybe even board one bound for London or some other far place. He could learn how to be a sailor and spend his life on board a ship, crossing the wide seas and exploring the great places of the world. But he had no sooner entered this world when he heard the breakfast gong and knew it was too late to do anything other than descend the stairs and take his place at the table.

Lord Dunmain and Miss Deakin were already at table when he entered. Smeadie put some smoked fish on his plate, but James could hardly look at it. He drank some tea, just to be doing something and not to draw attention to himself, but it made no difference, since both Lord Dunmain and Miss Deakin were staring hard at him. Miss Deakin sat up stiffly, the light pink of her dress contrasting with her dark expression. She looks like an eagle about to pounce on its prey, James thought. Lord Dunmain was making swift work of his herring while looking silently across at his son. All this silence was making James very nervous. Neither his father nor Miss Deakin were in the habit of saying much to James at the breakfast table on those occasions when all three were gathered together, which was certainly not every day. But his father could usually be relied on for a grunt or two, while Miss Deakin hardly ever stopped talking, not really to anyone, but just to the world at large.

'My lady would talk the hind legs off a donkey,' Mrs Rudge would mutter in the safety of her kitchen.

James could see the bonnet twitching on Miss Deakin's head, as if her brain was bubbling over with speech desperate to get out, and sure enough her lips soon began working hard. 'James, your father and I have been thinking about your future.'

James did not even dare to look at her.

'It's evident that this house is no place for a boy. Your father is taken up with his many concerns.'

And what were those? James wondered. Drinking, gambling, shouting, cursing? Lord Dunmain continued to eat. The fish was demolished. Now he was well through the beef.

'I have my own concerns and, much as I may like to, I can't be looking to the needs of a child ...'

'I'm not a child,' James found himself blurting out in spite of himself.

'You're barely twelve summers,' Lord Dunmain said, setting aside his fork. 'That's child enough for me. And I'd ask you to listen to Lady Dunmain.'

'My mother is not here.'

Why did he say that? Some things just say themselves. The whole room seemed startled at the affront. Even Smeadie froze like a statue as he brought another dish to Lord Dunmain.

'What did you say?' His father's voice was thunderous.

Miss Deakin, for James could not call her anything else, was white with anger and seemed temporarily robbed of the ability to speak. But it came back, in a choking, indignant gasp. 'William, will you let him speak of me so?'

Lord Dunmain rammed the handle of his knife on the table. 'How dare you dispute the honour of this lady. She is Lady Dunmain, James, and so she will remain. Your late mother does not enter into this.'

She is not my *late* mother, James said silently. He closed his eyes and saw his mother's face as it was on the day she left, drawn and tear-stained. Then he banished that image and thought of her when they had been alone together, talking softly. Sometimes she would read to him – he held now to the sound of her voice, trying to blot out the unpleasant voices of his father and Miss Deakin.

'He ought to be whipped,' Miss Deakin hissed. 'This is why he cannot stay here,' she added, as if she was only too glad James had furnished her with a reason to be rid of him.

'It is in your own best interest that we have decided you should reside under the guardianship of a most excellent gentleman, a relative of your step-mother. His name is Arthur Kavanagh. There is one other thing ...' Lord Dunmain paused and looked at Miss Deakin. James kept his eyes on his father. 'You will not be James Lovett there; you will be a simple boy and not the son of a lord, is that clear?'

James thought back to the conversation he had overheard.

They wanted him out of the way; they wanted to erase even his name.

'What of my school? Who will I be in Barnaby Dunn's?'

There was another pause as his father and Miss Deakin looked at each other again. Eventually Lord Dunmain spoke. 'There will be no school, for the moment. Later, perhaps, it may be possible to resume your education, but for now ...'

He didn't finish the sentence, but James understood that he was to become someone who didn't need schooling. He thought of his school, the crowded desks and the stern features of Barnaby Dunn, who was impatient but not unkind. It was peaceful to sit and write at a desk. James loved the feel of the quill and the flow of the black ink across the page, and he loved to look up at the big shelf where Barnaby kept his books, thinking about all the knowledge that was wrapped up in them, waiting to be discovered.

'What are you dreaming about now, young Lovett?' Barnaby Dunn would often ask.

He called James to his desk once when he was gathering his books to go home. 'You're a clever boy,' he said. 'And quick to learn. What do you think you'll be in life, other than a great lord?'

'An explorer,' James said. 'I want to see everything in the world.'

'Well,' Barnaby said, 'I can see you'll do great things.'

James felt his eyes stinging at the memory. How could he do great things if he wasn't allowed to learn? And to be in some other house, with a stranger, and without even his own name to comfort him – they couldn't mean it.

'I don't understand,' James said. 'How can I leave here?'

There was no reply. His father simply stared at him.

Smeadie hovered beside the table, offering more dishes, but Lord Dunmain waved him away and got up. Breakfast was over, and with it all discussion. The decision was made – there would be no appeal.

THREE

A Hurried Departure

The very fact that James's departure had been spoken of at breakfast seemed to demand that the plan be put into action at the earliest possible moment. Perhaps Miss Deakin felt that if the business wasn't concluded speedily, there was a danger that it might be postponed or simply forgotten. In any case, it was she who bustled about making the arrangements. She sent word to her relative and told Smeadie to pack a small bag for James with hardly anything in it but a spare shirt and some stockings. James hoped his new host would have a good supply of linen and extra coats should he need them, but he had no desire to make inquiries of Miss Deakin on the matter.

As soon as his bag was packed, Miss Deakin herself took him in hand and bundled him towards the door as if he were an old carpet.

'I must speak to my father,' James said, twisting out of her grip. 'I need to speak to Lord Dunmain now,' he insisted, as if the title might intimidate her. It didn't. He had to get to his father and straighten out this confusion. His father couldn't just forget him, after all. He thought of the moments they'd had, when Lord Dunmain wasn't maddened with drink or pestered by debtors. Then, he would seek James out for a playful wrestling match, or he'd sit on the edge of his bed and tell tall tales from his past. Even if he knew those moments would quickly pass, James loved them, and he knew his father cared for him, whatever anyone else might think.

'Do you dare defy me, foolish boy?' Miss Deakin said, pulling him firmly by the arm and slamming the door behind her, leaving James to lift the heavy brass knocker and bring it down repeatedly until the whole street must have heard the racket. But no one answered, and no one came to his aid. If his father heard, he gave no sign.

Once she pulled him away from the door, Miss Deakin flagged a hackney and dragged James into it.

'Stop fussing, boy,' she said. 'It will do no good.'

James sank into his seat and kept his eyes away from her. The hackney clattered away from the house and sped down in the direction of the river. When they got to the busy district near the castle Miss Deakin rapped on the roof with her cane and they descended into the crowd. James looked around desperately as if rescue might lie somewhere in the throng. But all he saw was the hectic life of the street: messengers running up and down with their baskets of groceries, hawkers standing in the middle of the street crying out their wares.

It was not easy to walk this street with its crowds and dirt, and the carriages that came thundering with their drivers shouting at people to get out of the way. Miss Deakin did not seem very comfortable here.

'Is it far?' James finally asked.

She didn't reply but kept on walking. An elderly woman hobbled towards them, carrying a basket of hot cakes.

'Buy one of me cakes, missus, diddle, diddle dumpling cakes. A cake for the young gentleman, missus. A handsome son indeed.'

Miss Deakin pushed by her impatiently, stung equally by the woman's brazenness as by her assumption that the boy was her son.

'Bad cess to you, missus,' the woman called after her.

Miss Deakin pulled James after her as she strode away. They passed through the narrow exit where the old walled city ended, and suddenly they were in the Liberties. Lying outside the city walls, this part of Dublin was a law unto itself, James had heard, but it was not a place he was familiar with. He was surprised how thronged it was. They came to a market with many stalls selling meat and fruit and greens and, in the middle, a ballad singer in full spate, something about a footpad on his way to the gallows. He was cheered on by a crowd of ragged onlookers. The herring-women were marching up to the throng, their red faces even angrier than usual.

'Would you buy a herrin' and not be blockin' the street listenin' to that racket?'

Some of those watching directed their attention to Miss

Deakin and James, looking them up and down.

'Part the Red Sea, lads,' said one, 'the quality is passin' through.'

Miss Deakin hesitated, as if put out by the attention, or as if she wasn't quite sure of the way. But she managed to push through the stalls, holding tight to James's arm until they came to a church. She glanced briefly at the facade and, satisfied by whatever she saw there, walked quickly past, more confident now, then turned down the lane at the side of the church. A gate off this lane led in to a little graveyard at the back of the building and this is where she led James.

What are we doing here? James looked around in confusion and fear. Miss Deakin walked among the gravestones, stopped in front of one and began to study it closely. *In memory of Jonathan Digges's beloved wife* ...

Out of nowhere, it seemed to James, as if he might have climbed out of one of the adjacent graves, a man appeared and tapped Miss Deakin on the shoulder. She started, and turned to him. He was a small man in a shabby coat, though his stockings were clean and his shoes were highly polished. Harry would have been proud of them. Maybe Harry had shone them. His wig had seen better days and his hat was grubby. The face beneath the hat and wig was angry and now engaged itself on looking Miss Deakin and James up and down.

'Master Kavanagh,' she began, but he waved all introduction aside.

A strange uncle, James thought.

'Have ye got the money?' he asked.

'Of course,' said Miss Deakin, a trace of irritation showing in her face.

'Boys are expensive. Always wantin' food or linen or the devil knows what. And I'm not in a position to be a provider of comfort to gentlemen.'

'Oh you don't need to trouble yourself about James,' Miss Deakin smiled. 'He needs no special treatment. And less of the gentlemen, if you please.'

The dancing master didn't reply, but satisfied himself by rubbing his thumb and forefinger together. Miss Deakin reached inside her coat and produced a bulging purse which she handed to Kavanagh. He weighed it in his palm and nodded, then opened it and glanced inside.

'It's all there,' Miss Deakin said.

His tone was obsequious now, 'Oh I'd never doubt you, ma'am.'

'Are you really her uncle?' James couldn't help asking.

Kavanagh raised his eyebrows and looked at Miss Deakin. 'Uncle, is it?' he said, seeming to measure the word in his mind. 'Uncle indeed. Of course I'm her uncle. And I'll be yours too now, boy. Come on, we can't be hangin' out in graveyards all day, the rector'll be out after us. I'll bid you good day so, Miss Deakin. Niece, I should say.'

But Miss Deakin had already turned on her heel and walked off without a word.

'No!' James said to her back. Vile as she was, James knew he was watching his home, his father and everything he had known vanish before him. A huge emptiness clutched at him as he heard the creak of the gate, worse than anything he had felt before.

'No,' he said again, more weakly this time. Maybe if he closed his eyes, he would find he had imagined this bleak scene. It would still be morning, and there would still be time to go and talk to his father. He opened his eyes. The grave-stones stared back at him.

'Come on,' his new master said roughly. 'Do you think I have all day?'

FOUR

A New Home

The dancing master and James passed through a warren of alleys and stinking laneways, constantly keeping an eye upward in case a torrent of filth should fall on their heads. A wild pig came careening down one lane, snorting and squealing as a gang of urchins came chasing after it. The daylight seemed to have been sucked out of this part of the city; it was a dark and frightening domain, and James felt he would never be able to find his way back out of it again.

Eventually they came to an alley as narrow and dirty as the rest. They entered a dilapidated building, but as soon as they stepped across the threshold and into the hall, James doubled over and reached out blindly as he felt himself falling in a dead faint. Kavanagh caught him roughly and pushed him upright again, and James gasped for breath as a horrible stench filled his nostrils. The hall seemed to be moving, as if it were somehow alive. As James's eyes grew used to the darkness, he saw that the passage was flooded with a bloody mess crawling with maggots. They would not be able to reach the stairs without wading through it, the thought of which made James retch.

Kavanagh swore. 'The shambles has leaked again,' he muttered. The adjoining house was a slaughterhouse, from where the foul animal blood had burst in through the back door. Kavanagh went back into the lane and retrieved a board that was lying upright against the brickwork. With this plank he made a rough bridge and they could cross to the stairs. As they climbed a steady stream of water poured down through the house.

'Broken roof,' Kavanagh said, as much to himself as to James.

James was still reeling from the stench of the hall. The stink of the rest of the house seemed to get worse with every step. They passed a room which had no door, and inside the small space James saw a large family sprawled on the floor over a meal of bread and soup.

'Where is the door?' he asked Kavanagh as they ascended.

'Didn't pay the rent,' he said. 'Landlord came and took away the door to make them quit the building. He was in a mad rage. The door was in such a state they could do nothin' with it but burn it afterwards. Didn't work, though, did it? He'll have to drag them out by the hair of their heads.'

The higher they rose in the building, the more James realised that he was unlikely to be greeted by much comfort when they arrived. In this he was right. They climbed until they reached the summit of the house, and Kavanagh led him into a sparsely furnished garret. There was a single chair and a small table, and in the corner a thin mattress. Against one wall stood a chest. James couldn't see anything else.

'Where is my room?' he asked.

Kavanagh laughed harshly. 'Why, my lord, this is it and you are in it.'

James put his bag on the floor and made no further comment. It was clear to him now what his father and Miss Deakin had planned, and that they had no intention of retrieving him. Of Miss Deakin he expected no better, but he did not expect it from his father, for all his brutishness and harshness.

That night he found himself sleeping with an empty belly on Master Kavanagh's hard floor, where Master Kavanagh's fleas were not slow to introduce themselves, and when the next morning he enquired when his hot water was coming he was rewarded with another harsh laugh.

'Can you dance, boy?' Kavanagh asked him.

'Not much,' James said. 'My mother taught me a little. Before she left ...'

'Well, you're no use to me unless you can move lightly on your feet. I am a professor of dance, a master of the minuet, the quadrille, the jig, the reel, a bringer of joy to the city.'

James wasn't sure he was convinced by this. There wasn't much joy in this room.

'I don't think I will be able to move at all, unless I eat something.'

'Don't think you're going to eat me out of house and home, boy.'

'Aren't you paid for it? By my father?'

The dancing master snarled. 'Your father!' he began, but went no further, going instead to the table where he cut a slice from a loaf and tossed it to James. The bread was hard enough to break teeth, but James devoured it. After this modest meal he made James show him what steps he knew, snorting with derision as James moved uneasily across the short space of his floor.

'An elephant would dance more gracefully.'

Then the master demonstrated his trade, moving effortlessly as he hummed tunes both quick and slow. His feet seemed to belong to a different body than their owner's upper parts. The upper body was quarrelsome and angry, but the feet had no quarrel with anyone; they moved lightly and happily and didn't grumble or growl.

His impromptu performance seemed to put Kavanagh in better humour and he announced that he was now ready to encounter the world again. He had once had, he told James, the best dancing school in the city, and he had taught the better half of the city how to dance before he fell on evil times. He didn't explain to James what brought the evil times, but James could guess as he watched Kavanagh take a swig from a bottle of gin. The dancing master pulled on his tattered wig and his hat, grabbed his cane and, with mock courtesy, took his leave.

'What should I do?' James asked as Kavanagh was leaving.

'My lord should do as he pleases,' the dancing master laughed, in a tone that made it clear that he really didn't care whether James lived or died.

Left to himself, James took stock of his new surroundings and his new position. Was this to be his new life, hidden away in a rancid garret? The walls and the poor furniture looked back at him blankly. James felt a tide of panic wash through his body. He must get some air. He went down the stairs at a run, pausing on the landing where there was the room without a door. A man sat at a table tapping at the side of a shoe. Patches of leather were spread beside him on the table, and several ragged young children sat around listlessly. The shoemaker looked up sharply as James stood outside.

'Who might you be?'

James had to think for a moment, as if this new life had robbed him of himself. 'James Lovett.'

'Well, James Lovett, what brings you to Coles Alley? You don't look as if you're related to the dancing master.'

'I'm not.'

The shoemaker invited him in and waved to an empty seat at the table. 'I'll warrant he doesn't have much more than gin in that room. You're hungry?'

James was starving. The shoemaker's wife brought him a bowl of broth. As James ate, the shoemaker cast a critical eye at his feet. James shifted uncomfortably under the gaze.

'Those are not the shoes of a street boy, are they, James Lovett?'

'They are now,' James replied. 'Since that is what I've become.'

• •

FIVE

A Terrible Discovery

As often as he could, James made his way out of the Liberties and back into the old city to seek out Harry down by the Custom House dock. If Harry was busy, James contented himself with watching his friend at work, smiling at the easy way Harry had with his customers, chatting away with them, sharing the news of the city.

Harry sat on his three-legged stool and the men would appear as if out of nowhere and place a foot on his lap. Harry would take his old knife – his spudd, he called it – and scrape off the dirt. Then he would fish out a mouldy old wig and wipe the boot with it. Finally it would be time for the polish, a mixture of lampblack and eggs, which Harry would ladle on with a paintbrush. The mix would dry quickly, leaving the boot looking as if it just been bought, but if you smelled the boot before it was completely dry, you'd nearly faint with the stink of rotten eggs.

'You know, Jim,' Harry said to him later as they leaned against the arch that gave onto the dock, 'I don't think you should lie down so easily under your burden.'

'What do you mean?' James asked.

'Just look at you. You're getting shabbier every day. Next time you come here someone might hold up his boot to you and expect you to polish it.'

'What am I supposed to do?

'Everyone knows where you belong. Everyone knows whose son you are. Have you ever gone back to the house?'

Since the day that Miss Deakin delivered him to his new life, James had never thought about returning. He had put the house out of his thoughts, which had been easier than he had expected. So much else was happening, his old life had shrunk back into a small corner at the back of his mind. If he kept it there, maybe the pain would shrink too, and he could learn to face whatever came his way. Yet he sometimes thought of his father, and then he would drift back to the time when they had lived in the house in Wexford, when his mother was still there, before the fighting started, before his mother was driven out and they came to the house in Dublin. He even imagined that his father still looked out for him in some strange and secretive way, asking about him, perhaps following him in disguise or looking out from a tavern or coffee house doorway as James passed in and out of the old city. He felt sure he had seen his father once or twice, in the distance and not very clearly but still unmistakably him. Maybe he wasn't completely abandoned; maybe there was a path back to the affections of his father.

Harry interrupted this thoughts. 'Have you really never gone back?'

'No,' James said.

'Well then, go, find out what's happening. Maybe your father has changed his mind.'

James hesitated. The word 'father' produced a strange sensation in him, a kind of sickening, in which fear and sorrow were the main ingredients. Was it really possible that there might be a way back to his old life? It had not been a happy life, but at least he knew where the next meal was coming from and where he would lay his head at night.

'Only if you come with me,' he said finally.

Later that evening, after Harry had finished his work for the day, the two boys crossed the river and made their way towards James's father's house. The streets were dark and lifeless, with just the occasional carriage trundling past. James grew more agitated the closer he came to his old home. He had no clear idea of what he would do when he got there, and was beginning to regret the impulse to go back. It did not feel as if he was coming home, but more like he was entering a dark cave full of hidden danger. He felt like Hansel following the bright stones back to the house where no welcome was waiting. He had to force himself onward. At last they arrived in the street. There was a sudden flurry of noise and activity as the coach from Newry pulled in and the passengers descended as the coachman set down their luggage. Harry and James hid in the shadows until the last passenger had gone, then James walked on the other side of the street, glancing across at the terrace where his father's house was. As he approached his old home James suddenly started. A black wreath hung on the front door. James's heart thumped uncontrollably. He walked past the house, then turned on his heel and went back again. It was the right house, and the wreath was still there.

'Looks like somebody has died,' Harry said.

James stood rooted to the pavement. In the upstairs windows he could see the glow of candles, but he couldn't make out any figures. He couldn't bring himself to knock on the front door.

'We'll go round the back,' he whispered to Harry, and led him to the laneway at the back at the houses until they came in by the stable and crept up to the kitchen window.

Mrs Rudge and Smeadie were sitting down to their supper at the table and James rapped on the windowpane to attract their attention. Both looked up at once, and James watched the colour drain from Mrs Rudge's face as she looked at him. After some hesitation, Smeadie opened the door a crack and hissed, 'What do you want?' He looked in distaste at Harry.

'Smeadie, it's me,' James said. 'And Harry is with me. Let us in, can't you?'

'It's more than my job's worth to let you in, sir.' Smeadie looked embarrassed by his confession, but he didn't open the door any further.

Then they heard Mrs Rudge's firm voice behind him. 'Let them in.'

Reluctantly, Smeadie admitted the two boys. Mrs Rudge took one look at them and sat them down at the table, without a word, then produced two bowls of steaming food and commanded them to eat. After they had swallowed a few mouthfuls, James asked about the black wreath he had seen on the door.

Smeadie and Mrs Rudge looked at each other awkwardly. Finally Mrs Rudge spoke. 'It's given out that you died, master. The wreath is for you.'

James almost choked on his stew. 'Dead? How can I be dead? Look at me!'

Smeadie gazed at him, as if not quite convinced that he was real and not a ghost returned to cause trouble for his master. 'His lordship was greatly distressed,' he said. 'It was said that you had drowned in the river in a most unfortunate accident.' He said this in such a way that James felt he had inconvenienced the household by not having the grace to perish quietly.

'I never believed it meself,' Mrs Rudge said. 'I always thought your going away was her doing, and since no body was ever produced I never believed you had gone to your reward.'

'Was there a ... funeral?' James asked, hardly daring to utter the word.

'Aye, there was,' said Smeadie, enlivened by the memory. He described it in some detail and with unmistakable relish: the solemn procession, the onlookers, the grave voice of the archbishop in the cathedral, the tears of Miss Deakin and his father.

'Oh be quiet man, can't you!' Mrs Rudge interrupted, irritated. 'Young James doesn't need to hear all that.'

'How shall a dead man live?' asked Harry, who had been

sitting quietly, eating and listening. His question was met with silence. But James wasn't defeated yet.

'It's a trick. They know I am alive. They know where I am.' He stopped suddenly, as if he had just realised something.

'The last thing they'll want is you turning up now,' Smeadie said.

'He's right,' Harry said. 'You're in great danger now you're ... dead. It would suit them very well to have the reality match the lie.'

'You must never come back here,' Mrs Rudge said.

'Can we trust you not to say anything?' Harry suddenly asked Smeadie.

'How dare you, you little get!' Smeadie spat back.

'He won't say anything, don't fret,' Mrs Rudge said. 'But you must take great care, Master James. Don't go down any dark alleys at night. Keep your wits about you and be careful who you talk to, and don't let anyone know who you are.'

Everyone knows who I am already, James thought to himself. I can't remove myself from their knowledge without destroying half the city.

He could see that Smeadie and Mrs Rudge were growing more uncomfortable the longer the visit lasted, so he got up from the table, thanked them and took his leave, and he and Harry slipped back down the lane and down by quiet streets towards the river.

SIX

The Faction Fighter

I t's hard to keep cheerful when you're dead. From the night of the black wreath onwards, James's life seemed to spiral downwards as if, being thought dead, the city had decided to wash its hands of him and no longer offer him any protection. But he wasn't dead, James told himself, even if there were those who wished it. For the first time in his life James realised what it meant to have enemies, deadly enemies who wished him harm. After they left the house, Harry and he kept clear of the main streets and avoided the bridge, crossing the river by ferry instead and making their way circuitously westwards.

'You can't go back to the dancing master's,' Harry insisted. 'He'd sell you for a quart of gin.'

'But where can I go?' James asked.

Harry indicated with his thumb a window at the top of a ramshackle house. James followed Harry upstairs to a garret not unlike the dancing master's but a good deal smaller. Harry's mother, a frail woman with a heavily lined face, and his two younger sisters were seated on the floor. There was no furniture that James could see.

'Who's this?' Harry's mother asked gruffly. 'And what's he doing here?'

'It's James, Lord Dunmain's boy,' Harry began explaining.

'Oh la deh da,' one of the girls piped up, suddenly interested.

'Spare some change, m'lud,' the other added.

'Don't mind them,' said Harry. 'He's in trouble, that's why he's here. They buried him in Christchurch last week.'

'That's what I call trouble,' the first sister grinned.

'Doesn't look too bad for a corpse, does he?' said the other.

'Dead or alive, he can't stay here,' Harry's mother was adamant. 'We don't keep a hotel here, your honour.'

Harry prevailed on his mother to let James stay for that night, but as soon as it was light, James rose and left, walking out into the still sleeping city. He felt a wave of hopelessness wash over him as he walked down the hill towards the river with no particular purpose in mind. How could his father have abandoned him so utterly? How could he have had the heart to attend his funeral service and accept the condolences of his friends and acquaintances as if his son were really dead? There could be no way back now; there was nowhere else for James to go. This was life now – this grey morning, these streets and whatever happened in them.

In the days that followed James learned the life of a street boy, prowling around the city from need to need. Hunger drove him towards the markets, hoping for a discarded hunk of bread or a stray piece of fruit. He earned the curses of the market women and, often, a hail of stones from the other boys who haunted the streets and whose territory he was encroaching on. Sometimes a milk woman might take pity on him and give him a ladle of milk, or a baker might toss him a loaf that was on its way to becoming a brick. He learned to live with constant hunger, and sleep with half an eye open. The nights were dangerous, as anyone sleeping in an exposed place was liable to attack by passing footpads or beggars, and James sought out the shelter of the Phoenix Park. Even here he had to be careful, as many criminals also found its seclusion irresistible. Under cover of darkness, he would move slowly from tree to tree until he found a spot where he could hear no voices or nothing that sounded like human footsteps in the undergrowth. Only when he had had sat for a long time in silence did he eventually allow sleep to take hold.

He often went to see Harry at his pitch. Sometimes, Harry would lend him his spudd, polish and wig and let him tout for customers. Some of his first customers complained that he wasn't quick enough and one or two clouted him about his ears for sloppy work, but he soon improved, and the pennies he got allowed him to buy bread and fruit. There was one brutish client James would not forget quickly. The man was well dressed, a nobleman of some kind, with straggly black hair and narrow eyes and a look of permanent disdain etched on his features. He looked like someone born to be cruel. He thrust his boot into James's lap as if he meant to injure him and, as he worked, James could feel the man's merciless eyes boring into him. The boots were of the best leather and didn't need much work, but the man was quick to find fault.

'Call yourself a shoeblack, you dirty little caffler. I'll blacken your eye for you!' He pulled his boot away and walked off, throwing a coin over his shoulder as he left, causing it to land right in the middle of a filthy puddle.

James felt himself sinking in this life. Every day he seemed to be filthier, more degraded. What would Master Naughton think of him now? He must find of way of getting back to the school, or he would live and die on the streets like so many of the beggar boys he saw every day. But how? When your life was changed for the worse, there didn't seem to be an easy way to change it back again. He was thinking these dark thoughts one morning as he stood on the quays watching the murky waters, when he became aware of a sudden commotion in the streets that led down to the river. He heard drums, whistles, and rhythmic chanting, and then suddenly they appeared, a long line of men bearing sticks and knives, including some men James recognised from his days with the dancing master. They were dressed in their work clothes: tailors, weavers, buckle-makers, farriers, but their faces seemed to belong to different men: they were hard and angry, set to a common purpose. These were the Liberty Boys, James realised, one of the city's most feared gangs, fired up now and spoiling for a fight.

'Up the Liberty Boys!' some shouted, and the chant was

taken up by the whole company. Without knowing exactly how it happened, James suddenly found himself caught up in the rush and swept along the quays, part of a menacing column of violent intent whose cause was mysterious to him, but to which he seemed, now, to belong. The anger that been welling up inside him for many weeks, as his life plunged remorselessly into the depths of the city, seemed to flow out of him all of a sudden, matching itself with the mood of the rushing crowd. As well as anger, there was a current of pure exhilaration. He was, now, a Liberty Boy, a fully functioning member of this streaming mass of clubs and knives and blood-thirsty howls. Whatever their purpose was, it was now his too and he was glad to be part of it.

'Come on, ye Liberty Boys!' He heard a strong voice raise itself out from the mass, and realised it was his.

He now became aware of another commotion, a low rumbling undercurrent as if the very streets were responding to the noise of the Liberty Boys. When he looked ahead, he could see that this was in a way the case, except that the noise was coming not from the streets but from a throng of butchers, all in aprons, brandishing cleavers and milling around one of the bridges in large numbers. Many of them also had stones, and these began to rain on the Liberty Boys.

James was frightened now, and wished he hadn't shouted out. He realised that the purpose he was caught up in was a bitter fight with these strong, armed and vicious-looking butchers. The Ormond Boys! Another gang, Catholics this time, and mortal enemies of the Protestant Liberty Boys. He was about to enter a battle between the most notorious factions in the city. He noticed that they seemed to have the city to themselves; all the shops were shuttered, the windows closed, and the stalls taken in from the street. There were no Charlies or redcoats to be seen. The streets were a battleground, deserted by everyone except the fighters. Stones landed on the column James was in; the man beside him screamed suddenly, his face an ugly mess of blood. Someone pulled him roughly to one side, and he lay on the quayside moaning. James's mouth was dry. Instinctively, he ducked as more missiles landed beside him. Men from behind him rushed forward, pushing him out of the way, and attacked the butchers head on with clubs, fists and knives. Screams tore at the air, blood spurted from legs, arms, faces. The bridge was a *melee* of bodies locked in combat. James could see white-aproned reinforcements coming from the direction of the Ormond Market. He wondered for a second if he would live to see the end of this day. He had no weapon to protect himself with and, although he had been happy to join the seething column of marchers, he had no particular desire to fling stones at the butchers on the bridge.

He didn't have to wait long before one of the butcher's apprentices saw him and made a sudden dash in his direction, brandishing a heavy axe-handle. James bent, found a stone and flung it at the apprentice's body as hard as he could. His aim was good, and the apprentice stopped dead, stunned by the blow. James made straight for him and relieved him of the axe-handle before the Ormond Boy had time to recover.

James raised the handle as if to strike the apprentice, but the boy came to his senses and ran back into the body of the butchers, much to James's relief. The battle for the bridge was becoming more intense by the second. The fighting was so close that the butchers hardly had room to swing their cleavers and much of the work was achieved by elbows and fists against eyes and noses. So great was the press of bodies behind him that James was forced towards the middle of the bridge, where he got several kicks and punches. Suddenly he felt himself grabbed by his shirt collar and then dragged along the ground by his arms.

'We've got one!' a shout went up.

'Bring him back to the market and show him how we treat Liberty Boys!'

Several more hands placed themselves under James's armpits, and he was dragged swiftly across the bridge. His heart raced and fear pulsed through his body. He had heard tales of the terrible things inflicted by the butchers on their captured victims. And he wasn't even a Liberty Boy! They were hardly likely to be convinced by that, and would take any denial as an act of the purest cowardice. He was now in the middle of Ormond Market. Apart from his captors, the stalls were deserted. Sides of beef and mutton hung from hooks on beams above the stalls, and trays of offal and cuts of meat were set on tables at the front. As he was being bundled towards one of the stalls another group of butchers dragged in a young man, his nose bleeding profusely.

'We got a college boy,' one of them yelled. 'And now we're going to educate him.'

The others whooped at this revelation. James felt the blood drain from his face.

'Let's do them side by side!' A roar went up, and the plan was instantly agreed to. James and the young man were bound together with ropes.

'Courage, boy,' the man whispered to James, 'don't let them see your fear.'

James clenched his teeth and looked directly at his captors. There were about six of them, and he recognised the apprentice whose nose he had bloodied earlier and who was now looking back at him with glee.

'Free the hooks,' ordered a butcher with a long thin face. He had a voice that other men listen to, and his dark expression was of complete absorption in the task. The other butchers lifted the sides of beef from two adjacent hooks and laid the meat on the table, and then pulled the table out of the way.

'Hook them.'

Hands moved to hoist them.

'At least spare the boy, can't you?' the college student said as they raised him towards the bloody meat hook.

The butchers who weren't engaged in the hoisting, including Thin Face, were sharpening knives. The noise echoed loudly in the enclosed market square.

Suddenly a new voice rang out. 'Wait!' An older butcher had entered the market and was making for the stall.

Thin Face looked up, displeasure narrowing his eyes. 'Purcell!' he hissed.

The others turned sharply and, seeing the older man, lowered their burdens. The one called Purcell looked them up and down. His manner was not friendly.

'Use the ropes,' he ordered. 'I want no deaths here today.' He walked up to Thin Face, so close the other must have felt his breath on his face. 'Put it away.'

Thin Face looked for a second as if he might be about to disagree, then slowly put down his knife.

James and his companion were hoisted again and lowered carefully onto the meat hooks so they hung suspended by the ropes around their chests. James felt the metal hook press painfully against his back. His feet were several inches off the ground. The butchers stood around admiring their handiwork.

Purcell made to leave the square. 'There's fighting to be done,' he said. 'Don't linger here.'

The butchers looked simultaneously relieved and disappointed – relieved that Purcell had gone, disappointed that they couldn't accomplish whatever they had originally intended. Thin Face wasn't finished yet, though. He picked up a stick and brought it down viciously on the dangling student and then, in a movement of equal deliberation, on James. James and the student both screamed with the pain and gasped for breath. The butchers laughed. Then Thin Face picked up his knife again and brought it up to their faces.

'It would an easy thing now to cut you open,' he said. He paused to relish the prospect, letting the blade graze their cheeks.

James forced himself not to flinch. He turned his eyes from

the blade and in that second felt the full force of another blow as the flat of the cleaver hit him on the side of his head. Everything went dark then, and when he came to his whole body ached. He looked down and saw the face of Purcell below him. The market was otherwise empty.

Purcell pulled a table close to them until their feet could rest on the top, and then he cut the ropes that bound them to the hooks. 'You're fortunate not to be carved in pieces. You wouldn't be the first Liberty Boys to suffer that fate. Now get out of here, and if you have any sense you won't go fighting the Ormond Boys again.' He pushed them down from the table, though his roughness seemed more feigned than real.

James wanted to thank him, but the butcher was already on his way out of the square. James and the student moved as quickly as they could, but their bodies were slow to respond, and it was with great sluggishness and pain that they left the square and moved eastward away from the cries of the battle, which was still continuing. They made their way to the ferry. As they walked, the student revealed himself as Jeremy McAllister of Trinity College. The college students often took the side of their fellow Protestant Liberty Boys against the Catholic butchers, though the conflict had long ceased to be about religion. No one knew the cause of the feud any more; it was just an established part of the city's life, and McAllister had gone out with a group of students more out of curiosity and mischief than from any particular conviction.

Once they were on the ferry, McAllister questioned James closely about his own life, and gave a soft whistle when he heard the tale. He was thoughtful for a moment.

'Why don't you come and work for me? I need a servant in college,' he said eventually. Seeing James hesitate, he added, 'I know, the pay wouldn't be much, but you'd have a roof over your head, and enough to eat.'

James was wary. He didn't have much trust left, and part of him had enjoyed the independence of his homeless life. But as the ferry docked, his stomach growled loudly, reminding him that he hadn't yet eaten that day. His spirit might lean towards unhindered freedom, but his body had its own ideas, and before he thought any more about it, he heard himself agreeing to the young man's proposal.

• • •

SEVEN

College Life

I'm not a boy, James thought as he looked out of McAllister's small window onto the courtyard below. I've seen too much for that. What does that make me? Not a man yet, that's certain. A lord, a thief, a servant, a ghost ...

Behind him, still abed, McAllister snored. He and his friend, Vandeleur, had been up all night drinking, and now was the snoring time. He'd miss this morning's lectures as he'd missed yesterday's. James felt a twinge of unease. He could sense the faintest whisper of danger on the air, the tiniest trembling of the wood beneath his feet with its suggestion that this world could also collapse, however solid it seemed now. Sometimes James felt as if he himself might collapse, as if he were nothing more than a bundle of flesh and bones thrown together with no particular design.

A lone pigeon pecked at the cobbles below. Who cared if that pigeon lived or died? Who cared whether it found a few meagre crumbs or flew home hungry? And who cared what happened to James Lovett in this grey city?

A bell summoned the students to their lectures; footsteps hurried across Library Square. Any minute now McAllister would wake and send him for a jug of milk and then for a basin of warm water. But for a few minutes more James could enjoy the spectacle of the college going about its morning business.

From a door in the other side of the square emerged the strange shape of Professor Jolin. His head looked as if it had been borrowed from the body of a man three times his size, and his wild white hair looked as if he had woken in the middle of the night and seen the most terrible ghost. It was said he never changed his linen, and certainly he was the smelliest man in the college. As he moved now, he held his hands in front of him, gesticulating enthusiastically and pausing occasionally in the middle of the square. He had begun his lecture just as he did every morning, whether or not he had reached the lecture theatre. Once the appointed hour came, even if he was still in bed, he would begin. And because he was often late his students would scratch their heads as they tried to catch his drift.

McAllister would sometimes let James sneak in to the lectures because it amused him to see his unusual servant further his patchy education. He had bought James a new suit of clothes and this, together with James's natural good looks, gave him the appearance of a student, although a very young one.

On cold days, after McAllister had spent all his generous

allowance on drinking and gambling, he would sent James out for a supply of books.

'A yard of books,' he'd say. 'The older and cheaper the better.'

So James would set out for the bookshops off Dame Street and come back with a heavy burden of tattered and unwanted books. These McAllister would consign to the fire, and they would sit in his room until they were well warmed by the flaming print.

All in all, James thought, McAllister wasn't a bad master. The duties were not too irksome; he was warm, dry and decently fed. McAllister was highly thought of in the college; it seemed great things were expected of him, and his easy-going nature made him popular with the students and professors. Yet, James worried about that same relaxed nature. McAllister had recently begun to show less enthusiasm for his studies, and to spend more and more time with Vandeleur. McAllister was the kind of person who, though without any badness himself, was very easily led into mischief by others. It was enough for Vandeleur to swagger into the room and announce some foolish plan for McAllister to drop whatever he was doing and place himself at his friend's command.

James didn't like Vandeleur much. He had seen many like him in his father's house, all bright clothes and mincing manners, men of title and money, with not a care in the world except what pleasure they might gain from it. Each time James saw him he was dressed more gaudily – the canary yellow waistcoat swapped for a green silken one, a purple topcoat for one in scarlet, or new boots, and if McAllister raised an eyebrow he always got the same reply. 'These are dressy times, McAllister. You won't amount to anything in this city unless you put your best foot forward.'

Vandeleur didn't care for James, regarding him as an interloper whose presence he put down to his friend's overly whimsical generosity. 'A filthy street boy, McAllister,' James had heard him say. 'What use can he possibly serve? You should have left him where you found him.'

James couldn't understand why these two were so inseparable, and put it down to his master's easy-going nature. Yet McAllister never revealed James's true identity to Vandeleur – this one thing he kept back from his friend, and James was grateful for it. Sometimes McAllister would talk to James about his father, suggesting that he should seek Lord Dunmain out privately and let his father acknowledge his son, even if only in secret. The bond between a father and son is not so easily broken, he tried to assure James, talking fondly about his own father and the many happy days they had spent together.

James would have none of it. 'It's too late now,' he said, over and over. 'It's too late for that.'

But McAllister's encouragement did at least keep alive a flicker of hope that one day James might be reconciled with his father, that he might wake up in his old bed and all of his life since he left his father's house would be swept away like so much dust. One morning when he came back to the room with a jug of milk, McAllister looked at him strangely.

'Have you heard anything?' he asked. 'I mean, about your father?'

James knew immediately something was not right. 'No. Why?'

McAllister looked uneasy. 'I was in the town. I heard talk. They say your father's dead.'

James stared at him, uncomprehending. 'What?'

'I'm sorry. There was an argument, I think, with someone who had lent him money. Hard words were spoken, and your father challenged him to a duel …'

James heard the words, but they didn't penetrate; they hung somewhere in the air outside him. He remembered his father's duelling pistols, their shine and heft. 'Feel the weight of that, boy. You won't be fit for society until you've blazed.' His father had blazed often – he was easily slighted – and he had always survived. He had strong opinions about duelling, as about everything else. The nature of the insult, the rules of engagement, the best places to fight. The challenged chooses his ground; the challenger chooses his distance; the seconds fix the time and terms of firing. James had heard it often enough.

'It seems his pistol misfired …'

James could hear no more. He ran from McAllister's room and right through the college until he emerged in College Green. He ran until he came to Harry's pitch near the Custom House. Harry was the only source of news he could trust without question. Nothing happened in the city that Harry didn't hear about. His friend was perched on his stool near the archway to the quayside, finishing off a merchant's boot. Harry nodded at James and when he had finished, he rushed up to his friend.

'You've heard, then,' he said. He could see how upset James was.

'So it's true.' James's whole body sagged. Now that the truth had been established there was no more hope, and all the life seemed to drain from him. He sat down on Harry's stool and slumped forward with his head in his hands. Harry put his hand on his shoulder.

'I'm sorry, Jim.'

Harry stood silently by his friend for a few moments.

'By the way, Jim, do you know your uncle?'

'Uncle? My father had a brother, I think. I never met him. I think he went to England.'

'He's back. He has assumed the title. A hard fellow by all accounts.'

James barely took the information in. Right now, he didn't care about any uncles, good or bad. He wanted to take his leave of his father before they put him in the ground.

EIGHT

A Funeral and a Fight

James crept into Christchurch cathedral and slid into a bench at the back, beside a group of townspeople who seemed to be there more out of curiosity than grief. At the front he could see the chief mourners: Miss Deakin — James would never call her anything else — arrayed in black like a rook, and beside her the man who must be his uncle. There was something strangely familiar about him; the dark cruel mouth, the straggly black hair, the way he stood, even here, as if he owned the cathedral and everything in it. Suddenly James felt his stomach lurching and his blood run cold. He recognised him: it was the man whose boots he had cleaned in Essex Street, who had cuffed him and abused him and thrown the coin to the ground as he marched off. This brute was his uncle? The knowledge sank into James's bones so that he felt exhausted. Every so often the man turned his head around to scan the congregation, coolly assessing the mourners at his brother's funeral. James ducked down into the pew when he saw the head move. He did not want to be seen by this strange new figure whose every gesture seemed calculated to arouse fear. He noticed Miss Deakin seemed very friendly with him, glancing and smiling in his direction at every opportunity.

At the side of the cathedral, some distance away from the proceedings, James saw a strange group of men. They were tall and loose-limbed and quite brutal in appearance, with rough, pocked faces and squashed noses that might have been broken several times. James half expected to see blood on their knuckles or a tear in the lapels of their coats, but if they had been engaged in fisticuffs lately there was no sign of it other than a flicker of malevolence in their eyes and the curl of their lips as they whispered and joked among themselves. No great respect for the dead had brought them here, that was sure. And why should they have respected my father? James thought. He was a cruel, careless man who lived for himself. And yet he was my father, and now he is dead. James felt a strange emptiness in the pit of his stomach. Part of him, part of his life, was gone forever. In spite of what his father had done, he felt grief tear at him. Who knows, maybe they would have been reconciled in the end, maybe they could one day have had a life together. As he looked at the coffin, he realised that now he was truly alone, now he truly belonged everywhere and nowhere.

His thoughts were disturbed by the whisperings beside him.

'Who are those men?' James nudged his neighbour.

'You wouldn't want to meet them on a dark night' came

the reply. 'Them's Richard Lovett's "Uglies", here to keep the creditors away now he's the lord, I wouldn't be surprised.'

Harry had been right: his uncle was a dangerous man with forces of violence at his command. He would have to be careful. Had his father spoken to Richard before he died? Did he explain that his son was not in fact dead but running around the city? James felt a sudden wave of anger sweep over him. He wanted to stand up in the aisle and call out his own name; he wanted to assert his rights, and one of his rights was to grieve for his father openly instead of crouching like an outcast in the shadows. James could feel his body move of its own accord, his hands on the rail of the pew, his knees beginning to rise from the kneeler. He was aware of the sudden interest of the people beside him, their glances curious and keen.

And then, as quickly as it had welled up, the impulse subsided and he sank down again. What was the point? He would only present an easy target for his uncle and his brutes, and the trouble would all be over. No one would mourn him. Had he not already been mourned in any case? He would be another homeless and entirely surplus boy to be heaped in the common pit.

He looked hard at his uncle as he shouldered his father's coffin down the aisle with the other pallbearers, burning the image into his brain so that he would be able to recall it at any time in the future. As the coffin passed his pew he averted his eyes, not wanting the least flicker of himself to be visible to his uncle. The coffin passed by, and he felt a sharp pang of grief. The end of the procession from the cathedral was brought up by the Uglies, whose slovenly gait barely allowed the minimum of respect, and they glared at those in the aisles as if to challenge any man or woman who might think their attitude unsuitable for the occasion. James paled at the sight of them.

When the procession left the church James crept out as quietly as he had entered and made his way back to the college. There at least he would be safe for a while.

'I'm sorry for you, James,' McAllister said. 'We don't get to choose our fathers, but we only get one, no matter how bad they might be. Can you remember any good times with him at all?'

'Yes,' James said, after thinking about it a while. 'Many years ago. I don't know if I dreamed it or if it really happened. It was in Wexford, in Dunmain. I can see the garden, the sun pouring through the trees. And my father, laughing, throwing me up in the air and catching me. And I can hear myself squealing and laughing.'

'Hold onto that, James,' McAllister said. 'Whenever you think of him, think of that.'

James settled with relief into the routines of college life. He fetched and carried and ate and slept and sometimes heard a lecture, hidden at the back of the hall. He learned a little Latin, a little French, a little Hebrew. It sometimes seemed to him that he would always be someone who got a little of everything: a little warmth, a little sustenance, a little life. One day, he told himself, there would be more than a little, and that was the day he must live for.

McAllister's easy ways got easier with every day. He now did very little work and rarely attended lectures. Vandeleur was around constantly, sitting in McAllister's rooms with his boots on the table, admiring their sheen. He would sometimes ask James to polish them and James felt like telling him to walk into town and get himself a shoeblack. If McAllister was present he would wave Vandeleur away. 'Leave the boy alone, he has enough to do.'

Once or twice, Vandeleur called when McAllister was still abed or had gone out somewhere, and then he presented his boots to James like a goad, and James was left with no choice. He performed the job as inexpertly as he could, ignoring all the knowledge of the art he had learned from Harry, until Vandeleur tired of his game. 'You really are a useless article, aren't you?' he sneered, before turning his attention to something else.

He and McAllister spent more and more of their time in the taverns and gaming houses and often came home drunk. Although the college authorities had forbidden it, Vandeleur usually went out with his sword, the end of whose scabbard he'd removed, just the way the Pinkindindies did it, hoping that he might be provoked into drawing a little blood.

McAllister had no interest in swords, but one evening when Vandeleur arrived in his friend's room he came bearing a gift. It was a sword, just like his own, in a scabbard with the end removed.

'Really, Vandeleur, you know I'm not going to go around with that thing.'

'Oh just this once, be a man for one night, and we'll speak no more of it.'

McAllister strapped on the sword, turning to James as he did so. 'It's possible that we might overdo things tonight ...'

Vandeleur snorted. 'Possible! It is entirely likely. We shall be gloriously drunk.'

'Could you come to the Bull's Head around midnight to escort us home? Do you know it?'

James nodded.

Vandeleur snorted again in obvious distaste. 'We don't need *him*,' he said. 'We're not mewling infants who need a nursemaid to come and fetch us home. Isn't that right, Nursey?'

James ignored him and spoke directly to McAllister. 'Of course I'll come,' he said.

With Vandeleur still muttering discontentedly, the two left the grounds of the college. As things were to turn out, James wished he hadn't been given this task. The two companions spent their evening in various taverns and finally ended up in the Bull's Head in Fishamble Street, where they drank to their companionship, and with pocket knives carved their names on the table; beside their names they carved, as a final flourish, *quis separabit*, who will separate us? There was an answer to that question, but they didn't know that yet.

By the time James got to the Bull's Head McAllister and Vandeleur were the worse for wear.

'Why James,' McAllister said, 'what brings you here?' He had evidently forgotten his request.

'Why don't you toddle off home?' Vandeleur said. 'You're not needed here.'

James was forced to wait until the two had exhausted their capacity for drink and talk. Finally they left the Bull's Head, with James attempting not very successfully to direct them. As they staggered up the hill, they managed to get into an argument with a man who had been in the tavern earlier. Maybe he had heard something he'd objected to, or maybe Vandeleur or McAllister had said something provocative. James wasn't sure what the cause was, and he could make no sense of the shouts from McAllister and Vandeleur.

'Come away,' he said, 'it's time to go home.'

Vandeleur pushed him roughly and James fell. As he got up, he saw that the argument had grown more heated. Angry words were tossed back and forth, and before James could make another attempt to get them to keep the peace, the man rushed at Vandeleur, who grabbed his sword so that the exposed end was pointing at the man's chest. Possibly Vandeleur just meant to frighten him, but however it happened the man, in his eagerness to hit Vandeleur, seemed to trip on the cobbles and his full weight fell on the student's blade. It all happened so quickly, James could hardly tell one part of the action from the other. All he knew was that at the end of it all, the man lay dead in the street.

NINE

The Pursuit

Vandeleur and McAllister ran, panic-stricken, back towards the safety of the college. For a moment, James felt he should stay and explain that what had happened was an unfortunate accident. But who would believe him? Instead, he backed away quickly, slipped into a laneway and walked back towards the college, making sure no one noticed him.

Vandeleur and McAllister had run down Dame Street and hadn't dared stop until the night porter had admitted them into the college. They'd run on towards Library Square and only when they had gained it did they come to a standstill.

'I think we're safe,' Vandeleur said, his breath coming in desperate gasps. 'No one there knew us'.

McAllister nodded, out of breath. His face was white, the horror of what they had done only now beginning to dawn on him. 'Is he dead, do you think?'

'Indubitably,' Vandeleur replied, not entirely without satis-faction.

McAllister groaned. 'If only we hadn't brought these damned swords!' He looked down and found that his coat was spattered with bloodstains.

'Quickly,' he shouted at Vandeleur. 'We must hurry!'

They ran to McAllister's room, where the young student immediately began to wipe at the stains on his clothes. Vandeleur, now that the initial excitement had abated, was less hurried; he seemed to want to contemplate the fruit of his actions a bit longer. When James arrived, he was dispatched to fetch hot water to try to remove the blood from their clothes. When he came back, Vandeleur still had made no attempt to clean his weapon. James looked at it with horror. He couldn't quite believe what had happened.

'My dear fellow,' Vandeleur was drawling to McAllister. 'I'm sure he was a man of no account. I don't know why you're troubling yourself.'

'He was a man!' McAllister shouted at him. 'Isn't that enough? We have taken a man's life?'

Vandeleur shrugged.

James asked leave to speak.

Vandeleur glared at him. 'Why do you keep this wretch?'

'Oh shut up, Vandeleur. Yes, James, speak up.'

'Did you meet anyone in the tavern? Did you talk to anyone?'

'I can't remember,' McAllister said.

'Did anyone see you leave?'

'Only the dead man,' McAllister said.

'And he won't be giving evidence to anyone,' Vandeleur said, a smile on his face.

As he said this, the blood drained suddenly even farther from McAllister's already pale face.

'Oh my God!'

'What is it?' Vandeleur looked up.

'*Quis separabit*! *Quis separabit*!' McAllister's words came out in a near-shriek.

'Ah,' Vandeleur said. He looked slightly less composed now. 'Our names on the table, carved for all to see.'

James saw at once how serious the situation was.

'There's no time to lose,' he said. 'Once anyone remembers you were there and sees your names, this is the first place they'll come looking. Who else but students would carve their names like that?'

'With a Latin inscription to boot,' McAllister acknowledged. 'We're doomed, then.' He sagged visibly, all animation banished from his features.

'You should go now,' James said. 'You should both go. And you shouldn't be seen together.'

'Go where?' Vandeleur snarled at James, but before James had a chance to reply there was a sudden commotion on the cobbles below. James rushed to the window. He saw four sheriff's men in the square outside, the college porter with them. They were making for the entrance to the building where Vandeleur's rooms were.

'They're here,' he said.

Vandeleur ran to the window and when he saw where they had gone his habitual composure seemed to desert him. 'Damn it,' he said, 'this is very inconvenient. Why on earth are they taking such trouble?' He became agitated as he furiously tried to work out the best course of action.

For a moment, James thought he might brazen it out and march up to them, but Vandeleur clearly wasn't as foolish as he sometimes seemed.

'I think a spell away from college is called for,' he said and, after the briefest of farewells, disappeared down the stairs.

James gathered up the two swords that were still on the floor.

'I'll put these in the attic, but in the meantime, sir, you will have to conceal yourself. I'll tell them you have not returned.'

With that, James raced upstairs to the attics and hid the swords in a roll of old carpet in a dusty corner, then raced back down. As he reached the landing outside McAllister's room he heard footsteps on the stairs below. He rushed into the room. McAllister stood frozen by the bed, an abject statue, rooted to the spot by fear. James had already chosen him a hiding place in his mind's eye as he was hiding the swords. On the wall beside McAllister's bed hung a large tapestry from his father's estate, a hunting scene, perhaps intended to remind him of home as he fell asleep. James had helped McAllister put it up. There was an alcove set in the wall, where the student had kept books and various personal effects, but there had been nowhere else to put the tapestry, so in the end McAllister had cleared out the alcove and they'd hung the tapestry over it.

'You never know,' James had said with a grin, 'You might need a secret place to store things.' He hadn't thought that the secret thing would be McAllister himself.

'Quickly,' he said now, pulling the tapestry aside. 'Get in and squeeze yourself as far back as you are able.'

McAllister mutely obeyed and climbed into the narrow space, and James smoothed over the tapestry as best he could, praying that the searchers' curiosity wouldn't extend to it.

The door burst open and the sheriff's men came thumping in, swords at the ready, followed by the porter.

'Where is he?' the first of the sheriff's men panted. He was quite out of breath from all his running, and the others weren't much better.

'Who are you?' one of the men asked, pointing his blade at James's chest, but James remained calm.

'Do you mean Master McAllister? He went out about an hour ago. He said he wouldn't be back until late this evening. He said he wanted to see the puppets in the Capel Street playhouse. I am his skivvy.'

'Puppets? Did you say puppets?' This information seemed to enrage the four swordsmen. Maybe it hadn't been such a good idea.

'I'll give him puppets when I see him!' the first said. With that, he lunged at the bed with his sword and ran the blade through the mattress, then ran the pillow through for good measure, scattering feathers all over the room. The other men began to search every corner, running the curtains through, emptying the clothes chest and spilling out McAllister's waistcoats, hose, smallclothes, wig, a hat, and various papers on the floor. They examined the papers. 'Poetry!' one of them said in disgust.

They lifted the rug from the floor and examined the floorboards; they scanned the ceiling, opened books and flung them to the ground.

James could feel the sweat sticking to the back of his shirt. He forced himself to stay calm in the maelstrom of searching and destruction. He kept his eyes away from the wall where the tapestry hung, terrified that even a glance might lead them to the hiding place.

'Nice picture,' he heard one of the men say suddenly, and his blood ran cold.

'Hunting,' another said. 'Very fitting. We'll run him to ground and no mistake, and someone can make a picture of that.'

'Does your master carry a sword?' one of the men asked abruptly.

As the sheriff's men turned their attention away from the tapestry, James nearly wept with relief.

'The carrying of swords is forbidden by the provost,' the porter said, speaking for the first time. James noted that he was eyeing the sheriff's men with some distaste. He looked James straight in the eye, and James saw something he couldn't quite interpret, a slight narrowing of the eyes, enough to indicate that whatever might happen in the city, the college was a

separate jurisdiction, and the officers of the city had no business floundering around and cutting up its bedlinen. Did the
porter suspect McAllister's whereabouts? James hardly dared
to return the man's gaze.

In the meantime, the sheriff's men had tired of their
ransacking.

'We're wasting time,' one said, 'we should seek him out at
the playhouse.'

The others seemed to think that this was a sensible suggestion, and the men began to leave. As they were doing so,
their leader suddenly lunged at James and caught him by the
neck so that the boy gasped for breath.

'If we don't find him, we'll be back for you. Mark my words,
you're not too young to swing for murder yourself.'

The sheriff's man flung James back on the bed, where he
lay until they had all left. Getting to his feet, James watched
from the window until he saw the men crossing the square,
and only then did he beckon to McAllister to come out from
behind the tapestry.

TEN

A Strange Meeting

His time in the college was over, as was McAllister's, and if they didn't act fast their very lives would be in danger.

'This is all a terrible mistake, James. I can barely recall what actually happened. There was an argument and then ... it all fades. If only I hadn't brought that damnable sword!'

McAllister went to the window and looked down forlornly at the square. 'It's all over now,' he said. 'I shouldn't have hidden. I should have given myself up. I am a gentlemen after all, and gentlemen don't cower under beds.'

James was disturbed by McAllister's mood. He seemed to be willing his own destruction. 'Better to cower in a hidey hole than swing at the end of a rope,' he said simply.

'What?' McAllister's eyes were wide, frightened.

'There's every chance they'll hang you for murder. It's not a pleasant death.'

'Nevertheless ...' McAllister's couldn't believe he would be found guilty.

'Look,' James said. 'A terrible thing was done. The wrong was more likely Vandeleur's than yours. But you're mixed up in it, and a trial might make little distinction between the two of you. And even if they don't hang you, your life will be over. You'll be disgraced forever. You may as well be dead.'

'But what am I to do then?' McAllister cried out.

'You must leave right now, before the sheriff's men return. Gather whatever you cannot do without and come with me.' James was surprised by his own decisiveness. He didn't have time to puzzle out the rights and wrongs of it. Someone else would have to do that. He didn't want McAllister to die, and that was all the justice he was concerned about.

'But where will I go?'

'Have you got money?' James asked. 'You'll need as much as you can get your hands on.'

McAllister nodded. He had a good deal of cash, and what he lacked he could depend on his bank to supply, if his family stood by him.

'You must go to the colonies, and you must leave immediately.'

James had no idea how this was to be accomplished; he only knew it had to happen. The first thing was to get McAllister out of the college, and the rest would somehow follow. Of his own future, after this day was out, he didn't dare think, but even as he spoke he could feel as if something in himself had shifted. Whatever happened, he knew that quick thinking and quick acting would be part of it, and that his only sure home would be in his own resourcefulness. It was a lonely idea, but there was hope in it too.

McAllister fell into the rhythm James had set, bundling a few clothes and private papers into a portmanteau.

'Right,' he said. 'I'm ready.'

They had, James reckoned, about half an hour before dawn would begin to shift the college into its morning life and the square below would begin to clack with footsteps and chatter. James went out onto the landing to make sure no eyes or ears were near, then beckoned McAllister. They went down the stairs and out the back door, and then along by the Anatomy House. From inside that grey building came a sudden sharp laugh that chilled both to the bone. They stopped dead and waited, but no one came out. They could hear a faint murmur of voices from within, but whoever was there was intent on their own business and had no interest in who might be passing outside.

'They must have a fresh body for dissecting,' McAllister whispered to James.

There was nothing unusual about this. McAllister had on several occasions gone to witness a dissection in the great theatre inside, but now the thought seemed to fill him with horror. They hurried past until they came to College Park.

McAllister, now full of urgency, made to run across the wide expanse of the park, but James pulled him back. 'What if we should be seen racing across the park like a pair of thieves? We should move swiftly but normally, as if it were our ordinary business to be here. That way, if we are observed, no note will be taken of it.'

McAllister seemed unconvinced, but agreed. They walked the tree-lined paths around the perimeter of the park. A faint light edged the trees as they walked down the avenue. They would soon reach the rear entrance gate, after which they could melt into the waking city. As they turned the corner at the bottom of the avenue, their spirits lifting at the prospect of escape from immediate danger, a figure suddenly appeared, as if from nowhere, on the path in front of them. McAllister moaned with fright. James stood transfixed, not daring to move any further forward. The figure was brown and somewhat stooped and was making straight for them. It had a cane in its right hand, which it now began waving at them.

'Who is it?' James hissed.

McAllister looked dead ahead, his body slumped from fear and exhaustion. 'It's the provost,' he managed to whisper from the side of his mouth.

Dr Baldwin! What was he doing here at this time of the morning? James had never met the provost but he had heard many fearsome stories about him, of parties broken up, students expelled for bad behaviour, terrible tongue-lashings, and even beatings, all administered by him. To meet him here, now, as the dawn began to come up over the college, was the worst possible fate that could befall two would-be escapees.

'What, who goes there? What fellows are you and what is your business in the park at this hour?' the shape shouted in a hoarse voice.

As the provost drew near, James made out a man of sixty or more years, his coat shabby, his stockings mud-spattered and clumps of thick grey hair sprouting from under his wig. The hand that held the cane was large and knobbly, and the arm looked strong enough to inflict a blow to remember.

'Well, are you deaf?' the provost raised his voice. 'Who are you, sir?'

'McAllister, sir, pensioner, Junior Sophister ...'

How much more information did he want to give? James wondered despairingly. Did he want to lead him back to his rooms and up to the attics to search for the tell-tale sword in its cut scabbard?

'And what are you doing here at this hour of the morning?' the provost continued. 'And with your portmanteau with you?' He tapped it with his cane.

'My father is taken ill, sir. I am summoned home.'

'And where is home?'

This is the time to use your imagination, James thought. But McAllister was not someone to whom imagination came readily in times of need.

'County Waterford, sir.'

There he goes, chapter and verse.

'Indeed,' the provost said, observing him keenly. 'And is this the way to the Waterford coach?'

McAllister looked on the point of giving up, as if he might confess everything and throw himself on the mercy of the provost. It was rumoured Dr Baldwin had killed a man himself once in his youth in England, but that didn't mean he would be likely to forgive the crime in others.

'Please sir, I asked my master if we might call by my aunt before we undertook our journey, since we may be gone some time. She lives nearby in St Patrick's Lane.' James knew this was a risk, but there was little time for elaborate invention.

The provost now turned his beady eyes on James, who had been, until that moment, as invisible as all servants are.

'I am sure your master can speak on his own behalf. Do you usually make so bold as to speak for him?'

'No sir, I am very sorry, sir.'

Dr Baldwin continued to eye them both balefully and looked in no way convinced by anything that he heard. Then his eyes lightened and lifted from them and, without another word, he moved off into the dawn, his cane clacking on the avenue.

McAllister immediately reached for a handkerchief to mop his brow. He was close to tears. 'I can't do this, James, I don't have the strength for it.'

'You must, sir. You mustn't give up. We're nearly out of the college now. And from now on, we'd better not be so quick with our names.'

McAllister nodded eagerly. 'Of course, you're right.'

Spurred on by their brush with danger, they walked quickly towards the gate that led out of College Park, and found themselves on the street where James had said his aunt lived.

'What if he had decided to verify your aunt's residence?' McAllister asked.

'No one's curiosity extends as far as servants,' James said simply.

McAllister gave him a sharp look but said nothing.

James led them on a circuitous northward route towards the river. In an alley off the quay they found an inn just opening for the day and they went inside the dark, tobacco-smelling room and called for food. As they were waiting, James inquired about the times of the packets to England.

'Ten shillings will get you to Holyhead,' he told McAllister on his return. 'There's a packet that leaves on the afternoon tide. But England will be dangerous; you'll need to get passage for the colonies as soon as possible.'

McAllister nodded. He didn't seem convinced.

'I have the feeling that all of this is happening to someone else,' he said. 'The old McAllister and his life have vanished forever, and I have no idea what will replace them.'

He looked at James. 'Would you come with me, James? You know you're more than a servant to me. What is this city to you after all?'

It was a good question. What was there in this city for James other than hardship and possibly worse? Why not take the packet with McAllister and meet whatever new life it would lead to? Why not try his luck in the colonies? But McAllister's question made James realise that, in spite of everything, his fate was bound up with this city. Only here could he claim his inheritance, when the time was right. Only here could he confront his uncle, only here could he find the justice that would restore him to his rightful position. After all, I am Lord

Dunmain, he thought to himself as he considered McAllister and his proposition. He didn't much feel like a lord right now as he ate his dish of cockles, and he didn't have as much as a roof over his head, but there was no doubt in his mind as he shook his head.

'No, I can't,' he said. 'I must stay here even if it seems hopeless now.'

He told McAllister to write to him at the bookshop in the piazzas; the owner would keep any letters safe for him.

'Best stay out of sight until it's time to take the packet. And be careful as you embark, in case they're watching.'

McAllister nodded and smiled a little ruefully.

'Stay well, James, and stay alive,' he said.

• • • •

ELEVEN

Dunmain's Man

Buy sweet whey; buy the pure sweet whey
Hard cruds here, hard cruds for the boys and girls!

The 'cruds and whey' woman moved slowly along the quay with her pannier on her head. A chimney sweep and his boy emerged from a side street, the boy weighed down with brushes and rods, both faces black even at this hour, and the shops and taverns were bustling into life as James walked slowly westward along the river, not sure where he was going. Everyone he saw was driven by a definite purpose, with a sure knowledge of where they were going and how, and where, their day was likely to end. Even the beggars assuming their positions along the quayside were working according to a plan as they stood or sprawled on the ground and whined for alms. And the seagulls crying above the ships knew what they were about and could, James felt, give a good account of themselves if they were asked. Only he had no clear destination in mind, and no notion of how or where his day might end.

He was woken from these gloomy thoughts when he noticed a man standing at the corner, a broad, hulking figure, leaning against the wall and scanning the quays like some beast of prey. Everything about him proclaimed malevolence, from the darkness of his eyes and the twist of his mouth to the long arms and pale fleshy hands that looked like they would be very happy squeezing a throat. James shuddered slightly at the sight of him. Something about him seemed strangely familiar, as if James had seen him before somewhere. But where? And then he saw him, in his mind's eye, walking down the aisle of the cathedral and looking over the mourners and onlookers with a glance of unconcealed contempt. He was one of the Uglies that his uncle employed to frighten anyone who might give him trouble, and do who knows what other evil deeds on his behalf. He looked like someone to whom violence came as easily as the leaves to the trees. What was he doing here? James could hardly stop looking at him, even though he knew it was foolish. The man seemed to have a force around him that could suck in the unwary.

Suddenly James felt the man's eyes on his own. James looked away quickly and continued walking along the quays, but he could feel the man's eyes boring into the back of his head. Then he heard the man's voice crash around his ears.

'You there! Little man, come here you, I want you!'

Whatever he wanted, James decided he was in no hurry to

find out. He kept walking briskly, and when he heard the man shout again and, looking over his shoulder, saw his great bulk begin to shift on the cobbles, he darted up the quay as fast as he could and slipped into a narrow laneway. The laneway was dark and empty, but as James ran he saw no place where he might conceal himself. Maybe the man hadn't seen him enter the laneway but had run past further up the quay. But that hope was dashed when a shadow darkened the lane even more and he heard the man running up the alleyway. For one so big he was surprisingly agile. 'Come back here, boy, or I'll throttle you!'

As he ran up the lane James saw a narrow gap between two warehouses, and without a second thought, dived into it. He found himself in a courtyard strewn with lumber and barrels, some completed and some still being worked on. There were tools and benches, though no workmen yet. With a surge of panic James realised there was no way out of the courtyard other than by the gap he had entered. He looked around but could see nowhere to hide. He crouched behind a barrel, then opened the lid and, finding the barrel empty, he clambered in and closed the lid after him. He had no sooner done that than he heard footsteps on the cobbles of the courtyard.

'I know you're here, you little scut. Come out now or it'll be the worse for you!'

Had he really seen him slip into the courtyard or was he bluffing? James was tempted to get out of the barrel and surrender before he was found there. Maybe the man wasn't as bad as he seemed, maybe he just wanted to ask him something and had been angered by his running away. Better to give up now than be caught and beaten black and blue by the brute. James was about to lift the lid when he heard the sound of barrels being kicked and rolling across the cobbles. If he could subject the barrels to such violence, what was he likely to do to James if he found him?

James crouched deeper into the barrel in the hope that he mightn't be seen should the lid be flung off. The kicking seemed to be nearer. James felt his stomach knot with fear and beads of sweat run down his back. Surely the man could smell him! He felt as if the stink of his fear must reach every corner of the yard. He hoped there were no dogs about, or they would surely sniff him out. He nearly cried out at the next blow, it was so near. It must be the barrel beside him. James braced himself for the blow which must come any second now, but then he heard other voices in the courtyard, angry voices calling out to the man.

'What's going on? What are you doing to our barrels? Who are you?'

The coopers must have come into their workshop. James's terror subsided a little.

'Have you seen the boy?' James heard.

'What boy? There's no boy here! Look at these barrels. A day's work destroyed! Who's going to pay for that?'

The man seemed to have calmed down, and was now trying to placate the angry coopers. James didn't dare move. He put his ear against the wood of the barrel as he strained to hear what was being said.

'A boy, fair-haired, maybe fourteen years or more ...'

'And what is he to you, this boy, whoever he might be?'

'Oh he's just a friend of a friend. I have some business with him.'

'A kicking business, a breaking business, to judge by the violence done here.'

'I'll pay for it. Compliments of Lord Dunmain.'

After another few moments, James didn't hear his voice any more, but still didn't dare move. He would stay here all day if he had to; he had no intention of moving until he was satisfied the brute was no longer in the courtyard.

Suddenly the lid was swept off the barrel, and James cowered, waiting for the blow.

But all that came was a voice, rough but kindly. 'It's alright, he's gone, you can come out now,' it said.

James looked up and saw a grinning face looking down at him.

'How did you know I was here?' James couldn't help asking.

'Because I know my own barrels,' the cooper said, helping him out. 'And I can tell a full one from an empty one.'

'You can?' James wasn't entirely convinced.

'And I can tell when a lid isn't down properly. I finished this barrel yesterday before knocking off. So what did your friend want you for?'

The other coopers gathered round him, wanting to hear his story. James was afraid one of them might take it into his head to run after the Ugly and fetch him back, but no one moved.

'Did you rob him?' asked one, eyeing James suspiciously.

'No,' James said. 'The robbing is all the other way. The brute belongs to my uncle, the man who calls himself Lord Dunmain.'

'What do you mean, calls hisself?'

'Because,' James said, surprising himself, 'I am Lord Dunmain.'

His words produced first a stunned silence, then a clamour of questioning.

'Wait, quiet everyone, let him speak,' said the cooper who had rescued him.

'Alright,' he said, turning to James, 'you'd better explain yourself. And it'd better be good. We don't take kindly to blather around here.'

'My father was William Lovett, Lord Dunmain. He died this year and my uncle assumed the title—'

'Where were you if you were the son?' The questioner sounded sceptical.

That didn't surprise James. He sometimes had trouble believing his story himself. 'My father abandoned me, he and Miss Deakin, whom he married though my mother is still alive. It was something to do with money; they couldn't have an heir in the way. So they farmed me out with a relative, who was no relative. And they gave out that I was dead.'

'Why didn't they just kill you, wouldn't that have been simpler?' It was the sceptical cooper again.

'I don't know,' James said. 'Maybe it's not so easy to kill a son. I don't think he was all bad.'

'Bad enough, from what I heard,' said another of the coopers.

'If it's hard to kill a son, I'll warrant it's a deal easier to kill a nephew,' said the kindly cooper. 'A man who surrounds himself with the likes of that bowsy wouldn't think twice about murder.'

'He was offering money,' the sceptical one reminded him. 'Maybe we should let the family work out their own business.'

'I wouldn't blame you if you wanted to give me up,' James said. 'And I can't offer you any money.'

'There'll be no talk of giving anyone up, or of money either. Not while Matt Brady is in this yard.'

James' stomach unknotted slightly at the man's words. The other coopers muttered their assent, even the sceptical one.

'Your father was a foolish and quarrelsome man,' Matt Brady said. 'He owed money all over the city, and if he hadn't got himself killed for his own pride, he might have got it some other way from someone with good reason. But your uncle is more than foolish, he's a dark-souled thug who they say has killed for the pleasure of it. What kind of man will you be, if you ever get that far?'

'I hope an honourable one,' James said. 'I mean to fight my uncle when the time is right.'

This statement was met with sniggers.

'Well, lad, you'll need to keep alive for that,' Brady said, and James remembered McAllister's words of only hours before. Staying alive was, he saw now, an even bigger challenge than he thought. How much did his uncle know? Had that brute really recognised him, and were they hunting for him throughout the city? He had been foolish to reveal his identity here.

What good could it possibly do him? It would take very little for word to get back to his uncle – a tale in a tavern, a casual mention to a friend. He was angry at the pride that tempted him to take an unnecessary risk, and silently swore that he wouldn't be so quick to reveal himself in future, but he was glad he had chosen Matt Brady's yard to hide himself in. For every evil he encountered there seemed to be an answering good. If only things could continue like that, he might be safe.

Matt Brady gave him some bread and a coin, and again told him to be careful. James thanked him, took his leave, and made his way cautiously to the top of the lane until he emerged into the bright light of Fleet Street. He had completed a large circle, and was now just around the corner from the front gate of Trinity College. He hurried in the opposite direction, scanning the streets for anyone who might be observing him, whether sheriff's men or his uncle's thugs. He hurried until he gained Essex Street and spied Harry at his station near the Custom House. Only then did he breathe easily again.

TWELVE

The Darcy Gang

'I t could be worse,' Harry said as they leaned against the wall of a shop in the piazzas. 'He could have caught you.'

They chewed their bread silently.

'You'll have to lie low for a while,' he continued thoughtfully.

'What else have I been doing?' James said as he stared at the pavement. 'I've been lying low ever since I left my father's house. But where can I go now?'

Harry had no answer for that. His own life was hard, and he had no shelter to offer James. In this city, those who had position could do as they wished; the rest had to spend their days in labour or take to the ways of vagabonding or crime. There were no inbetween places, and the problem for James was that he didn't belong to any class. His father had thrown him out of his house, but also out of the world he was born into. And now here he was, with no money, no trade, no foothold in the city. And the city didn't take kindly to that. You had to be someone, you had to stay in the place it gave you.

'I'll keep my ears open, in case anything turns up. Maybe I'll hear of a position somewhere.'

'As what, though?' James wondered. 'As stray, as dispossessed heir ... or maybe I should go for a chimney sweep.'

'No, you're too big for that,' Harry laughed. 'You'd just get stuck up a chimney.' James's friend thought for a minute. 'Where will you sleep?' he asked.

'Phoenix Park,' James said. He hadn't thought about it until Harry asked, but the park seemed like the obvious refuge now. He knew his way around it and he would be able to find somewhere to rest.

'There is one thing I can do for you,' Harry said.

'What?'

'Meet me here in an hour or so,' Harry said. 'I've some more boots to shine, and then I'll see what I can get.'

After he had left Harry, James whiled away some time in the bookshop at the sign of the Bible, and then he hung about in a corner of Custom House Quay, watching the boats land and the men unload their cargos, or simply staring down at the dark river. He wasn't sure how much time had gone by before Harry tapped him on the shoulder.

'Don't fall in,' his friend said with a grin.

Harry was carrying a closely wrapped bundle. 'It's nothing much,' he said. 'A blanket, a cap to keep the cold off, a bit of bread and cheese.'

James looked at Harry with emotion; he hardly knew what to say. He knew Harry had very little, and these gifts represented a fortune. James touched Harry's shoulder. 'Thanks, old friend,' he said. 'One day I'll repay you, you'll see.'

Harry smiled. 'Don't you worry about repaying me, you just worry about yourself.'

James took the little bundle and took his leave of his friend. Then he crossed the river and made his way westward until he reached the Phoenix Park. A little way in he came to the thickly wooded area he had stayed in before. At this hour in the afternoon the woods were quiet except for birdsong and the rustlings of small animals in the undergrowth. He walked a good way further in, until eventually he came to a small and, as far as James could see, unoccupied clearing. He began gathering branches and brushwood to elevate himself a little from the ground. He knew from his previous stay in these woods how quickly the earth sucked out the body's heat. When he had made a rough mattress, he unrolled his blanket. He broke off a piece of the cheese and ate some bread. Harry had even included a wine bottle with a little milk in it, with which he washed down his meal.

By now it was dark, and James wrapped the blanket around him as tightly as he could and lay down. It took him some time to adjust his senses to the noises of the woods, and he kept leaping up every time he heard a twig snapping or an unfamiliar rustling in the trees. Eventually, tiredness overcame his fears and he drifted into sleep.

Even though his sleep was light, he heard nothing. He

dreamed that the clearing was filled with sudden noise and that he was swept up from his makeshift bed by large and unfriendly arms which pressed him against a tree trunk while several blades hovered within inches of his throat.

'And who might you be?' a dream voice demanded harshly.

'Run away from the law, have you?' another shouted.

'Or come to spy on us and report us,' the first dream voice said.

'And we know what happens to spies, don't we lads?'

There was a cacophony of voices, all shouting together, vying with each other. James stared out of his sleep at the dream figures. They looked terrifying in the moonlight, like demons, wild-eyed and raucous and spoiling for a fight. As the noise went on and James tried to answer their queries as civilly as he could, explaining where he had come from and how he had got there, it began to dawn on him that this was no dream, and these were no dream-demons. They were real men with real voices and real daggers and he was in real danger from which there was no waking up. He tried blinking, just in case, but each time he opened his eyes the men were still there.

'I think we should hang him,' one was saying now. He couldn't have been any older than James, a skinny, half-nourished boy with big eyes and a baby face.

'Not a bad idea, Kitty, not a bad idea, if we had a bit of rope, but we'll have to wait until tomorrow to steal some.'

'We could just knife him. We have our hangers,' the one they called Kitty offered helpfully. 'Lovely blood,' he added with a leer. He drew close to James and touched his neck with the point of his short sword.

'Put your hanger away,' the first one barked. 'I think we've had enough excitement for one night. Help Kelly and Hare to put the stuff in the hide.'

James saw the two men and the boy make off into the darkness with a large sack.

The man who seemed to be the leader turned to James. 'The name is Jack Darcy.' He waited for this revelation to take its effect on James.

James obliged him by gasping. 'The highwayman?'

Darcy smiled, gratified. 'The very same. Best there ever was, highwayman, footpad, and … murderer when I have to be.' He looked hard at James, studying the lad.

He doesn't look much like a murderer, James was thinking. Or even a highwayman. His face was sinister up close in the weak moonlight, but it was fine featured and handsome, and his clothes were respectable, even foppish, with a good coat and fine boots, so far as James could judge by the light.

'So you worked in the college, did you? A boy of education. Let's hear you speak,' Darcy commanded. 'Say something for me!'

'What do you want me to say?'

'Anything you want. A rhyme or a recimitation, anything that shows us the cut of your voice.'

James flailed around in his mind, in search of something he might say. He remembered some lines McAllister was fond of reciting. James closed his eyes and let the words find their way out into the cold night air, shivering a little as he spoke.

When I consider every thing that grows
Holds in perfection but a little moment,
That this huge stage presenteth nought but shows
Whereon the stars in secret influence comment …

'I can't remember the rest,' James said.

'Oh that will do nicely,' Darcy said.

The others, who had re-emerged from the darkness, added shouts of mock appreciation and grandiose applause.

'Quiet, can't you,' Darcy said. 'What we have here is an employable asset.'

'A wha'?' said Kitty.

'Every business has to put its best foot forward,' Darcy said. 'To introduce itself to the public, if you get my meaning. And speaking of introductions, I'm nearly forgetting my manners. James, what did you say your second name was?'

'Brown,' James said. He was going to take no chances with his name here.

Darcy gave him his long stare again, as if he thought James Brown was a likely story indeed. But he let it pass.

'James Brown,' he placed sly emphasis on the surname. 'Meet Tom Kitt, known as Kitty, assistant to the company; Mr Joseph Hare, footpad, assistant highwayman; Mr Jonah Kelly, footpad, associate highwayman, swordsman first class.'

Kitty, Hare and Kelly all bowed elaborately, sweeping their hats through the air. James didn't like the look of any of the three. Kitty, he guessed, would slit his throat in the middle of the night with a squeal of pleasure and then think no more about it. Kelly and Hare looked exactly like what they were – common criminals with scaffold faces, pocked and unwashed.

'And now that you have found us,' Darcy continued, 'or rather, now that we have found you, you'll have to join us. Then we won't be obliged to kill you.'

James noted the look of disappointment on Kitty's face.

'How do you mean exactly, join you?' James asked, though he felt the foolishness of the question even as he asked it.

'We'll have to train you in, of course,' Darcy said, ignoring the question. 'Can't have a day's work spoiled by ignorance. You can help us with a bit of footpadding first, and then we'll see what else you're good for.'

James wanted to protest that he was no thief, but now did not seem to be the time to make his protest. He felt a wave of tiredness hit him like a blow and it was with great relief that he heard Darcy announce that they might as well get some sleep now. He would see what tomorrow brought before deciding anything. Who knows, he thought, as he fell down onto his bedding again and wrapped Harry's blanket around him, maybe this will all prove to have been a dream, and when I wake up there will be no one here.

• • • • •

THIRTEEN

In Red Molly's

Tomorrow did come but it brought no relief. When James opened his eyes, he was met with the sight of Jack Darcy's boots, inches from his face; the others sprawled nearby on rough beds of coats and branches. The sun was just starting to filter through the trees and the air was damp and cold. James shivered and eased himself up as quietly as he could. If he ran now, he might make it back to the city before any of the gang had woken up. But just as the thought occurred to him, he became aware of Darcy's half-opened eyes regarding him coolly.

'Thinking of bolting, James Brown?' he inquired softly, a hint of a smile on his lips.

'No,' James lied. 'Of course not. I've slept enough, that's all.'

'I'm glad to hear it. This is the first day of your new life. And the first order of business is the highwayman's breakfast, so why don't you gather some kindling and get a fire going.

And remember,' he said, as James nodded and turned to do his bidding, 'I have a dog's ears; I can hear a leaf rustle or a twig snap underfoot at fifty paces.'

James didn't doubt it, and set himself to his task without further thought of escape. When he came back, Kelly, Hare and Kitty were all up, shuffling around the clearing. Kitty was soon dispatched to fetch supplies from the hide and returned with a small sack from which he drew a little bacon, some pungent smoked herring and coffee. He also brought a cooking pot and a smaller pot with some water, which Darcy now used to brew some coffee.

'The finest thieves' coffee house in Dublin,' the highwayman announced. 'Kelly, work your wonders with the bacon and let's start the day as we mean to continue.'

In spite of his fears, James ate heartily. No matter what trouble he was in, his appetite rarely deserted him, and it sometimes seemed to him that the graver the circumstances, the hungrier he got. Once the meal was done and the plates and pots secreted back in their hiding place, Darcy was all action, instructing Hare and Kelly to take the wigs and coats and other valuables from last night's robbery to a tavern in the city, where they would all meet up later. He would keep the cash and the more precious pieces, and later that night, they would share out all the spoils.

'And now we will begin your education,' he turned to James when the others had left. 'Kitty, your hanger.'

Kitty reluctantly parted with his blade. James grabbed the handle.

'Hold it, feel its weight, swing it around, let it become part of you.'

James did as he was told, twirling the hanger round like a baton, slashing at the air. Kitty sniggered at his efforts.

Darcy made a sudden lunge for James. 'Have at you, boy!'

James stumbled and almost fell, then held his sword at arm's length. With a swift flick, Darcy knocked the blade from his hand and as James reached down for it, he brought the tip of his blade to James's throat.

'Give it to him, Jack,' urged Kitty.

'You were a dead man there,' Darcy said. 'Look, you need to parry, like this.' He brought his hanger up and held it firmly in front of him. 'Push forward with the end nearest the hilt, come on now, push.'

James leant forward and pushed with as much force as he could.

'Downward, downward,' shouted Darcy. 'Good. Alright, *en garde*, come on Brown, don't you know what *en garde* means? It's French for "watch yourself, or someone will have your guts for garters". Blade up, ready, don't turn your whole body towards me, side on, that's better, left arm up behind you. Alright, now I want you to lunge at me, like so.'

Darcy stood with his left arm hooked behind his head and extended his blade, then, faster than James could perceive, his right leg pounced and the blade was again at James's throat.

'Fight with your eyes, Brown. Your blade and your eye must be one, or you won't last.'

James practised on his own, determined to make himself

into a swordsman. After all, his father had been one, and he was sure his uncle was handy with a blade too. He had every reason to master this art. As he parried and lunged, he imagined he was locked in deathly combat with the usurping Lord Dunmain. *En garde*, parry, lunge; the blade cut straight through his coat and entered his black heart. James felt he was at one with his sword now, jigging and pouncing and swerving in the clearing as Kitty shook his head.

'Mad eejit.'

Darcy had disappeared into the trees, and came back with a small satchel.

'Time to go,' he said abruptly. 'Stay a little behind me and keep your eyes open.'

They walked through the woods and out of the park, crossing the river and climbing the hilly street that led up from it. The light was fading and the streets and river looked as if the life had been sucked from them. A thick cloud of smoke billowed over the city, and the wind scattered the noxious smells from the nearby dump all around the district so that James was close to retching until his nose and stomach acclimatised themselves.

About halfway up the street, Darcy paused and briefly indicated to the right, where a gap between the houses led into the dump. He himself passed by the gap and knocked on the door of the next house. Kitty and James slipped into the gap and walked a little way down a rough path. James shielded his nose with his palm.

'How long do you think he'll be?' he asked Kitty. The air

was cold, and he shivered.

Kitty shrugged. 'Depends who he meets in there. Could be an hour, could be three hours.'

Again James thought of escape. It would probably be easy enough to shake off Kitty in the gloom of the dump. He felt a hesitation in himself at the thought. It wasn't fear so much as a lack of attractive choices. He had no idea where he would run to.

Almost as if he was reading his mind, Kitty touched the hilt of his hanger. 'No ideas, fancy boy, or I'll lop your head clean off.'

You can try, James thought, and see how far you get. All the same, he was grateful to Kitty for his threat; it gave him another reason for inaction.

Suddenly there was a great commotion, which seemed to be coming from the street at the top of the hill. Shouts, a great many voices raised, and what sounded like a pistol shot.

'Entertainment,' grinned Kitty. 'Let's see what the cause is. If he hasn't come out now, he'll be there a lot longer. And remember ...' He touched the hilt of his hanger again.

One day, James thought, he and Kitty would come to blows, or worse, but for now he would have to endure him.

They climbed up to Thomas Street. There, by the Glib Market, stood the infamous Black Cart, surrounded by a mob. The cart was gathering beggars for the workhouse. Whoever had just been collected was protesting loudly from inside the cart, and the mob roared its disapproval of the cart wardens and pelted them with rotten vegetables and eggs from the market. Men, women and children joined the affray, and some students took advantage of the occasion to hurl stones at the wardens, egging each other on. The cart was now unable to move and the wardens were letting off their pistols to warn the crowd. This only provoked the mob further and they moved closer to the cart, as if they might crush it. Now the wardens were aiming their pieces directly at the crowd.

'Keep back!' they shouted. 'Or we'll open fire!' It was clear the situation would turn ugly. James wished they hadn't left the safety of the dump, but Kitty was wide-eyed with blissful excitement. Suddenly there was a scream and a young woman fell forward onto the cobbles. Her companions leant down and turned her around, but the shot had caught her on the temple and her body was lifeless.

'They've killed her!' the cry went up, and it ran through the crowd like a storm, shaking it up, hurling waves of fury at the cart and its protectors. More shots rang out and more fell wounded onto the street, but the crowd had the cart at its mercy now. Angry limbs tore the vehicle apart and liberated its prisoners: ragged men with clothes askew who stood like kings in the middle of the tumult, saluting their saviours with a bow. At least one warden that James could see lay dead on the street, the wheels of the cart on top of his chest. Another was bent double under a pummelling rain of kicks.

Kitty looked like he wanted to join in the kicking, but he was aware that it was getting late, and his fear of Darcy conquered his lust for blood, so he pulled James away from the scene of destruction in the Liberties and back down to the dump, where they resumed their positions.

James was dizzy with all he'd seen, and he felt as if someone had wrapped a strange new cloak of blackness around him that he hadn't the strength to cast off.

After they had endured another shivering vigil, Darcy reappeared, grinning. 'Enjoying the country air, are we, young Brown?'

James had to keep reminding himself of his newly acquired name. If he responded too late, he would be immediately caught by Darcy's sharp eye. He was sure Darcy only half-believed him in any case.

'What was that racket above?' Darcy wanted to know.

'The Black Cart,' Kitty said without further elaboration.

'And didn't you want a lift to your old house then?' Darcy asked him, but received in return just a silent scowl.

Darcy took his position at the head of the group again and they threaded their way across the labyrinth of the dump before finally emerging in a rancid laneway. They followed this into another lane, at the end of which was a tavern with no sign. Darcy banged on the door and they were admitted by a big, red-faced and red-haired woman, whose eyes pounced on James the instant they registered him.

'Who's this?' she asked Darcy. 'He doesn't look like any of yours. What's your name, boy?'

'James Brown, ma'am,' James answered.

Her eyes widened. 'Listen to you!' she shrieked. 'Quite the little gentleman. What fine house did you tumble out of?'

James felt himself flush, but Darcy pulled him away from the woman's curiosity into the interior of the tavern. The place was loud and closely packed, every table occupied and well supplied with beer, gin, wine and whiskey as well as plates of steaming food: roast mutton, potatoes, cockles, oysters, and great plates of pork and beef. The keen smells made James weak; he would endure anything now as long as he could fill his belly. At one of the tables he saw Kelly and Hare crouched intently over plates of mutton, a bottle of gin on the table between them.

Darcy hailed them. 'What manners are these, starting without us?'

Kelly and Hare squinted in their direction and grunted.

The red-haired woman bustled over to the table. 'What lovelies have you got for me?' she asked Darcy.

Darcy put his hand in his coat pocket and drew out a fine lace handkerchief.

She wrinkled her nose. 'Only a handkerchief? I have a chest full of handkerchiefs. You'll need to do better than that.'

As she inspected the handkerchief, her fingers felt something hard wrapped in the linen, and her eyebrows arched in anticipation. Greedily she opened out the handkerchief and saw a glittering brooch of amethyst and garnet. She cooed with pleasure at the sight and lifted the brooch to her eyes for closer examination. The other diners joined in the examination, some leaving their food to come and inspect the piece. There were shouts of appreciation, and glasses raised in toasts to Darcy.

'You'll have to marry Red Molly now,' someone shouted,

and the others joined in a raucous chorus.

Darcy laughed. 'Now Molly,' he said, 'our debts are discharged and our bellies can be filled for a long while yet.'

'You're an honest man, Jack Darcy,' Molly said. 'If only some others were as good,' she added, looking round the room and letting her eyes linger on some of the diners, who shifted in their seats and buried their heads in their food.

The rest of the evening saw a succession of dishes ferried to their table, and James ate and drank as if it were his last meal. He hardly remembered what happened next, but it seems that some point in the night the whole gang climbed the stairs and fell into one of the lodging rooms. As they struggled with their boots, an old servant put his head around the door.

'Clean sheets is three shillings, dirty ones are a shilling,' he announced. 'Which is it to be?'

Darcy threw one of his boots in his direction. 'It's on the account!' he roared. 'And the Darcy Gang would like the best sheets in the house, if you have to strip them off Molly's bed itself!'

• • • • •

FOURTEEN

A Robbery Planned

A weak light bled into the upper room through the grime of the one narrow window. The place was cramped, and most of it was occupied by the bed, on which lay the crumpled figures of Darcy, Kelly and Hare. Darcy lay on the inside with his face to the wall; Kelly and Hare lay twitching beside him, Kelly's arm across Hare's face, half smothering him; and Kitty was on the floor beside the bed, from which he had been ejected with a curse in the middle of the night. For the second morning in a row, James found himself looking at the sleeping gang. He watched from the floor near the window, where he'd crept from his own tiny portion of bed as soon as he woke up. Boots lay everywhere, like a fallen army, breathing their foul stink into the room. On a chair lay a mound of topcoats; otherwise everyone was fully clothed. It had been a long time since the small grate had seen a fire, and the room felt like an icy rain had crept in during the night. But it was inside, at least, James thought, remembering the cold of the night in the park.

He sat listening to the snores and grunts and thinking how harmless they seemed without their coats and boots, or their hangers, which also lay scattered on the floor. If the law were to raid the room at this moment, there would be no escape – they would all be led like babies to the cart, rubbing the sleep from their eyes. He saw how thin and frail Kitty appeared without his weapons and his bravado, looking just like what he was, a boy escaped from the workhouse. Maybe that was why he'd taken such pleasure in the destruction of the Black Cart.

It wasn't long before the gang shifted itself awake, like one groaning monster with a sore head and a bad temper. After a snatched breakfast, Darcy ordered everyone to make their way to the park separately, where the next action would be planned. Since he had some time before the meeting, James thought of slipping down along the quays to see Harry and let him know he was alright, but something prevented him. He realised that he didn't want Harry to know what company he had fallen into; he even felt his face redden at the thought. He knew his life had entered a shameful phase, but he knew equally that he was stuck to it for now.

He idled along the quays, staring at the ships, before crossing to the northern side and walking purposefully in the direction of the park. His route took him past the Bluecoat School and as he looked at the windows he could hear the low murmuring of the boys repeating their lessons. He felt a pang of envy, wishing himself off these street and onto the benches of the school in a blue tunic and cap. He looked with distaste at the faded and increasingly ragged glory of his own coat. His descent down the city's social ladder was all too evident.

When he got back to the hide the gang was sitting around inspecting their weapons. On the grass were spread out pistols, three short wooden clubs and a canvas tube which, when James examined it, turned out to filled with lead shot. Kelly grinned as James considered the tube.

'A good belt of that will keep a man quiet,' he said.

'Or woman, if needs be,' Kitty added.

'Are we doing pockets tonight?' Hare asked. He picked up one of the clubs and struck the air a couple of vicious blows before putting it in his coat.

Kelly licked his lips; the prospect obviously appealed to him too.

'What does it mean, doing pockets?' James asked. He knew it would have better for him to hold his tongue, but his curiosity got the better of him.

Darcy didn't seem so eager to answer.

'It's easy work,' Kitty said. 'Just got to find the right doxy.'

'And follow her somewhere nice and quiet,' Kelly added. 'The one holds her, and the other cuts out her pocket.'

James tried to hide his disgust, but his face must have betrayed him.

'Have we offended your feelings, poor thing?' Kelly taunted.

'Poor thing! Poor thing!' Kitty repeated.

'The boy's right,' Darcy suddenly interjected. His voice was edged with anger. 'Haven't you done enough of that? There's no honour in it, and no danger.'

'What do we want with honour?' Kelly asked. 'Where's the profit in that?'

Darcy continued to voice his feelings. 'I rode between my father's legs in the cart they hanged him from and I expect to die at the end of a rope and do you know what, I don't want to die for pocket snatching or frightening the life out of women.'

'It's all the same to me,' Hare snarled, 'I'm not fussy what they hang me for.'

Kitty put his hand around his own throat and mimed the action of a noose, his eyes bulging and his tongue hanging out.

Darcy punched him in the stomach, leaving him winded and gasping. He turned to Kelly and Hare. 'That's the difference between us,' Darcy said. 'I am fussy. It's not the dying I mind, but I'm damned if I won't die like a man for a man's crime.'

All this talk of dying threw a pall of gloom over the gang and they sat silently on the grass. Nobody wanted to tackle Darcy.

But if they weren't going be doing pockets, then what would they be doing? James wondered.

His question was soon answered. 'If it's robbing you want, we'll try the Green,' Darcy said quietly. 'It's a while since we were there, and the pickings are good.'

This didn't sound like much of an improvement on robbing

women to James. What part would he be expected to play?

Darcy seemed to read his mind. 'And we can blood the boy,' he said.

The others nodded their enthusiastic agreement.

'What does that mean?' James asked.

'What do you think it means?' Darcy snapped, anger edging his voice again. 'Do you think we keep you for a pet? You'll earn your keep, you'll do what you're told tonight, or you'll feel the cudgel on the back of your head.'

James said nothing, but sat scrutinising his muck-caked shoes.

They agreed to meet in the Quaker graveyard near Stephen's Green after dark that night. Kelly, Hare and Kitty sloped off then with a look of shifty sullenness about them, so that James didn't doubt that they had some side business of their own, and that some of it would certainly involve waylaying some unfortunate woman and robbing her pocket.

'Alright, boy, you and I will make a team,' Darcy said. 'Stay here and wait. I have some things to do. Meet me by Ormond Bridge around nine o'clock.'

He threw James a loaf and a thick slice of ham, much as an owner might throw his dog some scraps, James thought, but he ate nonetheless. Crime was hungry work, he was finding.

FIFTEEN

The Blooding of James

James waited a little way from the lantern on the bridge. He was learning, day by day, to melt into the shadows, to disappear into the folds of the city. Dublin at night in this district was a sinister place, filled with the songs and complaints of vagabonds, the hard laughter of shapes clustered in doorways, and the dark fury of coaches hurtling down the quays as fast as the coachman could drive the horses, in case anyone thought to stop them. It was a place where, at any moment, your life might be threatened or terminated with a few quick knife thrusts. How many grim-faced Kellys and Hares were lurking here now, waiting for their victims?

James froze as he felt a sudden hand on his shoulder, but it was only Darcy, who seemed to materialise out of nowhere like a spectre. He felt James start.

'Is James Brown frightened of his own shadow?' Darcy laughed. He led the way across the bridge, entered a tavern at the sign of the Bear, and called for gin. He drank swiftly and urged James to do the same.

'We'll need it this night,' he said. 'Courage, guile and warmth, all in a single bottle. It's a miracle, don't you find?'

James struggled with the drink, wishing he could spit it out.

Darcy enjoyed his clear discomfort. 'Can't drink either, James Brown? One of these days, if you live much longer, we'll find something you can do.'

They went out onto the street, climbed up the hill under the gaunt frowning cathedral and made their way through the narrow streets around the castle until they arrived at the Quaker graveyard. James shivered as they entered. He thought of the graveyard where Miss Deakin had brought him the day he left his father's house for the last time. That had been the beginning of his misfortune, and he didn't expect much good could come from this encounter. They stood behind some trees at the back and watched the entrance. They didn't have to wait long before they heard low voices and a soft whistle. Darcy whistled back and they could soon make out the shapes of Kelly, Hare and Kitty. Kelly and Hare didn't look too secure on their feet, James noticed, and as they approached he could smell enough drink on their breath to wake half the poor Quakers from their rest. Only Kitty was light on his feet, tense and ready for action.

'What's the plan?' he asked Darcy as soon as they reached the cover of the trees.

'To die rich,' Darcy said evenly. 'Tonight's lodgement will be provided by some stuffed buck who is about to stray from

The Beaux Walk, with a little help from our young and good-looking friend here.' He indicated James with a mock bow.

The Beaux Walk was one of the sides of Stephen's Green. James had often strolled there with his father in the days before he met Miss Deakin. That was when his father still wanted to be seen with a son.

Darcy then despatched the three Uglies, as James thought of Kelly, Hare and Kitty, to conceal themselves behind the pavilion in the centre of the green. A little later, he and James set out for the Walk. They kept out of sight of the avenue, working their way from tree to tree. The hour was late and it was dark, and surely no sensible person would be so foolish as to venture abroad on the walk now? But Darcy was cunning, and it seemed he knew his fellow man better than James; they weren't long in the Green before they saw a man coming towards them from the other end. Almost as if Darcy had invented him, he was portly and his walk was unsteady. He waved his cane in the air for no reason James could see, for he couldn't have seen them, and he was singing softly to himself.

'This is it,' Darcy whispered fiercely to James. 'We'll have him for supper, and maybe for breakfast and dinner too. Who knows what he might have with him? Now, James Brown, this is where you earn your onions. I want you to approach the gentleman in great distress, and tell him some boys have taken your unfortunate father and are even now robbing him just a little way from this very path. Mind you look convincing. Have you ever been to the theatre in Smock Alley?'

James had once, but he doubted if the acting he had seen there would be much use to him here.

'You must look pitiful, with weeping and wailing as if your poor little life depended on it. If he has any honour, he'll run to your aid. Go to it now, quickly.'

Darcy disappeared into the darkness and James stood hesitating a few yards from the path. All his instincts cried out to him to run the other way, to put as much distance as he could between himself and the clutches of the gang. But things had gone too far for that now. He had allowed himself to fall in with these men and he was afraid to go back. In any case, they would find him, and he shuddered to think what they would do to him when they did. He heard Darcy hissing fiercely from the shadows behind him, 'Get going, wretch!' Without thinking any more about it, James ran into the path towards the approaching gentleman. He waved his arms in the air and heard a voice that must have been his shout out in distress.

'Sir, please help me, won't you please help me, please sir!'

The portly man stopped his singing and looked up in fright. James ran to him.

'What is it? What's the matter, boy?' The man fixed his startled attention on James.

'Please, sir, it's my father!' James nearly choked on the words but he somehow got them out. 'They've got him, over there near the pavilion.'

'Who? Who has him?'

'Footpads, sir, they're robbing him even now.' James couldn't help noticing the fine silk waistcoat the man was wearing, and the gold chain that hung from one of its pockets. He wanted to warn him, but nothing came out.

The man looked at him dubiously. Maybe he won't believe me, James thought, maybe he'll simply walk away. They would never believe I didn't warn him, came the disturbing thought.

'Won't you help, sir?' he asked. 'They're bound to run away when they see you.'

This statement seemed to be decisive. He could see the man puff himself up proudly and though he carried no weapon his manner changed. 'Take me to them,' he commanded.

James did as he was bidden, and led him from the path into the heart of the park. As they neared the pavilion, James could see Darcy on the ground. Kelly held his arms fast while Hare grabbed his legs. Kitty appeared to be rifling his pockets.

'Help!' Darcy shouted piteously as he spied James and the man.

'Leave him be, you scoundrels!' the would-be rescuer shouted. 'Or I'll get the sheriff's men on you!'

The playacting stopped abruptly, and the 'victim' suddenly sprang to his feet, a cruel smile on his lips. 'Oh I don't think so,' he announced. 'I don't think you'll be getting anything for a while.'

'What?' said the man, looking amazed from one to the other. He seemed genuinely puzzled, as if he could not comprehend the situation.

Kelly ran to him and, without a word, cracked him over the head with his cudgel filled with shot. The man fell in a heap to the ground.

James stood staring in shock. 'There was no need for that,' he said.

Kelly lifted his cudgel again and made for James. 'Why, you damned whelp, I'll do you too!'

'We're wasting time,' Darcy barked. 'Get to work, and let's get out of here.'

They proceeded to strip the man of his coat and waistcoat. Darcy held his pocket watch aloft. 'Didn't I tell you? I knew he'd be a good one. Get the wig, Kitty.'

Kitty pulled the wig from the man's head. Blood dripped from it onto the man's face. He looked old. A few tangled strands of grey hair pressed on a wrinkled head. Kelly and Hare swept shoes and breeches off with a practised economy, while Kitty busied himself pulling a ring from his right index finger. When they had got all they wanted, Hare pulled out a knife and bent over the man, who was now coming to with loud groans.

'Will I finish him?' He looked up eagerly at Darcy, the knife trembling in his hand as if it couldn't wait to do its work. He let the blade touch the skin of his victim's neck.

James looked over at Darcy and caught his eye.

'No,' Darcy said, 'we don't want to upset Master Brown.'

Hare glared at James and pointed the tip of his blade in his direction. The prospect of a night without blood seemed to disgust him. Suddenly the knife was out of his hand and it landed within an inch of James's boot, embedded deep in the grass.

Darcy looked at the man impatiently. 'Don't forget it was

the boy who brought us this creature.' He indicated the groaning and nearly naked form on the ground. 'We all have our parts to play. He's one of us now.'

This pronouncement didn't appease Hare much. He retrieved his knife, put it away, and as they were slipping away into the night, he stepped back and kicked the helpless man several times in the head and body until the groans stopped.

• • • •

SIXTEEN

'One of us'

'*He's one of us now.*' The words continued to turn over in James's head. And Darcy had repeated it throughout that night as they sat in Red Molly's with their plates of beef and mutton, and their tankards of beer and jugs of the best claret. It seemed a large reward for a mean crime, but as James learned over the following weeks, every robbery, no matter how small the pickings, was celebrated in grand style in Red Molly's. Sometimes the crime didn't even pay for its celebration, and Darcy had to sign the chit at the end, promising to pay in the future.

'You know me, Molly,' he'd say, raising his glass to her. 'Jack Darcy always pays his way.'

It seemed to be that way with many of Red Molly's customers, so that every meal, every carousing night, every rental of her unclean sheets and flea-bitten beds provided another reason to rob. Even fleas had to be earned. This was the unending circle that defined their lives.

He's one of us now. What did that mean? Where was James Lovett, Lord Dunmain as he should be? What has he to do with James Brown, member of the Darcy gang, assistant footpad, deceiver of the innocent? He remembered how shocked he had been when Kelly had kicked the man in Stephen's Green, at the needlessness of it. He'd quickly sensed that for Hare, Kelly and Kitty, a large part of their excitement came less from the robbing than from the chance to kick, punch, cudgel or stab.

One night they went to Kilmainham where they waylaid a man in the field near the soldiers' hospital. Kelly and Hare began beating him severely even though the man offered no provocation. Kitty, meanwhile, thrust his pocket knife at the man's head and shouted, 'You dog, do you resent it?' The highwayman then cut then man so deeply James could see his skull under the flaps of skin.

'You don't need to do that,' James said. 'You have his money, isn't that enough?'

Kitty turned on him, snarling, his bloody knife an inch from James's throat.

'Are you going to tell me what to do? You isn't my nurse-maid, posh boy. I could slit you now.'

'Enough squabbling, children,' Darcy said. 'I'll be Daddy and Daddy says it's time to go home.'

'At least see if he's alright,' James said. 'He could bleed to death.'

'No time for that,' Darcy said.

All that for a wig, a coat and some little money. James couldn't get the bleeding man out of his mind as the gang made its way back to Red Molly's to toast their bravery and wash the blood from the wig and coat. The kitchen was often the first stop for the clients of the tavern, where they could be found scrubbing and scraping breeches, coats, wigs and boots, on the same table where the food was being prepared.

Lately, though, Darcy had grown weary of these small raids. It was not a question of blood or excitement for him, but of business, and he had little interest in coats, wigs or small change.

The low point for Darcy came on a dark day coming into winter when the gang had, on a whim, decided they needed new wigs. Since money was short, they went to the wigmaker's shop at the sign of the Peruke in Meath Street and waited for the hair-picker to come selling his wares. Kelly then stepped out of the shadows, grabbed the bundle of hair and sent the man on his way with a kick. Then they went in and presented the hair to the wigmaker, and asked for new wigs for all.

'That's not enough,' the wigmaker said, looking at the bundle of hair. 'That might buy you half a wig. For the rest, I'll need coin of the realm.'

Hare whipped out his hanger. 'Will this do?' he asked.

Darcy raised his hand apologetically. 'Forgive my friend,' he said smoothly. 'He is somewhat rash.'

The wigmaker eyed them closely. 'Very well,' he said at last. 'We understand that currency too.'

He disappeared into his workshop and, a little later, emerged with new wigs for Darcy, Hare, Kelly and Kitty. They preened in front of the mirrors and left well-satisfied. The gang went to a gin shop and when they came out some hours later a heavy shower greeted them, and by the time it had finished the wigs were a tangled mess – whatever the wigmaker had used, it was not human hair; the wigs lay like drowned rats on their heads. James tried hard not to smile. The men took them off in disgust.

'We should go back and slit that wigmaker's throat,' Hare said.

'We'll make him swallow the rat-hair he gave us,' Kelly added.

'It serves us right,' said Darcy. 'If you act like a pile of by-blows and dunghills, a shower of lobcocks and eejits, then you get what you deserve. What we need to do is show this damn town what we're made of, and the sooner the better.'

They stood in the rain and swore an oath to serious crime, and, from that day on, they'd kept their word. Darcy was like a man possessed as he coordinated their plans and not a day went by when they weren't engaged in some action. Apart from robbing on the streets, they stripped lead from vacant houses and began to try their hand at housebreaking.

James dreaded these expeditions. As the smallest in the gang, he was the first to enter the houses once Kelly and Hare had levered the window frame up or broken the panes and smashed in the bars between to make an opening just big enough for James to be pushed through. His first job was to open the rear door to let the others in, but those first moments alone in the house were terrifying. It was one thing to rob in the street; it was a terrible thing, but it happened in the open city and the gang could melt back into the streets within a moment of their actions, but if you were caught in a house there was no escape.

As James tiptoed through the drawing room of some fine house in the district where he himself had lived not so long ago, his heart beat violently.

In one particular house the gang decided that he should go in alone. James thought it strange at the time, though, afterwards, the reason was all too clear. Although it was daylight outside, the house was in darkness, with all the heavy drapes closed as if the place had been vacated. The only light was that streaming in from the fanlight over the front door; apart from the hall, the rooms were quite dark. James entered the drawing-room and, once his eyes had accustomed themselves to the gloom, he began to move around quietly, looking for goods to put in the sack he had brought with him. He found a pair of candlesticks and a silver tureen on a table.

Then he spotted what looked like a silver tankard on the mantelpiece and crept over for a closer look. The mantelpiece was high and he had to strain to reach it, but instead of grasping it securely he fumbled and the piece fell to the floor. The thud of the tankard on the floorboards was accompanied by another noise; a human noise, James realised to his horror, and he suddenly became aware of a human shape in the great wingback chair to the side of the fireplace.

'Who is it?' the voice shouted, and the shape leapt up from the chair. 'Who is in here?'

James dived under the table and then crawled to the window, where he concealed himself behind a thick drape. He could hear the man pacing around the room.

'What blackguard are you? Come out wherever you are, or I'll run you through.'

James didn't dare move, but he realised that his spot wasn't very secure since the man was bound to open the drapes to let in some light. Yet strangely the man didn't approach the window and seemed content to thrash around the dark room. James remained utterly still until he couldn't hear any more noise. The man must have left the room to search the rest of the house. Very slowly, James stepped outside the drape and stood still. The coast seemed to be clear.

He was about to edge toward the door when he suddenly saw two piercing eyes dead ahead of him, blazing like a fiend's with no body that he could see. James froze with fright and it felt like his own body was melting. But he forced his terror-stricken mind to think. The next thing he became aware of was a flash of steel as a sword lunged. James dropped to his knees and sprang out of the way, feeling the breath of the blade on his cheek. Then he raced for the door and managed to get out into the shocking glare of the hall, expecting the blade at any second to catch up with him. Yet no one came into the hall, and no one pursued James down the stairs to the basement or out through the broken window he had entered by. James hit the ground outside and immediately jumped up. As he raced around the corner he crashed into the bulk of a man. He cried out, but his screams were met with a laughter he recognised. It was Kelly he had run into.

'What's yer hurry, son?' Kelly wanted to know.

The others appeared from the laneway they'd been skulking in.

'I think James has met the demon,' Darcy laughed.

'What demon?' James asked. Now that he seemed to be safe, he could feel anger rising in him.

'This house is always dark,' Darcy said. 'They say the man who lives in it – if it is a man – can't bear light; that he can't see in the light. Some say he is the Devil himself.'

'The Devil wouldn't have missed me.' James said simply. He was angry because they had clearly sent him in knowing there was someone inside. He was not so much 'one of us' that they could resist toying with him when the mood took them.

* * *

And so their lives continued that winter, a constant cycle of theft and celebration, with nights spent in Red Molly's flea-bitten rooms or in other houses around the city where no one would think to look for them. How long can this go on for? James asked himself in the cold morning light as he listened to the snores of the others. The life of a thief was short and usually finished at the end of a rope or on a ship bound for slavery in the colonies. None of these thieves seemed to care much about their likely fate; indeed, it even seemed to James that, in a peculiar way, they lived for the end; they lived in full readiness for the death that, in all likelihood, would come to them. They sang songs about hangings; they went to Newgate to play cards with condemned men in their cells the night before they were executed. For a table they used the coffin which the gaolers had delivered to the cell to make the condemned man think of his fate. And they accompanied him to the gallows, cheering him along. Even when it involved someone they didn't know, they were drawn magnetically to these gruesome events.

One Saturday morning Darcy announced that they'd rest from robbery by going to the Green to see a hanging.

'It'll be a good one,' he said. 'Not often we get to see a student dangle.'

'What student?' James asked.

'The one that killed the man in Fishamble Street,' Darcy replied. 'They caught him down the country, boasting about it in his local tavern. Not much brains for a student.'

James paled. Could it be that McAllister had come back and been apprehended? But Darcy's description fitted Vandeleur better; James could easily imagine him bragging in a tavern and assuming no harm could ever come to him. He felt sick at the thought of Vandeleur, and sicker at the prospect of his awful fate. He didn't go with the gang to watch him die.

'His lordship's stomach is too delicate' had been Kitty's scornful dismissal.

But if James had no desire to see someone die at the end of a rope, he needed to know that it was in fact Vandeleur they meant. He set out to intercept the prison wagon near the castle. There he waited with a crowd of onlookers for the cart to pass on its way to the hanging tree in Stephen's Green. Much time went by without anything happening and the crowd was growing restive. Many shouted and hurled oaths. A ballad singer struck up but was shouted down by those near him.

A hawker went round with sheets of paper. 'Malefactor's confessions,' he half-sang, half-shouted. 'Fresh printed this morning.'

James noticed that many about him had missiles with them: rotten vegetables, eggs, sticks and even stones.

'Bring the bastard out!' the man beside him roared.

Eventually a rumbling could be heard in the distance and James heard a wave of jeering, faint at first, but swelling eastward until it filled every inch of Castle Street. James had never heard a noise like it; you couldn't make out any particular word. There was something savage in it. It was as if a hungry beast had entered the city and was baying for blood. James looked at the people around him and saw the beast in their faces, heard the beast in their roars.

A gang of boys pushed against him, shoving him out of the way in their hurry to get to the front. They craned their necks and raised their fists. They spat and shouted for all they were worth.

James was beginning to think he should leave when he saw Vandeleur, or what might have been Vandeleur's ghost. First came the horses with the sheriff and the men of the Watch, then the hangman and his assistants, and then the cart with the condemned man. He stood upright on the cart, leaning forward for support on his coffin. The form was the same, but James had to search hard to discern the face he once knew. Gone was the arrogant sneer, the always upturned lip. Instead, the face was white and haggard and twisted in the shape of pure fear. Vandeleur was dressed in his best finery: silk waistcoat, purple coat, fine breeches and stockings, but the clothes hung loose about his frame, as if they belonged to someone else. Around his neck was the rope, the long end of it coiled about his body.

Missiles fell all about him, and his fine clothes were already soiled by the mob's ritual fury. Vandeleur didn't look at the mob, but fixed his eyes at some distant space not in this world, as if he had managed to remove himself already from the earth he was about to leave. When an egg splattered on his cheek he made no effort to remove it but continued his staring, as if he had already taken his leave of his body.

James tried to catch his eye, thinking maybe the sight of someone he knew would be a small comfort. He had never liked Vandeleur, but he was going to a lonely and painful death, and James would have liked to offer him a token of human companionship. But what if Vandeleur recognised him and called out, 'He was there too, why do you hang him too?'

James shrank back, pulling out of the baying crowd. He leant against the wall of a shop, not trusting his legs to keep him upright. Imagine McAllister could just as easily be there! And what of him? James had helped them, after all; he had helped McAllister to leave the country: who knew what the punishment for that might be if anyone connected him with Vandeleur or McAllister? And who knew how long his current life would last before the law found him out, and he'd find himself trundling down these streets like a common criminal? He must change his life, he thought.

SEVENTEEN

A Visit to Newgate

I t can't be that hard to escape, James thought as he sat in the hide, whittling a stick with his knife. I could just walk out these woods and not come back. Avoid Red Molly's and dark alleys and try for a new life. That was where he kept getting stuck. Walking out was one thing; a new life was another, much harder thing. Where would he go? What would he do? He thought of the ships in the river. Maybe he could sneak onto one and hide in the hold until the ship was on the high seas. Then he would reveal himself and they'd let him become a sailor, and he would go ashore in strange new countries and see what life had to offer there. He had stripped the stick completely, and was climbing the mast to the crow's nest to look for land when Kitty came rushing in to the hide. For a second James thought he had spied into his head and seen his plans. He tightened his grip on his knife.

'Darcy's taken!' Kitty shouted. Kelly and Hare, who had

been slumped against a tree, shot up as if stung.

'Wha'?' they said with a single voice.

'He was drinking in the Ram when that man we attacked in Kilmainham spied him.'

'The one you cut up.' James couldn't help himself. The ship, the ocean, the exotic ports and all thought of escape had vanished.

Kitty glared at him. 'He asked for it.'

'Get on with it, we don't want your confession,' Hare snarled. 'How do you know what happened?'

'I was going there to meet him when I saw him being taken out by the sheriff's men and the cut man with him.'

Kelly looked at Kitty suspiciously. 'Strange how you happened to arrive after he was taken,' he said.

Kitty was indignant. 'There's nothing strange about it. And it was lucky I wasn't taken too — lucky for you that you have me to tell you the tale.'

'What will happen now?' James asked.

'The cut man will file charges with the magistrates,' Kelly answered. 'Then they'll prosecute Jack and if they find him guilty, he'll be sentenced to hang.'

'Then he's doomed,' James said. He wasn't sure what he felt about Jack Darcy, but he didn't relish the prospect of any man being hanged.

'Don't be so quick,' Kelly came back at him. 'Jack won't go down so easily. But we'll need to get to him quick. He won't thank us if we let him stew in Newgate. They'll already have taken what coin he had on him.'

'Who will get to him?' James often wished he wasn't so quick with his questions. This one was met with a thoughtful pause as all three looked long at him.

'He's perfect for it,' Hare said. 'No one there knows him.'

'No,' James began. 'I couldn't–'

'Oh, he's afraid, lads. Poor James is afraid of nasty Newgate,' Kitty interrupted.

'Why don't you go?' James asked.

'Do you think they'd ever let him out?' Kelly asked angrily. 'He's known all over the city for his knife-work.'

Kitty smiled with gratification.

'He'll need money for his rent and his penny pot,' Kelly continued. He seemed happy to slip into the role of leader in Darcy's absence.

James supposed all gangs must work like that, their members swapping roles interchangeably as the circumstances demanded. He couldn't imagine himself leading a gang, but then he didn't even really want to be in one.

He thought it strange that Darcy had to pay for his imprisonment but, this time, he kept his mouth shut. Then another thought occurred to him. 'Can we help him escape?'

Kelly snorted. 'This isn't some boy's adventure,' he said. He looked at James as if this question had been the height of idiocy. 'No one escapes from Newgate. It might have been possible once. The last keeper helped some lads escape for a handsome fee, but they got rid of him, and it would be more than Hawkins' job's worth to let anyone go.'

'The horrible Hawkins,' Hare added. 'Him and his harridan

wife who'd charge the fleas if they could.'

'Are we safe here?' Kitty suddenly asked. 'I mean, what if—'

Kelly broke in abruptly. 'What if what? Do you think Jack would lead them here?'

'No,' Kitty said, but he didn't sound convinced. 'What if Hawkins tortures him? They say he loves money more than anything. What if he made Jack tell where the hide was?'

'Jack wouldn't tell. He'd be too clever for him.' Kelly's voice was very definite, but he was rattled by Kitty's question, James could see.

'Maybe we should wait and see,' Hare said. 'See if anyone tries to come to the hide tonight.'

'Alright,' Kelly said at last. 'We'll wait one night and see what happens.'

They ate some bread and smoked fish and drank what small beer was left in the hide, then took turns as lookout through the night.

James tried to sleep, but it was bitterly cold and his mind was racing. He was terrified of the mission they had assigned him, and as he tossed and turned he began to wonder what might happen if he didn't stop at Newgate but fled westward through the gate and out along the great road that led into the heart of the country. Had he not said he must change his life? Why did life keep opposing his plans, putting fresh obstacles in his way at every turn? If he didn't go to the prison, what would happen? Darcy would be badly handled by the keepers, enough to kill him maybe, or he'd be hanged after his trial. What difference would his visit make? And if Darcy was dead, who would come after him? He saw the brutish faces of Kelly and Hare, and knew they wouldn't think twice about wringing his neck if they found him. Kitty he couldn't care less about; he'd relish the chance to fight him. But the three of them?

Yet it wasn't just his fear of what might happen if he fled that bothered him. He couldn't find it in himself to betray Jack, even if he was a ruthless thief he shouldn't care a fig about. It wasn't that Jack was a great friend of his, but still James looked up to him. It didn't make any sense, James thought, as he edged towards a fitful sleep.

It was still dark and very cold when Hare shook him awake to take his turn on watch. So far no one had come near the hide. James walked to the edge of the clearing and looked into the distance as far as he could. He could see nothing other than the vague shapes of trees, but there was plenty to be heard: bird-cries, the shufflings and brushings of unseen parallel lives, the stealthy night animals about their business in the dark – if they were animals, James thought, and not some other strange creatures – ghosts, maybe, desperate and desolate forms living out some demon life. James shivered. He couldn't decide if he wanted the grey light of a winter dawn to percolate through the trees or if he wanted to stand in this blackness forever, frozen in time.

* * *

James made his way down the northern quays. If his mind

had been racing last night, it was swimming now in a flood of information. There was the under-keeper, Bullard, to be paid, and he must also try to speak with, and offer money, to Hawkins the keeper. He was not to leave the prison until he had done so. The most important thing he learned in the schoolroom of the forest was that the prison ran on money, and the life of a prisoner depended on a plentiful supply of it finding its way into the hands of the gaolers.

As he crossed the river, he was nearly knocked down by a low cart pulled by two scrawny dogs.

'Get out o' the way, can't ye,' a cripple shouted from his cart, as James jumped awkwardly to one side.

'Have ye e'er a few pence for the King of the Beggars?' The cripple's voice was wheedling, yet confident enough to suggest he was successful more often than not. This was Hackball, a familiar figure who took up his position on the bridge and lived on what he could extract from those who had to cross it.

He was one of the reasons James tended to avoid the Old Bridge. Shrugging his shoulders, James showed his empty palms to the beggar, who let fly a stream of oaths so virulent that James felt their violence would cling to the back of his coat like a stain. James climbed up the hill with slow feet, every step bringing him deeper into the dark old city. He could hear the butchers calling out from the market square behind the houses on his left. It made his heart sink because it reminded him that he'd already reached the dismal district that housed Newgate and its sister-prison, the Black Dog, where debtors and many others languished. Some dreaded the

Black Dog more than Newgate itself because the gaolers were even greedier, and many who entered it had never come out again. At the border between the Liberties and the old city a heavy throng of people flowed in both directions. He stood there a few minutes watching the people and listening to the sellers from the Glib Market shouting their wares, gathering his courage. Finally, he turned into the narrow, crowded alley and arrived at the prison. As he stood in front of its mean-looking door, he again thought of bolting away, but he found his fist, almost of its own accord, banging on the wood. A slat shot back and a pair of eyes considered him.

'Please sir, I wish to see the prisoner Darcy. I have a message for Mr Bullard and Mr Hawkins.'

The slat was closed again and James heard the working of iron bolts from inside. The door opened and he was admitted to a dark antechamber. The gaoler looked him up and down. For a man in a position of authority, even if it was a low one, he looked dismayingly unkempt. His clothes were filthy and his face unshaven and grimy.

'Been here before?' he asked James.

James shook his head.

The gaoler seemed to find his response funny. He unlocked the inner door of the antechamber and they entered a corridor, at the end of which James could see another iron door. The stench hit him immediately – foul, stale air and rank human odours all mixed together. There was yet another door on the right about halfway down the corridor and the gaoler now stopped in front of it and unlocked it.

Inside was a throng of prisoners, men and women as well as children no older than James. They stood or sat or lay on the bare stone floor. There was no bedding that James could see, not so much as a handful of straw. If the stench in the corridor had been overwhelming, the stink coming out from this packed room was barely endurable. They looked at the gaoler and James without interest.

'This is the Felons' Room. Do ye see yer friend?' the gaoler asked James.

His voice was mocking, but even so James scanned the room to see if Darcy might be there. None of the ashen-faced, emaciated figures was familiar to him. They all seemed to have been rotting in this room for years. How long would it take it to look like one of these? James wondered. Suddenly one of the women prisoners lunged towards them, as if she meant to leave.

The gaoler lifted his arm. 'Get back out of it if you don't want the back of my hand on yer gob,' he said.

The woman halted abruptly, then turned on her heel, raising her middle finger at the gaoler as she slipped back towards the far wall.'

The gaoler stepped back and slammed the door.

'Well, maybe he's not there yet, but we'll save a place for him just in case,' he said.

'If I could see Mr Bullard,' James said. He willed his voice to be strong and clear, but he heard the hesitation in it as he spoke.

'Oh don't worry, you'll see him soon enough,' the gaoler said.

They went to the end of the corridor. The door was already open and James could hear the sounds of commotion inside. The gaoler led him in. The room was slightly less crowded than the other. A slit near the top allowed some light in and James noticed a covering of very thin straw on the floor. A short, stout man was berating and striking one of the prisoners, who was secured by two guards. Blood poured from the prisoner's nose. From the corner of his eye James saw Darcy in the far corner, sitting on the floor with his back to the wall. He didn't look too much the worse for wear. He raised an eyebrow at James, and James nodded slightly in return.

'This gentleman was asking for you, Mr Bullard,' the gaoler said, indicating James.

'Was he indeed?' Bullard replied without looking up.

He removed his coat, handed it to the gaoler who had brought James in, and rolled up the sleeves of his shirt. Then he began calmly and methodically to punch the prisoner in the stomach, ribs and face. The prisoner groaned.

'Did you think I was joking when I said the money was due today? Do you think you can stay here for nothing?'

Eventually he tired of beating the man. He rolled his sleeves down and the gaoler helped him put his coat back on.

'Get him out of here. Let him taste the comforts of the Felons' Room.'

The two gaolers who had been holding up the prisoner dragged him, feet first, out of the room and down the corridor.

Bullard now turned his attention to James. 'Who are you and what do you want?'

'I am here to see Mr Darcy, sir.'

'*Mister* Darcy? I don't think we have a *Mister* Darcy here. Anyone know of a *Mister* Darcy?' He addressed the question to the room; no one dared to answer.

Darcy remained sitting impassively where he was.

'Might you perhaps mean the thieving scum Jack Darcy?' Bullard asked him.

'Yes,' James said. 'Jack Darcy, sir.'

'Well then say it, boy, if you're not another deaf one. Who are you here to see?'

'The thieving scum Jack Darcy, sir.'

Bullard looked at him, as if trying to decide whether James was being insolent or properly deferential.

'Have you got his fees?'

James took the purse Kelly had given him from his pocket and counted out the week's rent, then added a shilling and fourpence for the penny pot, the alcohol ration which the gaolers doled out at great profit. Bullard took the money and pocketed it.

'Might I speak with him, sir?' James asked, the purse still in his hand. Bullard eyed the purse. James loosened another few coins from it and slipped them to him.

'Five minutes,' Bullard said, and left with the gaoler.

Darcy jumped up immediately and beckoned James over. There were no niceties or greetings.

'I have a lot to say,' he began in a low voice, 'and I want you to listen very carefully and miss nothing.' When he had finished, he made James whisper everything back to him directly into his ear, and when he was satisfied that James had retained all the information he'd given him, he told him to go.

'And don't forget to give Hawkins his due' were his last words.

The door swung open long before five minutes were up and the gaoler ushered James out. He had barely turned into the corridor when he met Hawkins, who had evidently been waiting for him.

Where Bullard was short and fat, Hawkins was tall and rangy. He was neatly dressed, and he put James in mind of a doctor or a lawyer from the Four Courts. He had none of the gruffness or obvious brutality of the under-keeper.

'So this is the young visitor?' He examined James closely. 'What do they call you?'

'James Brown, sir, and, if it please you, I have a message for you.'

Hawkins seemed not to have the slightest interest in what message James might have for him. He continued to peer intensely at James.

James could feel his cheeks flush under the pressure of the gaze.

'You're very well spoken for a thief, James Brown.' Like Darcy, Hawkins pronounced the surname as if he didn't believe it.

'I'm not a thief, sir.' James should probably have kept quiet. Had he not taken part in robberies? Had he not crept around houses in the city, putting silverware into a sack? I did not choose this life, he thought, but it seemed like a thin argument, and not one he could easily put to the keeper of Newgate.

'No, of course you're not,' Hawkins replied evenly. 'And everyone here is innocent; it is a house of saints, a holy sanctuary. And when your friend is hanged, it will a terrible injustice. The thought of it makes me want to weep.'

James said nothing. He took the purse from his pocket as casually as he could.

Without taking his eyes off James, Hawkins scooped the purse from James's hand and deposited it in his pocket.

'Yes,' he said, as if nothing had happened, 'it makes me want to weep my poor sentimental heart away.' And he turned on his heel and marched off.

The gaoler led James out the way he had come in and he found himself blinking in the sunlight of Cornmarket, like someone just woken from an unpleasant dream.

• • • • •

EIGHTEEN

The Trial

The courtroom was crowded. Most of the crowd was made up of friends and relatives of the accused, as well as a few who seemed to be there out of simple curiosity. A good many of them were friends of Jack. Well, maybe friends was too strong a word. James recognised many of them from Red Molly's, including some who were rather better dressed than they usually were. That was part of the plan, of course. James had to admit it was a good plan, even an ingenious one, but he knew that even elaborate and beautiful plans can go wrong, often.

At least he had done his part. Once he was released into the light again he had rushed down the street and didn't stop running until he came to Red Molly's. Molly herself admitted him and he immediately began to babble out Darcy's instructions.

'Calm down, boy,' she laughed, 'if it's urgent business, you must tell it to me calmly.'

She was different during the day, James noticed, despite his agitation; less excitable, gentler even. She took him into a small room off the kitchen and sat him down, then poured him a glass of port and insisted he drink it before speaking. James felt himself warm towards this woman as he drank. His eyes moistened, as they always did when anyone showed him kindness, but he blinked rapidly to shoo the tears away.

'Now tell me about it, nice and slowly, and we'll see what must be done,' she said.

She knew that Darcy had been taken, and had been expecting James. 'I knew he'd send the only one of his crew with something between his ears.'

James blushed, as he always did when someone praised him.

Molly smiled. 'How does a boy like you get mixed up with Jack Darcy?'

Maybe someday James might be able to explain. But the question went unanswered for now, and he just shrugged his shoulders before telling her everything that Darcy had told him. When he'd finished, she was silent for a while.

Then she was all bustle. 'Alright, we'd better get to it. A doctor, an apothecary, and the apothecary's assistant. Are you sure no one saw you that night?'

'Pretty sure. I stood back, and it was pitch dark there.'

Darcy's plan was to deny the charge and insist it was a case of mistaken identity. He had been ill on the night in question, and he had the witnesses to prove it. It seemed a risky strategy to James, but then what choice did Darcy have? Molly took it all in her stride, part of a day's work. She seemed to like Jack

Darcy, but there was no shortage of Jack Darcys in the city, and if one were undone, another would immediately step up to take his place. And there is probably a plentiful supply of James Lovetts too, James thought; boys down on their luck, cast out from their families and fending for themselves in the dark alleys of the city.

* * *

The gaolers brought in the morning's prisoners, two men, a young woman, a boy not much older than James, and lastly Darcy, more expressionless than James had ever seen him and looking, in that group, like just one more prisoner.

James remembered the boy and the woman from the Felons' Room in Newgate. All four of them looked wretched and bore the signs of their time in prison. The woman smiled weakly at the public gallery, where there were some who knew her. The men and the boy stared out from the dock at the empty bench where the judge would sit, as if already anticipating the judgement that would be passed on them, and avoided the eyes of the witnesses gathered in the witness box, where James sat, and the jury on its bench.

James knew enough of Chief Justice Norwood's reputation to know that the gloomy aspect of the prisoners was probably very well justified. He wondered what was going through Darcy's mind as he stood with the other prisoners.

As the time drew near for the start of the session, James could feel the tension sweeping across the room. All eyes were fixed on the clerk, who now called out, 'All rise!'

A great shifting and shuffling filled the room, accompanied by the sound of a door opening and closing, as the solemn figure of Lord Norwood approached the bench preceded by his tipstaff. There was a collective intake of breath at his approach, as if just the sight of him was powerful enough to fill the room with apprehension. He was a large and powerful man, swathed in red and with a full, luxurious wig. His face was broad and, strangely enough, not unkind. There was nothing evil or twisted about the features, nothing demonic. It looked like the face of a kindly uncle, full of humour and fun.

Is this really him? James wondered. Maybe people were mistaken about him.

His thoughts were interrupted by the clerk reading out the first charge against one of the men, who answered 'Not guilty'. His prosecutor was a tavern-keeper, and he told the court how two gentleman had come to his house for a glass of claret and thrown down their coats on a table by the window. Later that night, as the tavern-keeper was filling their glasses, he saw the coats suddenly moving out through the curtained window. He ran outside, where he saw the accused run up the alley bearing the coats. He cried 'Stop thief!' and the man was apprehended by a neighbour, who happened to be passing.

The judge asked the neighbour to verify the story, which he did.

The accused denied all knowledge of the events, and swore that he had never been in Swan Alley in his life.

The judge asked the jury for their verdict.

They huddled together for no more than a minute before their foreman turned to the judge. 'Guilty, my lord,' he announced.

The gentlemen whose coats had been stolen clapped enthusiastically until the judge silenced them.

The second case was disposed of equally swiftly. This time it was a burglary, and the man had been caught red-handed with a sack full of goods. James began to tremble as he watched him, remembering his own near-capture. The jury found him guilty.

Then it was the boy's turn. Stealing a gold watch, which he then pawned. Verified by Mr Smith the pawnbroker. Guilty.

The girl was accused of stealing a crêpe hatband, value of sixpence, the goods of Thomas Clarke, here present. Thomas Clarke was not very convincing. There seemed to be some personal animus motivating his charge. He fumed and spluttered and introduced further charges, which the judge impatiently ruled out of order.

'If you waste my time any further I'll have you clapped in irons in the Black Dog,' he barked.

The jury hardly needed to huddle before finding her not guilty.

At last, it was Darcy's turn, but the judge was showing signs of impatience. 'Is this likely to take long?' he asked the clerk.

'I believe there are a number of witnesses who contest the prosecutor's case, my lord.'

'No, that won't do,' Norwood said emphatically. 'There are three guilty men here who want sentencing. I'll sentence them now.'

James wasn't sure whether his haste came from compassion or some darker motive, but he could feel a sudden stiffening in the room as the judge placed a small black cap on his head and turned to the first of the defendants.

'Joseph Tomelty, you have been found guilty in the matter of grand larceny, and I mean to show you that you trifle with the property of others at your peril. Are we to fear for our very clothes now? May we not take refuge in an inn or a coffee house without fear of attack? The sentence of this court is that you be returned to the prison whence you came and from there be taken to a place of execution and hanged by the neck until you are dead.'

The crowd gasped. They had not expected Joseph Tomelty would have to pay the full price for the failed theft of two coats. The men whose coats were at issue didn't clap or cheer this time.

Joseph lurched forward and leant on the rail of the dock. He looked as if he might collapse. 'Please, my lord,' he began, his voice barely above a whisper. 'Have mercy on a poor man.'

'Take him down,' Norwood commanded, and the gaolers came at once to remove him.

The burglar was the next to receive the full glare of the judge's attention. James found himself transfixed by the piercing blue eyes that bored into the man. It was more than a look; those eyes were like knives reaching in to the bone, and anyone who suffered them could be in little doubt about his fate.

If the judge had been angry at the theft of the coats, the

full vent of his fury was reserved for the crime of entering a property with intent to plunder it.

'What does it mean, to break a window or force a door and slip into a house to remove a few pieces of silver or gold? Is it so very important? Is it any worse than grabbing a coat or a hatband or a watch or a bundle of linen?'

He said this in a way that the tension in the room softened, and something like relief swept through it, as if maybe the deed wasn't so bad after all. The judge waited for the tension to reach its lowest point before resuming.

'I'll tell you what it means,' he began. 'It is nothing less than an attack of the very basest kind on the entire fabric of our city. It is not just a crime against the owner or the keeper of the house, though it is most certainly that, and a grave injury to that party. But have we set out the streets of this city and laboured to build its houses so that vermin …' Here he raised his hand and pointed at the prisoner with such contempt it seemed his hand could hardly bear to perform the action. 'So that vermin like this can scuttle in and commit their filth there, and shit over everything we have built, everything we stand for?'

The tension was now stretched so taut again it seemed something would rupture, or that the prisoner would simply evaporate under the hot fury of the judge.

'Hanging is too good for you,' he continued. 'Though it is all the law prescribes. But your miserable body will be anatomised by the city's surgeons after your death, and thus you may return some benefit to the place you desecrated.'

The burglar remained impassive, and did not plea for mercy. His fate must have been clear to him the moment he was caught, for no burglar had ever been spared.

When it came to the boy, the judge had regained his composure. He treated him with indifference, and then, almost as an afterthought, sentenced him to hang. When all three had been taken down, he removed the black cap, but set it down in front of him on the desk, in the knowledge that he would soon need it again, an action not lost on his audience. James felt his stomach tighten with fear as he thought about the part he had to play.

The clerk read out the charge against Darcy and asked him how he pleaded.

'Not guilty,' Darcy replied. His voice was clear and strong.

Lord Norwood snorted. 'Where is the prosecutor?' he demanded.

The prosecutor made himself known.

James flinched when he saw the man. His face was deeply scarred where Kitty's blade had scored him.

'Do you see the man who did that to your face?' the judge asked him.

'I do not,' he said, 'but this man was with him.' He indicated Jack.

'Somebody is lying,' the judge said. 'And my money is on you, Darcy.'

'My lord, I do not pretend to be a good man, and God knows I have made many mistakes in my life, but I like to think that if I am indicted for a crime I have committed, I will not be loathe to confess it. I like to think that I am a man of honour, my lord.'

His declaration seemed only to have the effect of irritating the judge.

'I'm not very interested in your honour. The truth is what interests me, and nothing else.'

'But that's just it,' Darcy continued in the same reasonable tone. 'The truth of it is that on the night in question I could not have assaulted anyone, even if I were so inclined, because I was gravely ill all of that night and the next day. I had the gripe, my lord. I'm a martyr to it, if the truth be known ...'

'Maybe a warmer employment is what you need. I've heard the gripe is very common among footpads and high-waymen.'

The judge was beginning to enjoy himself. James didn't like the sound of it. He was like a cat playing with a mouse, which he would, when he tired of the game, casually destroy.

Darcy persisted in his mild and reasonable manner, until Norwood leant forward. 'Is there anyone in this room who can verify this nonsense?'

There was a shuffling in the witness stand and eventually a hand was raised. Now it was time for Doctor Bob to do his part. He was a regular at Red Molly's, and was even, it was said, a real doctor. But he had somehow disgraced himself in London and found his way to the second city, where he had set up a practice in the Liberties in which medicine played only a small part.

Molly had told James all of this with a grin. 'And he owes

me money,' she added, 'which makes him all the more reliable a witness.'

James hadn't argued. Money accounted for everything, it seemed; there was nothing in the city that could be accomplished without it, and nothing that couldn't be suffered for the want of it.

Now, in the courtroom, Doctor Bob came forward in a new coat and well-shined shoes, and the clerk swore him in. He testified in his cultivated English voice that on the night the prosecutor was attacked by villains near Kilmainham his patient had been confined to bed in his lodgings in Thomas Court with a bad fever caused by the gripe. He had sent to the apothecary down the street for fennel seeds and figs, and the apothecary had despatched his boy to the house with the remedy. Both were here present today and could testify to that effect.

'You are English?' There was interest in the judge's voice.

'Yes, my lord,' Doctor Bob said. His voice grew oilier with every sentence, it seemed to James, but if its intent was to soften the judge, it seemed to be working. 'London. Oxford. If you please, my lord.'

'What I don't understand,' said Lord Norwood softly, after this polite exchange, 'is why someone as cultivated as yourself is defending scum like this. What have you done, I wonder, that men like this are your clients?'

Again the listeners had been lulled into a sense of security by seeming politeness, and again the shaft had been loosened suddenly and caught the whole room by surprise. James could see that Doctor Bob was rattled, though he kept his composure. Beads of perspiration had begun to appear on his forehead.

The eagle-eyed Norwood spied it. 'I'm sorry, is our room too warm for you, doctor? Should I summon your apothecary?'

'No, my lord, it's quite alright, I— '

'I think I will summon him, though not on your account. Where is he?'

Now it was the apothecary's turn to raise his hand weakly. He was beckoned forward and sworn in.

'This man says he sent to you for a cure for his patient. What was the remedy you sent?'

'If it please my lord, I sent my boy with tar water.'

'Tar water? What on earth is tar water?'

'You mix it with water, your honour, work it with a flat stick, let it stand then pour off the water. A pint every hour for fever, but it should cure just about every disease, smallpox, scurvy, ulcers ...'

Lord Norwood looked as if he could bear no further information. 'Who brought this concoction to the prisoner?'

'My apprentice, sir.'

'And is he here?'

This was it. James could feel the back of his neck prickling. He put his hand up.

Norwood looked at him long and hard, and waited for the clerk to swear him in. 'So you're an apothecary's apprentice, are you?'

'Yes, my lord.'

The judge looked at him as if he thought this was extremely unlikely. 'I'm troubled by a cold. What would you prescribe?'

James had spent an evening in the apothecary's shop trying to learn the essentials of that trade. He pictured the shelves in the shop. 'A little ground ivy tea, my lord, sweetened with syrup of horehound before retiring at night.'

Then he abandoned the shop and was back in Wexford with his mother's hand on his forehead. 'Or you could make a hole through a lemon and fill it with honey, then roast it and catch the juice. Take a teaspoonful of this frequently.'

'Oh yes?' Norwood said blandly. 'And what herbs do you recommend for consumption?'

Again, James tried to picture the shelves and the labelled drawers of herbs. But which were for consumption?

'Mugwort, nettles, foxglove, spearmint ... a little cinnamon.'

The judge took no notice of what he said, but continued to stare at James, as if the very force of his gaze could compel the truth from him.

'Falling sickness?'

James closed his eyes and pictured the shelves again. He knew that the real enemy was silence. He remembered how quickly the apothecary talked, how a great part of medicine seemed to lie in speed of reply, matching the ingredients until a clear and indisputable remedy appeared.

'Valerian, peony, mugwort again, thorn-apple, common henbane, mistletoe, belladonna, foxglove, bitter orange and Peruvian bark.'

As he opened his eyes, he could see the torn and angry

face of the prosecutor. Norwood looked at James with a flicker of interest, as if he might pursue him to the end of his knowledge, but it was getting late. It was past lunchtime already and justice cannot be dispensed on an empty stomach.

'You are either an excellent apprentice or an excellent liar,' he said. 'We'll find out soon enough.'

He waved his hand in a gesture of dismissal and James returned to the witness box. At last, he could breathe. He saw Kelly at the back of the public gallery. What was he doing here? Was he not afraid he might be recognised?

Suddenly, the blood drained from James's face. There was a man sitting beside Kelly, tall, bulky, dark-eyed, and staring straight at James. He turned and whispered something to Kelly and Kelly nodded. It was Dunmain's man, the one who had chased him into the coopers' yard. What was he doing here? He gave no indication that he had recognised James, but the force of his stare was not kindly, and James felt sure that they were discussing him.

The judge ordered the jury to deliver their verdict on Darcy. They huddled a little longer this time. James could see the strain on Darcy's face; maybe he wasn't as brave or as sure as he seemed. If they found him guilty, he would be sentenced to death, like his father before him. And his witnesses might find themselves arrested for perjury.

The crowd in the public gallery grew restive. As the jury huddled, a scattering of talk broke out. Some began to move towards the door at the back of the gallery. Kelly and his companion were no longer there. Maybe Kelly feared what might happen to *him* if Darcy was found guilty and someone should recognise him as one of Darcy's men.

The foreman stood and delivered the verdict. Not guilty. There was some clapping and cheering.

The prosecutor pointed to his face and shouted, 'This is what they did!'

The judge shouted for order and the room was silenced. His face was dark with displeasure. He looked down at his black cap as if he itched to put it on. He seized it with his hand and rolled it up in a tight ball as he addressed Darcy. 'You were born to hang, and you will hang. You may have cheated the rope today, but you'll be back in this room before long.' He unrolled the black cap. 'And this will be waiting for you; the tree in Stephen's Green has your name on it. And your companions will perish with you.' His eyes swept past the doctor and the apothecary, coming to rest again on James. And then he billowed out of the room behind his tipstaff.

NINETEEN

A Meeting

Red Molly's was packed. There wasn't an inch of the place free from the press of human flesh caught up in an endless round of eating and drinking. The tables were awash with beer and gin and claret, and weighed down with sides of beef and pork, plates of rabbit and codfish, and just about any other food you could think of.

Doctor Bob clapped James on the back so hard he nearly fell forward into his food. 'God but I wouldn't mind having you as my own apprentice. You sounded like you knew the remedy for every ailment under the sun.'

'A trick of memory,' James replied, resisting the man's praise. 'Nothing more than that.'

'You're too modest, boy,' Darcy called out to him.

Even though Darcy was just across the table, the din was so loud it was hard to hear him. Darcy raised his tankard in a toast to James, and the doctor loudly followed.

Kelly and Hare were slumped against a wall in a corner of the room. Hare looked stupefied with drink, but Kelly's eyes were sharp and calculating. James had not forgotten his courtroom companion. He'd also noticed that Kelly seemed less joyous than everyone else at Darcy's restoration, even though he'd played a large part in it. But it meant he was no longer leader of the gang, and Kelly was the kind of man who, when he got a taste of power, found it very hard to let it go again.

Kitty, meanwhile, was standing on a table, dancing madly and swinging his hanger above his head until Molly appeared and ordered him down if he didn't want to feel the back of her hand. Someone asked for a song from the dead man. 'Come on, Lazarus, give us a tune!' and the cry was taken up by the whole company.

Darcy bowed in acknowledgement, then stood on his chair and demanded silence. 'A song,' he said, 'for the lady of the house'.

This was met with great applause, and then the room fell quiet as Darcy sang.

Och! It's how I'm in love
Like a beautiful dove
That sits cooing above
In the boughs of a tree;
It's myself I'll soon smother
In something or other
Unless I can bother
Your heart to love me,
Sweet Molly, sweet Molly Malone,
Sweet Molly, sweet Molly Malone.

When it came to the chorus, the whole room took it up, and it seemed to James that the rafters might tumble down under the weight of so much singing.

Molly herself was redder in the face than ever, but James could tell she was pleased. 'Just don't think your song will pay the bill, Jack Darcy,' she said.

'Oh, the devil will pay the reckoning,' Darcy shouted. 'And it's the devil will be back on the streets with a brace of pistols and a merry crew!'

For a man who had just escaped hanging, this seemed to be tempting fate, James thought. But crime was no longer a choice for Jack Darcy; it *was* him, and he didn't care where it led. It wasn't in his nature to be cautious, or to think of consequences.

'Your problem is you think too much,' he often said to James.

That might be true: James did think about everything. He tossed and turned at night, and often woke to see Jack stretched out peacefully, not a sign of worry to be seen on his mild face.

The carousing went on in Red Molly's until nearly dawn. And then Darcy got up and announced that he had business elsewhere. He didn't say where he was going, but he told James they'd meet again in the Phoenix Park. James was anxious at his going; he felt safer with Darcy around, but the inn was so full of good cheer that he felt no harm could come to him here. Kelly and Hare seemed to have disappeared; they must have gone with Darcy or collapsed in one of the rooms upstairs. What was it the servant had said the first time James had slept there? 'Clean sheets is three shillings, dirty ones are a shilling.' James smiled at the memory. Life wasn't all bad; he even found himself dancing a jig on the table to Doctor Bob's violin and the roaring encouragement of the drinkers. He felt that he was dancing all the worry of the last few days out of his body. At the end of it, he was exhausted but happier than he'd been in a while.

The birds had already started singing when Kitty came over to the table. His face was flushed with drink or excitement, or maybe a combination of both. But when he spoke to James his manner was businesslike.

'You're to meet Darcy in the dump,' he said. 'He's calling all the gang together.'

James looked hard at Kitty, but apart from the flush of excitement that had been there when he arrived, his features were impassive. James wondered why Darcy hadn't said anything earlier about a meeting.

'Why now?' he asked Kitty.

'He doesn't tell me his plans,' Kitty said. 'He said something has come up, something unexpected that needs action now.'

'He's only just out of gaol,' James said. 'I don't see why he can't wait.'

'I'll tell him that, will I?' Kitty's face was twisted into his usual sneer.

'No,' James said, 'I'll come. But I want to take my leave of Doctor Bob first. I'll see you outside in five minutes.'

Kitty looked at him distrustfully, but finally nodded. 'Alright,' he said. 'But no longer.'

When he left, James went to find Doctor Bob. 'I'm not sure what's happening,' he said. 'But can I borrow your sword?'

'Can you use it?' the doctor asked. 'It won't do you much good otherwise. I've seen plenty killed who grabbed a blade they couldn't wield.'

'I can use it well enough. I hope I won't have to.'

Doctor Bob considered James carefully. James could read the question in his gaze, the one that was often there when people looked at him. Who is this boy? the gaze asked, and how does he come to be here? If the question was in his mind, the doctor chose not to articulate it. He handed James the sword and scabbard and, as James thanked him and turned to go, he touched his shoulder gently.

'Be careful, my friend,' he said.

Before he stepped outside, James unsheathed the sword and put it inside his belt, then wrapped his cloak around his coat to conceal it.

Kitty was stamping his feet in the cold outside. His eyes brightened a little when he saw James, but his expression was neutral. The morning was grey and cold, the bricks damp in the mist. A large rat scurried off in the direction of the dump. A good enough guide, James thought, as they moved off behind the rat until they came to the dump. It seemed as if all the rats of the city were congregated here this morning; everywhere James looked he saw their fat bodies twisting and darting. Gulls screeched above and came down to inspect the rubbish. No other humans walked the rough path through the dump. It looked like a long-deserted place, a rat-and-gull kingdom. James spotted a couple of fist-sized stones on the path and scooped them up quickly, secreting them in his breeches pocket. They trudged on past mounds of stinking rubbish until they came to a clump of bushes in the corner of the dump.

'This is the place,' Kitty announced.

James noticed his companion's hand had gone to the hilt of his hanger as he spoke, and under the cloak he reached quietly for the hilt of his own blade. He wasn't entirely surprised when Kelly and Hare stepped out from the cover of the bushes.

'Where's Darcy?' he said, though he knew the question was pointless.

'Who?' said Kelly. 'Jack Darcy, do you mean? I imagine he's well tucked up in bed with his floozy. Were you expecting him?'

Kitty went for his hanger, his eyes shining now as if all his wishes had come true at once.

'Nothing like a cock-fight to warm us up on a winter morning. Better than breakfast, if you ask me,' Kelly said. He reached into his pocket for his cudgel. 'Isn't that right, my lord?'

So they knew who he was. James didn't wait to find out what they knew exactly or what their intention was. He whipped the sword from his cloak and lunged at Kitty before Kitty knew what was happening. The blade went into his shoulder and he dropped his hanger and cried out.

'You should have expected that, Kitty.' Kelly shook his head.

'Don't you know these gentlemen were born with their hand on a sword, the better to teach the lower orders some manners?'

Kitty lay groaning on the ground. James backed away and held his sword in front of him. Kelly and Hare began to circle him, Kelly with his cudgel ready and Hare with hanger and dagger pointed at him, keen for his blood. James switched the sword to his left hand, and with his right he pulled one of the stones from his pocket and launched it at Hare. It hit him on the side of the head. He fell, but got up again, blood trickling from under his wig.

'You little bastard,' he shouted. 'I'll cut you so many ways you won't be able to tell what's skin and what's scar.' He ran at James with a mad fury, waving both his weapons.

James managed to fend him off but had to spin violently to avoid the dagger. As he spun around to take up his position again, he found Kelly waiting for him with his cudgel raised. He ducked and hacked at Kelly's shins. Kelly doubled over in pain but it made no difference, for Hare had him now, his hand around James's throat as he kicked the sword away.

This is it, James thought, there's nothing more I can do.

He closed his eyes and waited for Hare to do his worst, but, as he did so, he suddenly felt the man's grip slacken and at the same time he heard the report of a pistol. Hare slumped to the ground and James saw Kelly look around quickly in confusion.

A figure in a long cloak was approaching down the path with a second pistol cocked and aimed. Kelly bolted towards a mound of filthy rubbish and disappeared among the rats and gulls. James had never seen a man move so fast. The figure with the pistol came nearer and James recognised him. It was Doctor Bob. He bent over Hare, then turned him on his back.

'He's dead,' he said simply.

Kitty had managed to get himself up and was shuffling away towards the street, but the doctor caught up with him in a couple of strides. He took an object from his pocket, some sort of cosh or baton from what James could see, and landed a single sharp blow at the base of Kitty's neck. Kitty fell in a heap.

'Not dead,' the doctor said as James caught him up. 'Just out of action for a few hours. He'll need to get his shoulder seen to then. Your handiwork, I take it?'

'Yes,' said James, 'though not so notable as yours. How did you come to be here?'

'No one who is not in danger borrows a sword. I left Red Molly's to follow you, and in my haste went down to the river. It only then occurred to me that you might have gone this way. A more private place for murder, with only rats and gulls as witnesses.'

'You think they meant to kill me?' James asked.

'Maybe,' the doctor replied. 'I didn't have time to inquire.'

He paused a little as he looked at James. 'This is a densely packed city,' he said at last. 'An easy place to lose yourself in, for you to feel you can hide in it and no one will really know who you are. But there's always someone who knows the truth, or who finds it out, especially if there's profit in finding it out.'

'You know who I am then?' James felt a great relief as he asked this. He was tired of being James Brown; he had had enough of it. From now on he would be the man he was born to be, no matter what the price.

'I knew your father a little. He wasn't entirely a bad man, though God knows he was bad enough.'

'I think my uncle wants me dead,' James said.

'Lord Dunmain?'

'I am Lord Dunmain,' James said calmly. And he felt it too: they were not just words.

'Of course,' Doctor Bob said. 'By rights you are. And that's what makes you so dangerous.'

'One day, if I live that long, I mean to claim my inheritance.'

The doctor didn't reply. Maybe he didn't think this was a likely outcome. Maybe he just didn't want James to lose heart. 'What will you do now?'

'If this were a tale, I'd say I'll go and seek my fortune. Or I'll go into the forest and kill the dragon and return to the cheering crowd. But all I can do is, as you say, sink deeper into the city, into some corner of it, where those that want me dead can't find me.'

'You must never return to Red Molly's. This whole district is dangerous for you now. You understand that?'

'Yes,' James said. 'What about the Darcy gang? Will they pursue you now?'

'What gang?' He looked at Hare and Kitty. 'A wounded boy and a dead thug, and another scrambling around in the dirt like a rat. Gangs come and go; they're temporary alliances which break asunder at the slightest provocation. Do you know how many have been hanged on the evidence of their companions? Darcy himself has little loyalty to his gang; his first loyalty is to himself, and it's not in his interest to pursue me, or you.'

James hoped Doctor Bob was right. As the doctor made ready to leave, James returned his sword.

'Have you no weapon?' the doctor asked. 'Take this at least.' He took the cosh from his pocket, but James shook his head.

'No, I've robbed and fought and seen men brutally beaten. I don't want to live like that any more. I mean to do without knives or sticks or cudgels.'

'Then I wish you well,' the doctor said. 'But remember, others may not be so kind.'

James turned around and made his way back. The day was dark and spitting rain and the wind gusted the stench of the dump mingled with the stink of the tanneries in that district. He walked past the still unconscious form of Kitty, and out onto the street. Aware that Kelly might still be lurking in the neighbourhood, he turned away from the river and crossed eastward through a series of narrow and foul-smelling lanes until he emerged at Wormwood Gate and went down to the old bridge. He was tired and hungry and he had no idea where he was going.

• • • •

TWENTY

Respite

L ater, James could not remember exactly what happened. He remembered leaving the dump and crossing the river, but after that everything became a blur. There was a graveyard with cold stones; there was the hot stink of a market. Straw, cattle dealers, butchers, the noises of cattle and commerce. One minute there was all this great din, as if all the noise of the city had flown to this one spot and settled here, and then there was silence, his body crumpling, his head emptying itself of noise and putting itself to sleep. Maybe it was the shock of the fight, or maybe he had been carrying it inside him for many days, but a fever had burst on him with a force he couldn't resist. So he lay down right in the marketplace, the strangest bed in the city. He was woken by voices.

'Who are you? What are you doing here?'

He tried to answer, but nothing would come. The questions sank down into a marsh inside him and no matter how he tried he couldn't retrieve them.

The different voices resolved themselves into one voice: kindly, concerned. 'I'll take him.'

A man lifted him from the ground; his face was pressed against the fibres of a coarse shirt. Odour of dirt and blood. He felt sick, then everything was gone again. He fell down through the ground, through layer after layer, into cellars and pits and dank corridors, where he was chased by ugly forms. He heard his uncle's cruel laughter. He screamed. There was the sound of footsteps on the stairs, the door burst open. Then a wet cloth was placed on his forehead, a hand touched his cheek, cooling words came out of the darkness.

Gradually, the broken pieces of the world began to reassemble themselves again. A little more light fell into the room. His head began to feel as if it belonged to him again and his body pulled back from the desert heat.

Each day the room in which he lay became a little less mysterious to him. He even found out where he was: Phoenix Street. It wasn't far from Smithfield, the market where, it seemed, he had collapsed. The man who brought him home was none other than the butcher from the Ormond Market who had cut McAllister and him from the hooks on the day of the terrible battle between the butchers and the Liberty Boys. James could hardly believe his eyes when he walked into the room.

'I didn't think I'd see you back again, Liberty Boy,' the butcher had said, when James had been able to sit up and drink a little soup.

'Oh leave him be, John,' the woman of the house said – the

one who had placed the cloth on his forehead and put her own hand on it to test his furious heat. She was John's wife, and her name was Nancy. Hers was the voice he had heard, breaking through the muddle of his fever.

'The poor creature! Where does he come from, John?'

There was a third voice, quieter and heard less often. This was Sylvia Purcell, their daughter, of an age with James. She sometimes brought him water and soup but she didn't fuss or ask about his sickness or where he might have come from. She looked at him a little warily, James thought, as if she was waiting to make up her mind about him.

'I'm no Liberty Boy,' James said to the butcher. His voice still seemed to belong to someone else. 'I got caught up in the madness that day, I hardly knew what was happening. It seems a long time ago.'

'No more talking now,' Nancy said. 'Now isn't the time to be worrying about who did what. Plenty of rest and nourishment is what you need now.' Her voice wasn't much louder than her daughter's, but it carried weight.

'You're in safe hands here,' her husband said, smiling.

Day by day his strength came back. He began to feel hungry and was able to eat all the meat and potatoes he was given. One day he felt well enough to get out of his bed. He looked down into the street below, watching people pass by. A fish woman walked slowly with her creel on her head, shouting out her wares. A few small children played with a hoop. A man trundled a cart heaped with vegetables. Everyone moved with a purpose, and James longed to find a real purpose too. In a few days, when he felt strong again, he'd find some useful work.

He panicked suddenly as he gazed out. What did he know about useful work? What if they found out that he'd been a common thief, that he'd hung around with a band of notorious robbers, that he had lied through his teeth in the Four Courts to get a footpad off the hook? That wasn't me, he thought, not the real me. But who was he really? He thought of his words to Doctor Bob as they had stood in the grey light of the dawn: 'I am Lord Dunmain'. He remembered how proud the words had made him feel, even if they amounted to a claim he couldn't assert or prove. If he wasn't Lord Dunmain, who was he? An urchin adrift in a dark city, dependent on the kindness of others.

No, he thought, his eyes fixed on the street, I mustn't forget who I am or what I have to do, though even as the thought formed in his mind he realised that his main task for the moment would be just to survive. Dead men don't claim inheritances.

He needn't have worried so much about his recent adventures. The Purcells didn't ask him who he was or where he had come from. All they knew was his first name. It wasn't that they were not interested; just, James realised, that they were waiting for him to tell them himself, in his own time.

The day finally came when he was well enough to take his meal downstairs with the family. It was a slightly awkward occasion, though everyone did their best to hide it. The family were greatly relieved that he had come through his sickness, but now that the urgency had passed his position had shifted from rescued waif to something else, someone who sat down at the same table and ate the same food. Sylvia was quiet, but he could feel a particular tension from her direction. And the butcher was not by nature a talkative man. But Nancy made up for both, bustling and fussing and talking. Whenever James had eaten a few mouthfuls she heaped more onto his plate.

'You need your strength, dear,' she said.

'I'm very grateful to all of you,' James said. 'And I'm sorry to be such trouble.'

'It's no trouble at all,' Nancy said emphatically. 'And you must stay here as long as you like, mustn't he John?'

The butcher pushed his plate back. 'What's ours is yours, young fella,' he said. 'Four mouths is as easy to feed as three, and it'll be a great novelty to have a boy about the place. Not that we've exhausted the delights of womankind.' He grinned at Nancy and gave Sylvia a little pinch on her arm.

Sylvia flushed. 'Stop it, Da,' she said. 'Don't mortify me.'

James felt a pang of guilt. What if his presence should bring misfortune on this family? Shouldn't they at least know what they were dealing with? Maybe then they might be less open-hearted; they might even ask him to leave. In spite of this, he felt his name furiously racing around his head as if it wanted to leap into the room.

'You may not like me so much when you know who I am,' James said quietly.

John Purcell raised his eyebrows. Sylvia and Nancy looked at him curiously. Nancy made to speak, but her husband raised a hands to his lips.

'I am James Lovett—'

John Purcell interrupted him. 'Lord Dunmain's boy? Him that's dead, I mean?'

'Yes,' James said. 'You knew my father?'

'All Dublin knew him in some form or other, though not for the best of reasons, saving your presence.'

'That's alright,' James said. 'I know the kind of man he was.'

John Purcell looked worried.

'But I thought ...' he said. 'I mean, it was given out that his son was dead. Many thought he had done away with him.'

'They, I mean Miss Deakin and he – he abandoned my mother and let it be thought that she was dead – sent me away. Something to do with money he was borrowing, but I think Miss Deakin must have had a deal to do with it too. And then my father died, and my uncle assumed the title.'

'And does your uncle know you're still alive?' Purcell asked quickly.

'Yes, and that's the trouble. I fear my uncle is a much worse man even than my father,' James said.

'You don't have to do too much to better them,' Purcell said.

'John!' Nancy said, as if she might be afraid James's feelings would be hurt.

'The lad knows it, Nancy. But he's made of finer stuff, I'll bet.'

Sylvia was looking at James with sharp interest. 'I knew you were no ordinary boy,' she said. 'Those hands haven't seen much hard labour.'

James looked at his hands and laughed. 'Maybe not, but they can wield a sword—'

Purcell broke in, an impatient edge to his voice. 'There'll be no talk of swords in this house,' he said. 'Swordplay is nothing to be proud of, if you ask me.

'I'm sorry,' James said. 'I meant nothing by it.'

'You've been leading one kind of life, James,' Purcell said, his voice quiet but determined, 'but now it may be time to learn another.'

Purcell's words would echo often in James's mind in the months that followed. Every day he spent in the house in Phoenix Street was a step away from the life he had been leading and a step into an unfamiliar world. The small routines of the house were as strange to him as the most distant jungle and he felt like a rough explorer with only the dimmest knowledge of the territory. He was surprised at the amount of industry a house demanded. There were endless tasks to be performed: provisions to be bought in the market, meals to be prepared, bread to be baked, floors to be swept and mopped, the fire to be lit and tended. When they weren't bustling around the house, Nancy and Sylvia would be busy in their chairs with sewing and mending, their eyes narrowed in concentration. For a while, as he built up his strength, James was content to watch all this labour, but he soon realised that it was no good standing on the edge of things. Learning another life must mean being right in it, he thought.

'Let me help,' he said to Nancy. 'There must be something I can do.'

'Hold your arms out then,' Nancy said. 'You can be the wool holder.'

James held out his arms. She put an untwisted skein of wool around them and then began to wind it slowly into a ball. James liked this because it meant standing close to her, but he had to keep his wits about him so the wool didn't slip off his hands. He kept a close eye on Nancy to see which end the wool would be wound from next and move that arm towards her. It was a strange thing to match your movements to another's like this, an intimate thing. He had never stood close to his mother like this and found himself envying Sylvia's easy familiarity with Nancy. This is what a family should be like, he thought.

'Not bad for a wild boy,' Nancy teased.

'Next he'll be sewing and embroidering,' Sylvia added coolly, and James felt his face burn. It made him want to drop the skein and run out into the street. He couldn't decide if Sylvia liked him or not. He was annoyed at himself that her opinion seemed to matter to him; he found himself trying to make her think well of him. If swords were forbidden, then maybe his independence might win favour.

'I know well how to sew,' he said. 'I learned it in the woods …' He paused, seeing Nancy frown. 'I mean I've often had to darn and mend. I'd be a sad sight if I didn't.'

'A sadder sight,' Sylvia said.

James ignored this. 'I wasn't very good at it,' he said. 'I'd like to do it better. There are so many things I don't know.'

'Then we must be your school,' Nancy said. 'We'll teach

you what we know, and, in exchange, you can tell us some of your adventures.' She suddenly frowned, looking over at Sylvia and back at James. 'Only those suitable for our ears,' she added. 'We don't want to be scandalised.'

'Speak for yourself!' Sylvia said, grinning merrily.

It was a fair bargain. Over the next couple of weeks James told them of his early life in Wexford and Dublin, his life with his father and then Miss Deakin, and his life in the streets. He didn't tell Nancy about his time with the Darcy gang, but Sylvia's constant questioning whenever they were alone drew it from him.

'You could have died, you know that, don't you? They could have hanged you.'

She was especially horrified at the story of the trial and his own role in it.

'What if Lord Norwood should see you now? He'll know you're a perjurer and might send the watchmen after you.' She paled at the thought of the thuggish watchmen coming into the house.

She looked at him thoughtfully. 'You are quite recognisable, you know,' she said, 'with your soft voice and yellow hair.'

'So are you,' James couldn't help himself blurting out. But it was true. It was not that she stood out in any obvious way. She was not startlingly pretty, but her sharp brown eyes seemed to draw James farther out of himself than anyone else had ever done.

They were both silent after their observations, but James didn't think she was entirely displeased.

In return for his stories, James began to be an expert in the indoor life. He could bake a loaf that wouldn't shame a baker as well as prepare the meat that John Purcell brought home and make a passable stew. And he could mend his stockings with a bit more finesse. He began to accompany Sylvia on her errands and soon got to know the stallholders and shopkeepers of the district. They were curious about him and it wasn't long before everyone knew at least part of his story.

'Aren't you afraid that your uncle will find you?' Sylvia said.

Of course I am, James thought, but he also knew secrecy had offered him little enough protection. What would have happened if he hadn't managed to escape the clutches of Kitty, Kelly and Hare? They would have delivered him to his uncle or his uncle's henchmen. I would be dead by now, he said to himself.

'He'll find me whatever I do,' James said. 'But if I am well enough known, maybe that very fact will persuade him to leave me alone.'

Nancy didn't look convinced, but she held her tongue. Sylvia had often asked him the same question, but she couldn't deny that walking around the neighbourhood with a young lord, even if an abandoned and disinherited one, was a lot more exciting than her usual round of errands.

'Anyway,' she said, 'a person should tell the truth. If you live a lie, at the end of the day you will be no one.'

'Just now,' James said, 'all I want to be is the boy from Phoenix Street.'

TWENTY-ONE

A Visitor

James was kneading dough when John Purcell came home. James's arms were covered with flour and he had managed to sprinkle liberal amounts of it on all of his clothes.

Sylvia was watching him with amusement. 'Faster,' she said. 'Imagine there's a line of impatient customers with empty bellies outside the door.'

Purcell took in the scene and shook his head. 'Is this what you're at?' he asked, a note of genuine bewilderment in his voice. His own stout arms were sprinkled with blood from the day's work at his butcher's stall. He took off his deeply stained apron and hung it on the back of the door. 'Well, I suppose you can always get a job as a cook's maid if all else fails.'

'Or a baker's boy,' Sylvia chipped in.

'And is that enough, do you think?' Purcell asked.

James looked at him. He supposed Purcell thought his work not manly enough and maybe he thought James was wasting his time at home with the women all day. It was certainly true that he preferred this indoor world to the life he had been leading. 'I like to be busy,' he said simply.

'I've been thinking about you, you see,' Purcell said. 'One of my customers is Dr Smith, the master of the Bluecoat School. I told him about you, and he said there might be a place.'

James looked at him in surprise. It was a long time since he had thought about school. He rubbed the flour from his arms. 'I'm not sure,' he said.

'You're not like us,' Purcell said. 'You weren't born to be a butcher or a baker, or a runabout urchin. And if you're to be a proper lord, you'll need to know how to acquit yourself in high society.' He grinned. 'So it's hard benches and long books for you, lad.'

'What about me?' Sylvia asked, a small trace of jealousy in her voice.

'You can have my books,' James said, 'and my long nights poring over them.'

And so James found himself inside the building he had looked at when he passed it on his way to the hide in the Phoenix Park. There was a stir in the large room full of boys when James was brought in. He wriggled in the uncomfortable blue tunic and felt his face redden under the scrutiny of so many new faces. The master was a grave, thin man in a dark coat, perched on a high desk, and he barely nodded at James, stretching out a bony finger to indicate the desk where James should sit.

'I am told you are a savage ignoramus,' the master said when

James had taken his place.

The remark was greeted with a titter. James felt himself redden again and beads of perspiration pricked the small of his back.

'I hope I'm not an ignoramus,' he said.

The master regarded him evenly. 'Very well,' he said. 'We shall see. You are familiar with arithmetic?

James nodded.

'Well then, imagine you are a farmer. You do know what a farmer is, don't you?'

More titters. James nodded again.

'A farmer mingles twenty bushels of wheat at five shillings per bushel, and thirty-six bushels of rye at three shillings per bushel, with forty bushels of barley at two shillings per bushel; now I desire to know what one bushel of that mixture is worth?'

James thought hard. Twenty plus thirty-six plus forty makes ninety-six bushels. One hundred shillings plus one hundred and eight shillings plus eighty shillings makes two hundred and eighty-eight shillings. Two hundred and eighty-eight divided by ninety-six ...

'Today, if possible,' the master said to more sniggers, though there was nervousness there too. A tense silence followed.

'Three shillings,' James said. 'Each bushel is worth three shillings.'

The master nodded, with a slight reluctance it seemed to James. 'Very well,' he said. 'Perhaps there is hope for you after all.'

The best part of school was sharing what he learned there with Sylvia in the evenings. Her appetite for study was greater than his, and it made him feel he must try as hard as he could for her sake, not to disappoint her. They sat at the kitchen table poring over arithmetic, Latin and Greek. If he seemed a little less ignorant under the frowning gaze of Master Casson, it was because Sylvia had schooled him.

One day, after school had finished, he set out to find Harry. He was slightly nervous when he reached the bridge, as he hadn't crossed the river since the day he'd tumbled into Smith-field and he was afraid of encountering someone who knew him from his former life. But in his blue tunic and cap he looked like any Bluecoat boy and he reckoned no one was likely to give him a second glance. He was more nervous of meeting Harry. So much had happened since the last time he'd seen him. There had been so many changes in his own life, he couldn't be sure Harry's life hadn't also been changed severely. James had been so used to Harry always being there at his pitch by the Custom House Quay that he never thought his friend could be elsewhere, but he viewed life differently now. James knew that everything could change in an instant, and what you thought was your life could be swept away forever and some other life put in front of you that there was no escape from.

But he needn't have worried. As he turned into Essex Street he saw Harry in his old spot. He was busy polishing the shoes of a stout merchant. Harry had a particular way of moving and polishing that James recognised immediately, but he noticed that his coat seemed to hang more loosely on him than before.

James waited until the merchant stood himself up with the help of his cane and Harry's shoulder, and then walked over. Shyly, he tapped Harry on the back. Harry turned and looked at him.

'Want yer shoes polished, is it?' he said, his voice flat and weary.

'Harry, don't you recognise me? It's James!'

Harry's eyes narrowed as he looked closely at the boy in the blue tunic. It was only when James took off his cap that a smile flickered on Harry's face.

'Don't you scrub up well?' he said. Yet his smile was strained.

'How have you been?' James asked.

'Busy, but not so busy as you, it seems.'

James noticed the chilliness in his voice. 'How do you mean? I know it's a long time since I've been to see you, but don't think I didn't want to.'

'But thieving's an absorbing profession, I suppose,' Harry said.

'What?' James said, surprised at Harry's tone.

'Isn't that what Jack Darcy's gang does?' Harry asked.

The name came as a shock to James. It was as if it belonged to another life, not his. Since he had been living in Phoenix Street he hadn't thought any more about Jack Darcy or his gang. He had put the experience out of his mind and lived as if he had always been in Phoenix Street with Nancy, Sylvia and John Purcell. Harry's words fell like stones on shallow ice.

'I couldn't help that, Harry,' he said. 'I had no choice.'

'You always have a choice,' Harry said. 'Do you think I couldn't have chosen to rob? Do you think I don't need money? That I don't have mouths to feed?'

'I didn't do it for money,' James said, feeling how hollow his voice sounded. 'I did it to survive. If I didn't join them, I wouldn't be here today. I'd be lying in a ditch in the Phoenix Park.'

'I saw you with them,' Harry said. 'All standing on the street together. You didn't look too uncomfortable.'

'Maybe you're right, Harry, maybe I should have run away. I did get away in the end. But I had to think about my future. I mean to claim my inheritance, I mean to be the true Lord Dunmain.'

'And what kind of lord will you be, Jim?'

James looked closely at Harry. 'What do you mean?'

'The city is full of lords. Your own father was one. Your uncle's a false one. Being a lord is no great recommendation, it seems to me.'

James tensed with anger. Why was Harry so unreasonable? 'You think I should forget who I am?' he said with more passion than he intended.

'No,' Harry said simply. 'I just think *who* you are isn't as important as *what* you are.'

Of course he was right, just like the Purcells were right. They didn't care what name he bore; they looked beyond that into who he really was, just as Harry had always done. James laughed suddenly. 'Maybe that's why "the who" is so important, Harry. Maybe I want to show that not everyone of my name is evil. But I have to get there first.'

'Just mind how you get there, will you?' Harry said.

It was getting late by the time James had finished talking to Harry. He had treated his friend to mutton pie and small beer in a chophouse nearby. It's always easier to talk with a full stomach.

'Let's not leave it so long again,' he said to Harry as they ate the last of the meal.

Harry jabbed his blue tunic. 'You keep changing, Jim,' he said. 'You appear and disappear again like a strange spirit. What will you be wearing the next time I see you?'

'No,' James said, smiling. 'That's over now. Things are settled now. I mean to stay where I am until I'm old enough to be taken seriously by the law.'

Harry said nothing. They left the chophouse and James escorted Harry back to his pitch.

'You just see how soon I'll be back,' he said, but Harry already had a customer, and he was setting to work with his spudd and rag, scraping and rubbing as if he'd never left his stool.

Before crossing the river, James called into the bookseller's in the piazzas to inquire if any mail had come for him. The bookseller looked at him curiously and James removed his cap and told the man his name.

'It's a long time since you've been round here, Master Lovett, but, as it happens, a letter came here for you some weeks ago.' He went to fetch it. After some rummaging he returned with the sealed package. 'It's a miracle it got here all the way from the New World,' he said.

'How much is the postage?' James asked, suddenly worried he wouldn't have enough money to pay for the letter.

'There was another sealed package with it, addressed to me,' the man explained. 'And it contained the cost, so you don't owe me anything.'

Relieved, James took the letter and thanked the bookseller. Outside, he broke the seal and read the contents. It was from McAllister, though he did not use that name now, but called himself Baldwin in honour of his former provost, the same man who had almost scuppered their escape that night in College Park. He had made it safely to the New World and was now employed with a shipping merchant in Philadelphia. He was happy in his new life, though he was still greatly saddened by the circumstances that had driven him there, which he referred to only in the most indirect manner. He asked after James, and gave him the name of the business he worked for but asked him to let no one else know of it. Although he didn't say it in as many words – he must have feared it could all too easily fall into the wrong hands – James understood clearly that he must destroy the letter and commit McAllister's new name and address to memory. He seemed not to have learned of Vandeleur's fate, but James thought it was better to leave him in ignorance of it.

It was almost dark when James turned off the quay and made his way to the Purcells' house. As he entered Phoenix Street he realised how much these streets were home for him now. In a short time the area around the great marketplace and the people he passed on his way through it had come to seem as familiar and beloved to him as if he had grown up among them. Maybe this was the life he should lead, maybe this was his natural home, and all the rest a kind of unhappy dream. He walked up the street with a light step and knocked on the door. Sylvia opened it. James thought she had a strange look in her face. She looked at him but didn't speak. A dog growled in the parlour. James stepped in.

'Hello, James,' a voice said.

TWENTY-TWO

A Family Matter

James stood transfixed in the room. A black dog bigger than any he had ever seen snarled and moved towards him.

'Down, Caesar,' his uncle called, and the dog froze and sat immediately, contenting himself with glaring at James, his pointed ears spiked to attention to let James know he was still under full scrutiny.

'Once he gets to know you, he'll be sweetness itself,' his uncle said in a treacly voice.

Black, poison treacle, James thought, as he stared at him. He hadn't seen his uncle since that day in the cathedral and he looked as evil now as he did then – hollow-cheeked, black-eyed, an eternal smile about his lips, the smile that was a signal of triumph past and future more than an expression of any pleasure. He sat at his ease in the Purcells' small parlour, which his presence and bright rich finery had the effect of shrinking further. John Purcell was standing, as was Nancy, and Sylvia took up a position beside James and put her hand on his elbow as if to give him strength to face the demon, whose smile now flashed into a full grin.

'Don't they teach you any manners in the Bluecoat School, James?' he asked mildly. 'I have always heard such good reports of that institution. I hope I have not been mistaken.'

'I'm sure James is just overcome with surprise,' Nancy said. 'He can't have expected to see you here.'

'Not see his own uncle, his own flesh and blood?' Always the perceptible sneer in the voice.

'His own flesh and blood that abandoned him and made out he was dead,' John said. He didn't look in any way cowed by the grand figure in his parlour.

For his part, Richard Lovett, the man who called himself Lord Dunmain, wasn't in the least troubled by the butcher's observation.

'His father indeed has much to answer for,' he said. 'But who can be his brother's keeper? I myself have always thought of James with the greatest fondness.'

'Strange way of showing it,' Purcell said.

'What do you want?' James asked at last. 'Am I to be resurrected?'

His uncle considered this, or pretended to. 'Ah, you haven't lost your wits. I'm greatly relieved to hear it. But no, I don't think resurrection is quite the word. You were never buried in my mind, or in my heart.'

No, but you wanted me dead or captured at the very least, James thought.

'But I had no idea where you were or indeed if you were alive,' his uncle continued. 'Only one of my assistants chanced to hear of a young man near Smithfield who claimed to be a relative.'

'I claimed no such thing,' James said.

'No, well, perhaps not exactly.' His uncle rolled his palm on the silver top of his cane. 'You claimed to be Lord Dunmain, which is one way of indicating a relationship, I suppose.'

James said nothing, and nobody else spoke either.

'You can imagine my joy at discovering that my long-lost nephew was so near, and so well looked after, if I may say so.' He inclined his head fractionally and extended a gloved palm in the direction of the Purcells.

'James has made his home here,' Nancy said. She spoke like a woman who had no intention of allowing those circumstances to be altered.

'Of course he has,' his uncle said. 'Your kindness does you much honour, ma'am, and it is my own turn, now that I have found him again, to assume the burden of this poor boy's care.'

James felt Sylvia's grip on his arm tighten. 'No,' she said. 'This is where James belongs. Isn't it, Mother?'

Nancy nodded. 'We think of the boy as one of our own,' she said.

A faint trace of irritation showed itself at the corner of Dunmain's smile. 'Yes, of course you do, and he must continue to be a frequent visitor. All the same he must take up his rightful place in society.' His uncle looked around, his eyes narrowing and his nose wrinkling. 'Unless you mean to be a butcher, James?'

'I mean to be what I am already,' James said, 'Lord Dunmain.'

'Ah, indeed, the complications of family life ...' His uncle sighed, but seemed reluctant to elaborate further.

'These are details,' he said finally, 'matters to be resolved in the fullness of time and with the help of the lawyers. Your father, James, did not leave an orderly estate. Why don't you come with me now, and we can discuss these matters further?'

There was a sudden commotion at the door. Purcell went to investigate. James heard shouting and then a man entered the room whom James recognised immediately as one of his uncle's thugs, the same one who had chased and almost caught him in the coopers' yard. He was followed by Purcell, his face red with anger.

'Who is this man who pushes me out of the way in my own house?'

'You must forgive Grady,' Dunmain said. 'He suffers some-times from an excess of zeal.'

'What's he doing here?' James asked.

The thug was staring at him, his eyes blazing with recogni-tion.

'How shall I put it?' Dunmain asked. 'He's here to ensure an orderly resolution of our discussion.'

'Are you threatening me?' Purcell said. He was at the very limit of his self-control, James could see.

Dunmain smiled.

His smiles are like knife-thrusts, James thought, but they're also the smiles of a man who will never have to rely on his own strength. The dog was climbing up the thug's legs, demanding attention, and the thug patted him, one black animal to another.

James felt he couldn't put the Purcells in any more danger. 'I'll go with you, if that's what you want.'

'Excellent,' his uncle said. 'You won't regret it.'

'James is going nowhere.'

James was surprised at how absolute Purcell sounded.

Without waiting for orders from his master, Grady put his huge hand around Purcell's throat. Purcell gagged for breath. James ran to help him and the thug paused briefly to swat James away with the back of his hand as if he were no more than a fly. James fell back on the floor. Nancy screamed. She began to pummel Grady's back with her fists. He ignored her blows. Dunmain watched the scene with interest before calling off his thug. James noticed that Sylvia wasn't in the room; he was relieved she didn't have to see this.

'Now, I think that's settled. James, are you ready?'

James went to Purcell and Nancy. 'I'm sorry about this,' he said.

There was more commotion at the front door.

'More of your thugs?' Purcell asked Dunmain.

Dunmain looked puzzled. 'Grady, see what's afoot.'

The thug moved for the door, but James was surprised to see him suddenly fall back in and topple onto the floor. He was followed by several substantial men in bloodied aprons, carrying meat cleavers. Sylvia came after them. She smiled at James. The dog barked furiously and lunged at a butcher.

'Are you the man who threatened John Purcell?' one of the other butchers asked.

'That's him,' Sylvia said.

'A family matter,' Dunmain said, no trace of a smile on his lips now. 'I am merely trying to return this boy to the bosom of his family.'

'I think we know what you have in mind for the boy,' Purcell said. 'No family I know brings their baboons with them on a visit.'

The baboon stirred and began to heave himself up from the floor. A butcher put a foot on his chest. 'Take yer ease there awhile, friend,' he said.

'It's alright, Grady,' Dunmain said. 'I think we shall adjourn our discussion.' He stood up and smoothed his clothes, as if to remove any trace of the Purcell household from them.

'I wish you good day, sir,' he said to Purcell. 'And ladies.' He bowed with elaborate ceremony towards Sylvia and Nancy, who failed to return the honour.

'Dear nephew,' he said to James. 'I hope our paths will cross again under happier circumstances.'

The butcher who had his foot on Grady released him, and the two men left the Purcells' house with as much dignity as they could muster.

The house soon resumed its normal tranquillity. Purcell went back to the Ormond Market with the butchers and James stayed at home with Sylvia and Nancy. The doors were well bolted, and they were under strict instruction not to venture outside. Purcell had slipped a few pennies to a boy in the street to come and fetch him at once if any stranger showed himself near the house.

'That was close,' Sylvia murmured.

'If it hadn't been for your quick thinking, I'd be in his house now.'

'Or dead,' Sylvia blurted out.

'Sylvia!' Nancy was shocked.

'Well, who knows what that monster would have done with him?' Sylvia said. 'He didn't come here to rescue James, you can be sure of that.'

'You're going to have to be very careful,' Nancy warned. 'He didn't look the kind to give up too easily.'

'Perhaps I shouldn't stay here,' James said. 'I'm afraid it will be dangerous for you.'

'Don't be foolish, James. This is your home, you can't think of leaving it now.'

'We won't let you, will we, mother?' Sylvia laughed, but there was anxiety in the voice too. She didn't want to lose James.

James felt almost ashamed of their concern, as if he didn't deserve it. But he was glad – the very last thing he wanted was to leave Phoenix Street.

After that, James didn't move through the streets so freely. The Bluecoat School and the Ormond Market were his westerly and easterly boundaries. He didn't dare venture any farther. Sylvia was convinced the most dangerous parts of the day were the trips to and from the school. She took to accompanying James every morning and waiting for him in the afternoon. Part of James felt he should resist her impulse to protect him and assert his independence, but the truth was that he liked to be in Sylvia's company. He wouldn't let her go right to the door of the school, not wanting to expose them both to the taunts of his fellows.

Sylvia went as far as the corner of Haymarket and Queen Street and then watched James make the short trip to the school. In the afternoons, she came to the same corner to wait for him. James was always glad to see her. As they walked home he would regale her with the adventures of the day and tell her what he had learned.

'Do you think we'll always be able to talk like this?' he asked one day as they made their way home.

Sylvia paused a little, and glanced at him. 'I don't see why not,' she said.

'I don't think I could bear it if we couldn't,' James said. He looked directly at Sylvia, and found her eyes meeting his with an intensity he hadn't seen before.

She took his hand and squeezed it tightly. 'That won't happen,' she said softly.

TWENTY-THREE

A House Near the City

Sylvia waited at their usual corner. She looked up and down the street. It was a busy thoroughfare: carriages came and went in both directions; beggars and street sellers tried their luck; maidservants carried baskets of fruit and vegetables back to their houses; men ducked in and out of taverns; and those who emerged wrapped their cloaks tightly around them against the bitter February cold. The sky was overcast, with that sharp frowning grey that seemed to press down against the streets. It was not a day to be outside if you could help it. Sylvia shivered.

A coachman shouted a series of obscenities at a black carriage that had pulled over not far from the school. He only just managed to avoid crashing into it. 'Are you a complete eejit?' he shouted at the rival coachman who, in reply, calmly raised his middle finger.

Sylvia looked away. James would be here soon. Already a

line of blue-coated boys were beginning to file down from the school. Suddenly she saw him, his fair hair visible under the schoolboy cap. Sylvia smiled, but knew better than to wave. She ducked back around the corner into the Haymarket. It was a game they played: he would come around the corner whistling to himself as if he didn't expect to see anyone, and she would stand with her back to him and then turn around as if surprised.

'James Lovett, is it really you?' she'd say, her eyes wide.

'*Mademoiselle Purcell*,' he'd reply. '*Quel plaisir!*'

She was wondering what he might say today, when she became aware of the commotion surrounding the carriage. From where she stood she could see the heads of the first pair of horses rearing in protest at being pulled up so suddenly earlier. Curious, she went back to the corner. There, she saw the door of the black carriage, the same one she had seen outside the school, slam shut, and heard what sounded like the rap of a cane on the roof. Hearing the noise, the coachman cracked his whip and shouted, and the horses moved off swiftly. The carriage thundered along the cobbles far faster than it should have been travelling on that crowded road, and Sylvia could see irate walkers racing for the shelter of the farthest edge.

And then it was gone. She looked back up the street, where just minutes ago she had seen James walking towards her, but he was nowhere to be seen. Maybe he was playing her game, and hiding to make her come and look for him, but that was unlike James. Games had to wait until he was out of sight of the school; he was very unlikely to try to tempt her to go where they might be seen.

Nonetheless, she turned into the street and walked hesitantly in the direction of the school. She passed the point where she had seen James, but there was no sign of him. Sylvia scoured doorways and alleyways but to no avail. She even went up to the door of the Bluecoat School in case the boy she had seen hadn't been James after all and James had been kept in for some reason. When a porter finally answered her knock, he told her that every boy had left the school long since. Then, fighting off the anxiety that lay in wait at the back of her mind, she thought she might have missed him somehow, and that he had gone home without her.

She raced back to Phoenix Street and was out of breath when she rushed in the door.

'What's wrong, girl?' her mother asked as Sylvia almost knocked her down.

'Is James here?'

Her mother looked at her in surprise. 'Isn't he with you?'

Sylvia kept looking past her mother as if James might be somewhere behind her.

'Maybe he went with one of his friends,' Nancy said.

'No, he was there, and then he wasn't. There was a carriage, a black carriage.'

As she said the words Sylvia knew with absolute clarity that James had been bundled into the carriage and she had no doubt that he had been taken to his uncle's house. 'Oh mother,' she wailed, 'what are we to do?'

* * *

As soon as they got him into the carriage they tied a gag around his mouth and bound his hands behind his back. The carriage hurtled through the city so fast James would have fallen from his seat if he hadn't been held fast by the man who had bundled him in from the street. Across from him, the unmistakable form of the chief Ugly leaning forward so that his large face was only inches from James.

'Not so brave now, are you, without your butcher friends?'

He slapped James hard across the face, in case his words might not be trusted to do their work. James reeled from the blow and again only the other man's arms saved him from plunging to the floor. Grady prepared to strike him once more but the other man raised his arm.

'Let him be,' he said. 'Or there could be trouble when we get there.'

Grady held his arm in mid-air for a moment, as if he couldn't decide whether to complete the blow or let it drop. Through the expressions in his face James could read the ponderous machinery of his brain considering the problem. At last, with painful reluctance, he let his arm return to its place.

'You just wait,' he said. 'You just wait and see.'

James tried to make out where they were going, but Grady, delighted to be able to do something to frustrate him, pulled the blinds down on the carriage windows. James knew they had been headed south when they took him, and the carriage hadn't turned, so they must have crossed the river. He felt the carriage slow as it climbed a hill and then turn to the right and pick up speed again. It must be Thomas Street, James thought. We must be headed westward out of the city. He pictured the city in his mind. From Thomas Street they would go past the workhouse towards Kilmainham, unless they went near the Royal Hospital.

James gave it up. What did it matter? It was not as if he might send out a signal to the butchers of Ormond Market to let them know where he was. Still the carriage kept hurtling on, out of James's map of the city. When eventually it stopped, he calculated that they must be deep in some country place full of fields and trees. Well, they could provide cover enough for escape. Wherever they were bringing him, they would not succeed in keeping him long, he would make sure of that.

'Journey's end,' Grady announced, pulling a black cloth from his pocket and binding it with unnecessary force across James's eyes so that he could see nothing. He felt himself being manhandled roughly out of the carriage and carried into some building. Then his stomach lurched as he felt Grady descend a flight of steep steps. Cold, damp air filled his nostrils, reminding him of Newgate. He could hardly ...? But no, they had travelled too far for that. He was set down on a cold stone floor and heard the clink of a chain as his left hand was grabbed and shackled. His gag was removed, and Grady gave a snort of pleased laughter as he looked down on his handiwork.

'Can't you at least remove the blindfold and unbind my arms?' James said, and immediately regretted it.

'Poor diddums,' Grady said. 'Aren't you comfy?'

He found this so funny he almost choked on his laughter before James heard the sound of a heavy door closing.

☀ ☀ ☀

John Purcell tried to console his daughter. 'He can't be far away,' he said, though in his heart he knew James didn't have to be very far away to be entirely out of the reach of his family. But he knew his daughter, and knew she wouldn't be satisfied with general remarks.

'I'll find out,' he said. 'Someone must have seen something, and the city is full of wagging tongues. I'll start in Queen Street.'

'Let me come with you,' Sylvia said, and Purcell nodded. It was better that she be out doing something than fretting at home.

✳ ✳ ✳

The door opened. James heard footsteps approach. He steeled himself for a blow, but none came.

'Wakey, wakey' came the voice of the thug as he pulled the blindfold off and removed the gag. Finally, he unbound James's arms and removed the shackle.

'Where am I?' James said.

'Hell,' Grady said as he grabbed him by the collar of his coat and dragged him up the steps.

The cellar steps led up into a kitchen and James was amazed to see Mrs Rudge and Smeadie standing in front of him.

'The poor creature,' Mrs Rudge said. 'What have they done to you?'

Smeadie contented himself with a non-committal nod.

'Haven't you work to attend to?' Grady barked, pulling James out of the kitchen.

They entered a wide, stone-flagged hall. A few paces down, they came to a high double door. Grady knocked and James heard his uncle's mild voice commanding them to enter.

He was standing in front of a blazing fire. Miss Deakin sat in a chair beside the fire, her small eyes fastened on James.

'Nephew,' Dunmain said. 'Welcome to our house. How was school today?'

'What am I doing here?' James asked, ignoring the taunting civility.

'Your mouth has brought you here,' Miss Deakin hissed from her chair.

'What do you mean?' James said.

'Running around the city telling every ragamuffin and fish-wife that you're the real Lord Dunmain,' she said.

Dunmain raised his hand. 'We mustn't quarrel,' he said.

'Is it the fact that I say it, or that it's true that grieves you?'

'Do you hear the boy, Richard, how impudently he addresses me?'

Dunmain sighed. 'Understand this, James: while I live you will never be Lord Dunmain.' The civility was gone, his voice now pure steel. 'Surely that much is obvious? You're a clever boy, after all.'

'Not just while you live, either. The boy will never come into the title.'

Dunmain frowned impatiently at this intervention.

'I plan to remain alive for some time yet,' he said.

James still couldn't see what he was doing there. Unless ... No, he pushed the thought away. But it wouldn't go away.

'Do you plan to kill me then? To get me out of the way of your plans?'

James realised that this would be the perfect solution. Was this to be the end, then? His heart raced, and he saw that his hands were trembling. He didn't want to die.

Dunmain eyed James, as if considering this possibility carefully. 'It would be one solution, wouldn't it, James? And it would be hardly noticed. Do you know how many boys die in this city every week, every day even? Typhus, pox, fever, starvation, falling under the wheels of a carriage ... You could spend your time going to their funerals.'

'The Purcells would notice. The Ormond Market butchers would notice ...'

James found it hard to believe he was even having this conversation. For the first time he had a clear realisation of just how much danger he was in. More than any displays of fury or violence, it was his uncle's calmness that disturbed him. He seemed to be the kind of man who could contemplate anything without flinching, without so much as raising an eyebrow. He thought of Sylvia waiting for him at the Haymarket. He felt a sharp stab of pain when it came to him that he might not see her again.

'Yes,' he heard his uncle saying, 'your butcher friends are a slight nuisance, but a band of Popish troublemakers will not cause as much difficulty as you might think. Death is not an unreasonable, or even an unusual outcome.'

He let the words sink in. 'As it happens, it is not entirely necessary.'

James had no idea what he meant by that.

'The world is a big place, and great distance can easily achieve what only death might once have done,' Dunmain said.

He examined James's school uniform. 'I hope you made the best of your scholarship,' he said. 'For your school days are over now. It's time for new horizons. Isn't that right, Grady?'

James had forgotten that Grady was in the room. He turned around to see the grinning thug coming straight towards him. James instinctively put his arm up, but the blow had connected before he saw it. He felt his head spin around and the image of Miss Deakin's widened eyes flashed into his brain before the room exploded with bright lights and then he saw nothing more.

• • • • • • •

TWENTY-FOUR

The Crossing

The room was dark and was pitching around violently as if some malevolent creature had grabbed the house and was now tossing it as hard as he could from one hand to the other. James felt his whole body revolt against the movement and suddenly, as well as retching, he felt a sharp pain as his head banged against the wood that lay behind him. He was now fully, sickeningly awake. In the dim light he could make out other shapes, also retching and reeling, and emitting low desperate groans like him.

'What Hell is this?' James found himself asking, convinced that he must have died and woken up in a dark and unforgiving underworld.

The shape nearest to him turned its head in his direction. 'A stormy Hell,' the voice croaked. 'Let's hope this cursed ship can take it, or we'll perish in the freezing ocean.'

James looked at him with horror. Ship? Freezing ocean?

The salty smell of the sea water leaking through the deck into the hold hit his nostrils. So his uncle had put him aboard a ship. He tried to remember what had happened but all he could see was the sneering face of his uncle telling him the world was a big place. So that was what he was thinking. How long had he been unconscious? His head ached horribly where his uncle's thug had stuck him. They must have bundled him straight to the docks and into this ship, or maybe they slipped him a potion to keep him asleep for days. He had no idea how much time had passed since he stood in his uncle's house. His head felt as if it belonged to someone else, someone much slower and heavier.

'Where are we bound?' he shouted as the vessel lurched in the swell.

It was some time before he heard an answer. 'The New World.'

The voice that spoke didn't carry much hope, as if the New World was not likely to be a great improvement on the old one. The dark hold plummeted into a deep trench, leaving their insides somewhere above them, then as quickly rose again, throwing the crowded bodies against each other. The smell of frightened flesh and vomit-drenched clothes caused James's stomach to rebel again; he produced sounds he never knew his body was capable of and felt his throat burning. Those who could speak began to pray and, hearing them, many other voices followed until the hold was filled with the sound of low desperate praying.

Then the hold shifted again and James closed his eyes, as if by refusing to look he might somehow make the situation more bearable. There seemed to be a multitude in this cramped and filthy space, and he was amazed to see many young children, but he had no curiosity about them now, no inclination to ask any further questions. He touched the tender spot on the back of his head and winced in pain. Then he slumped back into the darkness he had recently woken from.

When he came to again, the storm was still raging and the chorus of low prayers could still be heard. Some of the children were crying with fear, and it was all that James could do to stop himself joining their lamentations. He caught the eye of the man nearest to him.

'What kind of journey is this?' he asked him. 'And why are there so many of us crammed in here like fish in a barrel?'

The man looked at him strangely. 'Do you really not know? Or did a spirit lure you?'

'A spirit?'

'Yes,' the man said. 'The spirits often lure the young ones, filling their heads with all sorts of stories and giving them fruits and sweetmeats. Children make good servants, and fetch a good price in the New World.'

James stared at him blankly. 'Servants?' He looked as closely as the light would allow at the people around him. He noted the poor clothes, the worn faces, the eyes that seemed to hold a hundred miseries.

'Indentured servants,' his neighbour said. 'A few years' slavery for the chance of freedom in a new land. It pays for the cost of our passage too, and for the little food we'll get here and beyond, if we make it that far.'

'If it keeps on like this, the sea will get all our servitude.' The speaker was a burly man, wider and stronger than James and the other man put together.

James was still trying to take in the information. 'Not everyone here is a servant, surely?'

The burly man looked at James and raised his eyebrows. 'No,' he said. 'Some of us is princes, and some of us is fancy quality just wantin' to see how others live before we get back to our riches and our burstin' tables. Like you, by the cut of your jib.'

'I'm no rich man, as you can well see,' James said hotly. 'But I'm no servant either.'

'You are now,' the first man told James as the ship again lurched in the swell. 'However it happened.'

The labouring of the ship was too violent for the conversation to continue and James was thrown back against the side of the hold. He didn't try to get up again, but crouched where he lay, thinking of what he had heard. He knew he should not be surprised that his uncle's treachery would have stretched to this, but he could scarcely believe what was happening to him now. It seemed too much like a nightmare to be true, but he knew that if he blinked or shook himself the foul world of the hold would still be there. The wailing of a child reminded him that the nightmare wasn't only his. Everyone in this place was suffering terribly, yet a great many had come here willingly. The world was a pitiless place, but there was no comfort to be had in that thought.

For another whole day the storm pummelled the ship and tossed the occupants of the hold from side to side like shoals caught in a swinging net. When finally the weather settled down and the ship's progress through the waves was a little steadier, a crewman came below and barked out an order to go on deck.

The passengers shuffled awkwardly up out of the purgatorial hold into the cold shock of the wind-lashed deck. James tried to steady his footing but fell forward twice before reaching the side. He stared down at the churning sea and retched yet again.

'Not got yer sea legs, sonny?' one of the crew laughed.

'It's a mistake,' James said as he tried to straighten up. 'I'm not supposed to be here. I'd like to speak to the captain immediately.'

'Immediately, would yer? And who might you be, if I may be so bold as to ask, begging yer pardon like?'

'My name is James Lovett,' James said.

There was little point adding to that information now. One of the other crew members was shouting at them to get back down into the hold.

The crew member James had spoken to was bowing in mockery. 'I shall inform the captain immediately, yer honour, and sooner if I can manage it.'

They were ordered to line up on deck and an officer stood back from them, as if in extreme distaste, and shouted that they would now be given their fortnightly ration. 'And God help anyone that doesn't make it last,' he said. 'Because there won't be another scrap given out before two full weeks have gone by, even if you're at death's door itself.'

The crew began to distribute the rations, and if the officer's words had made James think they would be receiving a large hamper of supplies, the meagre fare that was being given out chilled him. A large loaf of bread, some rotten biscuits, and water that hardly seemed fit to drink – it didn't seem enough to keep body and soul together a week, let alone two. As soon as the food was distributed, James found himself bundled back down into the stinking hold with his companions. He tore a piece of bread from his loaf and sank his teeth into it. It was hard enough to pull the teeth from his head. But the bread reminded him that he hadn't eaten for days, and the hunger that had been kept at bay by the storm and the filth of the hold now came back with a vengeance. He tore another piece off and ate ravenously.

A strong arm pulled at his elbow. 'Mind how you go,' the burly man said. 'Don't give in to hunger if you want to live. Remember what he said above. He meant every word of it. They'd rather let you die than give you an extra morsel.'

The man's name was Reilly and he was a cooper, he told James. The first man was a tailor called Byrne and he nodded now in agreement.

'It's their profit,' he said. 'They won't give a crumb more than they have to.'

Reluctantly, James set aside his loaf and took a slug of dark water, wincing with distaste as he drank.

Some days later, when he was back up on the deck, one of

the crew approached him.

'Are you the one they call Lovett?'

James nodded.

'Yer to follow me,' the sailor said, and led James towards the quarterdeck where a door led down into the captain's quarters. James could hardly believe the space he now entered was in any way a part of the same ship in whose foul belly he lay cooped up. The captain's cabin was neatness itself; painted a light pea green with gold beading, it was elegantly fitted out: with a bed and curtains of the richest Madras chintz, a fine dressing table and a beautiful bureau and book-case. It was as if he had stepped into another, altogether more pleasant domain, though the motion of the waves reminded him that he hadn't after all escaped the ship or his unexpected journey. That, and the eyes of the captain boring into him.

'You were asking for me, I believe.'

The captain looked at him evenly. He was a neat man, as carefully arranged and tidy as his room. James could see neither kindness nor malice in the eyes that examined him, just a mild curiosity that, in its way, was more frightening than a threat. The man didn't seem to attach any great importance to James or his plight.

'I don't know how I got here,' James began, 'but I have a pretty good idea that it was my uncle's doing. You must understand that I don't belong on this ship.'

The captain pointed at the large charts spread out on his table. 'I understand these,' he said. 'I know how to plot a course. I know how to make provisions for a voyage. I understand a little of business and the markets. Other things don't concern me much.' He shrugged. 'I'm kept busy enough.'

'Has my uncle paid you off, is that it? Have you been paid to deliver me into slavery?'

'Hardly slavery,' the captain said mildly. 'Indentured servitude is a respectable business.'

He seemed to soften a fraction. 'What's a few years to a boy like you? You'll still be a young man when you get your liberty; you just have to work hard and please your master.'

'I am my own master!' James was indignant. 'My father was Lord Dunmain, and I am heir to his title, and no servant to any master.'

The captain's eyes narrowed. 'That's all as may be,' he said, 'but it's no concern of mine.' He looked at his charts again. 'If you would be so kind as to excuse me, I must return to my navigation.'

James began to shout. 'But I have been kidnapped. I must return to Dublin!'

But the captain was already rapping on the cabin door and two of his officers came in immediately. 'This conversation is over,' he announced. 'Take the boy below.'

James was manhandled and quickly despatched back down to the hold, still protesting. The other passengers looked at him curiously, but James would look at no one. He sat down, put his head in his hands and would neither speak nor be spoken to. He felt hunger gnaw at his belly, but in a strange way he relished the pain since it expressed perfectly what he was feeling. Why should he let himself be taken across the ocean against his will, as if his life was of no account? He might as well be at the bottom of the sea as living the life of a slave in some godforsaken wilderness. At least his body was his own; no one could stop him controlling that. And so, for two more days James ate not a morsel of his ration, contenting himself only with sips of foul water.

By the third day he was weak and lightheaded and his stomach was protesting with all its might, but he wouldn't listen. He lay back and listened to the incessant noises of the hold: the crying of the young ones, the moaning of the sick, and the piercing shrieks that seemed to come from a woman in the stern. This was the most troubling noise; it seemed to come from some dark pit of suffering. He heard other voices trying to soothe the woman, but they hadn't the slightest effect. Through the night it went on, rising above the labouring of the ship, till James wondered if the voice was real and not something inside himself, a waking nightmare his hunger and dizziness had conjured. Then he seemed to doze off and float free of all the hold's commotion.

He woke to the harsh voices of the cooper and tailor. He felt drops of the fetid water on his face and moved his arm to wipe the liquid off. His arm seemed to take an age to perform the task.

'What are you at, boy?' Reilly asked roughly. 'Have you a yen to die?'

The other man was holding a crust of bread to his lips. James shook his head. He noticed that the screaming from the stern had stopped. That at least was something.

'You haven't been eating, have you?' The voice was Byrne's, gentler than the cooper's, but with an edge of impatience in it.

James didn't answer. It was too complicated to explain. He heard a sudden commotion from the stern of the ship; voices were raised.

One voice separated itself from the crowd. 'She's too heavy to go aloft, and she can't stay here. She'll have to go out.'

The voice was met with more arguing and loud wailing. Then silence followed by the sounds of activity.

'Any strong men here?'

Reilly left James and went towards the stern.

'What's happening?' James asked, his voice not much above a whisper.

'The woman who was crying out,' Byrne said. 'The one who was with child. She died in the night.'

So it was real, James thought. He heard the sound of curses and great effort, and then great blasts of cold air swirled though the hold. In the midst of this the cooper's voice rang out harshly.

'Bring the boy over!'

The tailor helped James to his feet and half-carried him in the direction of the voice. A group of men had managed to manoeuvre the dead woman's body to an upper bunk near the stern and were now pushing it through the porthole.

Reilly, his face dripping with sweat, looked angrily at James.

'Do you see what happens here?' he shouted. 'This woman would have given anything for a chance of life for her and her child, but here she is now on her way to the bottom of the ocean.'

James watched with shock as the woman's body disappeared through the porthole. There was no report at the other end, or it could not be heard above the labouring of the ship; she seemed to slip silently out of the world, as if she had never been in it. Watching the blank porthole that had marked her last ghostly journey, James began to feel ashamed of his wilful hunger. The support of the tailor was suddenly no longer enough to hold him, and he fell down in a dead faint. When he awoke he asked for bread and water.

TWENTY-FIVE

New Horizons

J ames lifted the axe and struck again. Then he went around the other side and cut a notch a little higher than the first. He returned to the first notch and cut again as hard he could. He could feel the sweat trickling down his back. The sun poured hot and heavy through the trees, but more than the sun James felt his owner's eyes boring into him.

'Put your back into it, can't ye?' Mackenzie barked at the boy. 'Ye'll get no easy ride here.'

James mopped the sweat from his forehead. His hair clung damply to his face and his rough shirt chafed against his skin. His arms ached, but the ache was duller now than it had been when he first started working for Mackenzie. Mackenzie had come aboard the ship when it docked to see if he could spy a bargain and, sure enough, a 'fifteen-year-old boy with seven years' indentured servitude' was to be had at a good price.

James was weak and ill-nourished from the voyage. He

could hardly keep upright on the deck when the captain summoned the servants and slaves, who were capable of standing, for inspection. Mackenzie had managed to get himself on board with the agents, and ran his shrewd eyes along the line until they fell on James. He looked him up and down, prodding him with his stick.

'What's your trade?' he asked as he prodded.

Gentleman, James wanted to say, but he'd learned enough by now to control his tongue. 'No trade,' he said. 'Common labourer.'

'You don't look like a labourer. You don't look like you've done much.'

James didn't respond. He didn't care whether Mackenzie wanted him or not. He had seven years of servitude ahead of him, if he survived that long, and one master was sure to be the same as another. His uncle's mocking words about new horizons went round in his head, as they had done ever since the moment he woke to find himself in the hold of the ship as it laboured across the ocean. James thought bitterly of all the times he had stood on the quayside watching the ships unload, imagining journeys to exotic lands. Now here he was in the dank hold of one of those selfsame ships on his way to a life of slavery in the colonies.

Mackenzie continued his scrutiny.

'You don't say much, do you? I though you Irish never stopped gabbing.'

James shrugged.

Mackenzie began to haggle with the captain over the price.

James didn't listen. He had no control over the transaction; he had lost control over his life the second he was bundled into the black carriage. And his uncle must be pretty confident that the colonies were as good as a coffin for his purposes and that the last thing he needed to do any more was fret about the doings of Lord Bluecoat. There would be no Lord Bluecoat here, just a scrawny Irish labourer to be ordered hither and thither and barely kept alive as reward.

After Mackenzie's bargain was done and the agents had finished examining the others who had survived the voyage, they were marched down the gangplank onto the quay. Crowds of men, carts and wagons swarmed around, loading and unloading ships. Merchants and buyers examined exhausted groups of servants and slaves from other ships. After so long at sea, James and the others in his group could hardly find their land legs, and they hobbled and wobbled behind the captain along the crowded quay and up the steep riverbank to a big building, where they were registered. It was hot, and James felt faint. Outside, Mackenzie was waiting with a horse and cart. It was all James could do to clamber up onto the cart before his new master drove off on the long journey from the town.

* * *

How long ago was that? How long had he been here aiming his axe at Mackenzie's trees in the blazing sun? How long had Mackenzie been standing behind him, cursing him and complaining at the quality of his labour, reminding James of the small fortune he had expended on him and raining blows on his back to make the boy work harder? James converted the tree into Mackenzie's neck in his mind, and it took some of the pain out of the blows and the work itself.

Eventually Mackenzie would tire of standing in the sun and retreat to his house. His absence didn't allow for any let-up in the work, though. He would come back after his lunch to inspect what work James had done in the meantime, his viciousness renewed by a hearty meal. He was a man quick to anger; indeed, he seemed to live for that emotion.

The evening after James arrived he had been summoned, along with the other servants and slaves, to the apple tree near their quarters. There, a servant called Connolly, who had escaped and been brought back after only a day, was suspended by his hands with a rope thrown over a branch, so that he stood on tiptoes. His back was bare and Mackenzie stood behind him with a cowhide whip. He looked at his audience, his eyes burning.

'You can see now what happens to any servant or slave who runs away from Robert Mackenzie.'

Then he began to lash the man with all his force until the blood streamed from his back and gathered in pools at his feet. James lost count of the number of lashes, but they told him later it was past fifty. Mackenzie only stopped when his arm was too exhausted to continue. When Mackenzie went back to the house, they brought Connolly into the hut the male servants and slaves shared, and a slave called Amelia came with some salve for his back.

Connolly couldn't move for a week after that, and James was surprised that he survived his ordeal. His back was a tangled mess of scars and another beating would surely kill him.

James hacked at the wood until he felt his arms would drop, praying for the relief of darkness when he might be allowed to rest and appease his hunger. At least the darkness came quicker here than in Ireland. A bowl of corn mush and a pitcher of water was little enough to look forward to, but the food at least stopped the pain in his belly for a few hours. As he hunched over his bowl, he would allow his mind to drift back to Phoenix Street and the Purcells. He let himself imagine he was walking home from the Bluecoat School with Sylvia, though the happiness the picture gave him was matched by an equal stab of desolation. How could he ever see her again? He might as well try to leap onto the moon. He'd be better forgetting her and all of his life before now. There was only this eternal present of trees and sweat and hunger. As day followed day, he became more and more sure of one thing: he would not make it to the end of his appointed time. He would not be able to endure seven years of Mackenzie's farm.

In his first weeks at the farm James turned himself into a tree-felling machine and took little notice of his companions. It was as if he didn't want to be touched by the human world of the farm but preferred to be alone in his private hell. If he admitted that he wasn't alone, it would mean that the world he was in now was real, and the people in it real people who deserved his attention. He didn't want to accept that Mackenzie's farm was his whole world now. But he found he couldn't stay blind to those around him. He couldn't ignore John Connolly, the skinny pockmarked man from the north of Ireland who lay in the bed next to his with his back on fire from Mackenzie's cowhide. But it was Amelia who began to break through the wall he'd put up around himself.

'It's hard to think this is life,' she said. 'It's hard to think this place is the world. And it isn't, but it's our world for now, and we have to live in it as best we can. And don't forget, you're indentured. That means you can be free one day. We're not all that lucky.'

'How did you get to be here, Amelia?' James asked her, a little ashamed he hadn't thought to enquire before.

Amelia didn't look like she wanted to answer him. 'What's the use of talking about that?' she said.

'Please,' said James. 'I'd like to know.'

Amelia looked at him. James knew that if she told him, it would be a sign of trust between them.

'I was eleven years old,' she began. 'My father had a big family in Africa. He even had many slaves.' She smiled thinly. 'It seems strange now,' she said. 'My father had many sons, and I was the only daughter, and the youngest, which made me a great favourite. One day, when the grown-up people were at their work far away in the fields, I stayed at home with the youngest of my brothers to mind the house. Suddenly, two men and a woman leaped over the walls and grabbed us before we could even think to shout out. They stopped our mouths and ran off with us to the woods nearby. There they tied our hands and led us away as far as they could until night fell. We reached a small house, where we rested for the night. It went on like that for many days, walking all day and only resting when night came on. And then one morning when we woke they were pulling my brother from my arms ...' Amelia stopped, her eyes red.

'What happened to him?' James asked gently.

'We pleaded with them not to separate us, but they didn't listen. They sold my brother to some other traders. I never saw him again.'

'And what about you?'

Amelia hesitated before continuing. 'Then they took me to the coast and I saw the ship. That filled me with astonishment, to see such a thing, but when they carried me onto it, I thought I would surely die, I thought the light-skinned men with their loose long hair meant to sacrifice me. I thought I had wandered into a world of bad spirits. When I saw everywhere black people chained together, their faces twisted with terror and misery, I fell down in a faint on the deck.'

A look of pain came over Amelia then, and she stopped talking.

'I cannot speak of it any more,' she said. 'The thought of that journey and what came after is unbearable. We can't look back, James.'

James thought of his own journey in the stinking hold.

'You and I are alike, Amelia,' he said. He had already told her his own story.

'Yes, James, we are alike, and not alike. We've left our better lives behind us and now we must make our way through a world of bad spirits.'

Amelia's words were often in James's mind as he laboured on Mackenzie's farm. But, even if it might make his life easier to bear, he couldn't accept that the boundaries of this farm were the boundaries of his heart and mind from now on. He talked to Connolly, whose back still burned from Mackenzie's lashing, as they were digging out the roots of the felled trees. He was only ten years older than James, but he looked like a man twice his age.

'Was that the first time you ran away?' James asked.

Connolly didn't look up from his work, and waited so long to reply that James thought he was ignoring the question. Eventually he spoke, though he didn't look at James or pause in his work. 'No,' he said. 'I ran away before, and that's why I was sold to Mackenzie. I got farther that time, near six months before I was turned in. Five pounds they got for me.'

'Why did you run?'

Connolly shot James a contemptuous look before turning back to his work. 'I got tired of living in luxury,' he said with a snarl.

He stopped digging and turned to James. 'Why are you asking me anyway? What's it to you?'

'I'm sorry,' James said. 'I didn't mean anything by it.' His words seemed only to inflame Connolly.

'Didn't mean anything by it? Where did you get your fancy voice from, Blondie?'

'What does it matter?' James said wearily. 'I'm here just as the same as you, chopping down the same trees, cutting out the same roots, using up the same life's blood.'

Connolly grunted, but made no more objections.

'There has to be a way out of this,' James said, as much to himself as to his companion.

Connolly didn't reply.

* * *

A summer of hard work turned to an autumn of work no easier. James rose with the sun and slept soon after nightfall. In between was tree cutting and clearing, timber to be brought to the sawmill, fenceposts to be readied and driven into the boundaries, animals to be watched and crops to be tended. James learned how to smith a horseshoe, to tan leather and make bricks. He fixed and mended fences, barn walls, even furniture. He moved from field to wagon to house to barn, always busy, with an unending set of tasks that changed with the season.

Always at the back of his mind was the thought of escape, but he knew that escape was very often followed by recapture and worse conditions than before and, cruellest of all, a term added to the years of servitude. The countryside beyond the farm seemed to promise great hope of a new life. It looked like it could hide a man forever, but it was not like a city where you could disappear and never be found. However wide the countryside, it was still full of those who could tell an escaped servant at a hundred paces and if you didn't have a pass or the papers of a free man you'd be clapped in gaol until the reward could be claimed. James had seen the advertisements in Mackenzie's discarded newspapers. Ran away this August a servant man, slender, of middle height, a neat-made impudent Irishman. He had on a large hat, a brown wig, a dark-coloured old coat, a pair of linen breeches and a silver-hilted sword. Whoever shall bring him to me shall have four pounds in gold reward, plus reasonable charges …

James looked at his clothes, imagining his hat and poor shirt set out in print, and wondered what the reward for his capture might be.

And yet, he thought, there might be a way. He had not forgotten the day he had picked up the letter from McAllister in the bookshop at the sign of the Bible. He hadn't kept the letter but he had committed McAllister's particulars to his memory, and they were still lodged securely there. What if he were to get a letter to McAllister? Maybe he could find some way of helping him. Who knows, he might even be able to persuade Mackenzie to let McAllister buy him, and then James would be free at last to make his way home to Dublin. But how would he get the letter to McAllister? It was one thing to have the address, but Mackenzie didn't provide a postal service for his servants and slaves. James would have to find someone to bring the letter from the farm to some place where it could be conveyed to McAllister. He couldn't think of anyone who might be likely to provide that service for him, yet he must be ready in case the opportunity should arise.

It took some time for James to get his hands on some old paper, and to make ink from a mix of tea leaves, boiling water and gum. When the ink was ready, he wrote to McAllister telling him all that had happened to him and giving him as much detail as he could about the place he was now in. He pleaded with him to do what he could to come to his aid, for he didn't think he had the strength to last much longer in this wild prison. When he had finished, he sealed the letter with some wax from his candle and hid the letter under the thin pallet that served as his bed. Now he only had to find someone to give it to.

TWENTY-SIX

Indelible Affection

Sylvia wasn't familiar with this part of the city. She usually kept within the comfort of her own district and had no fear of walking alone there. But today she had walked down to the river and across the old bridge. She was accosted by beggars as she went by but she kept moving swiftly, walking as though she knew exactly where she was going. The din of the crowded Glib Market filled her with fear at first, but she told herself it was just another market, and if the Liberties was an unfamiliar quarter to her, it was not after all another planet. The traders, the buyers, the beggars were not so different from those she was used to. And anyway, if she could manage Red Molly's, she could manage this. She pushed on, her definite steps more certain than she was, until she found the church and the graveyard behind it, exactly as the woman had described.

It had taken some doing to get this far. She and her father

hadn't been able to find out much on the day that James disappeared. Many people had seen a carriage travel by at speed, but there was nothing particularly unusual about that. The city was full of carriages that often raced through the streets without regard for who might be in their path. They could only guess that he must have been taken to his uncle's house. Through many enquiries they had found out that Lord Dunmain had taken a house outside the city and Sylvia and her father had immediately made their way there.

But James's uncle hadn't forgotten the indignity of his visit to Phoenix Street, and he treated them with amused contempt.

'No, I'm afraid I haven't seen my nephew since that day in your charming house. Don't tell me you've lost him.'

'There are those who care for his welfare, and they are more numerous than you might think,' Sylvia's father had said.

'Oh dear, should I be afraid?' Dunmain retorted.

He made it clear that he was lying through his teeth and that there was not a thing they could do about it.

'How is your meat, Purcell?' he'd said before dismissing them. 'Perhaps you might send a sample to my cook. We can always be doing with a good butcher.'

Sylvia had been desolate on the long walk back to Phoenix Street. Her mind was filled with the terrible things that might have happened to James, but she wasn't prepared to give up the search, even if it meant finding his dead body. She would know what became of him if it was the last thing she did.

James had told her of his time with the Darcy gang and

though she had been shocked at the time, she began to think that it would take someone like Jack Darcy to find out what had become of James. But how would she find him? You didn't just walk around the streets asking for a notorious criminal. James had also told her about his friend Harry and she decided to pay him a visit.

'I don't know where you'd find Jack Darcy,' Harry said. 'Footpads like him are always on the move, they don't sleep two nights in the same place if they can help it. But I've heard of a tavern they go to, Red Molly's near Watling Street.'

Sylvia didn't like the sound of the tavern or the street. But if that's what it took ...

'I'll come with you, if you like,' Harry said suddenly, and Sylvia smiled in relief.

And so, one afternoon, Sylvia slipped out of the house and went to meet Harry, and they made their way to Red Molly's. Even with Harry beside her, Sylvia was nervous. The lane stank and she started as she saw a huge rat scurry down the middle of the lane as if he owned it.

It was Molly herself who answered the door, and she looked the two of them up and down. 'No beggars or children here,' she said.

How could James have been in a place like this, with a woman like this? Sylvia wondered.

'We're here about the boy who used to be with Jack Darcy,' Harry said.

Molly's eyes narrowed.

'A fair-haired, well-spoken boy,' Sylvia added.

Molly considered her. 'What's it to you?' she said.

Sylvia flushed. 'He was staying with us. My family took him in. And now he's been abducted.'

Molly's tone softened. 'You better come in,' she said.

When she heard them out, she agreed that Jack Darcy would be the best person to help. 'If he's so inclined,' she added. 'James did kill one of his men, don't forget.'

'He had no choice,' Sylvia rushed to defend him. 'It was that or be killed.'

Molly gave her a long look. 'It's like that, is it?'

Again Sylvia flushed. Was it so obvious? She could hardly explain her own feelings to herself; she was afraid to consider too closely the rush of warmth she felt when James's image came into her mind. All she knew now was she wanted him back.

Molly agreed to arrange for Jack to meet Sylvia.

'I don't promise anything,' she said. 'I can't even say that he'll turn up. But I think he liked the boy, so you just might be lucky.'

And so here she was, on the appointed day at the appointed hour, staring at a headstone in the little graveyard with a tight knot of fear in her stomach. The bells of all the churches in the district rang out the hour and fell silent again. No one entered the graveyard. Sylvia walked slowly among the head-stones, scrutinising each one to keep her from the possibility that her journey had been for nothing.

Hereunder lieth the corps of Robart Bagot and his wife Ellenor. Here lyeth the body of Mrs Allice Brown. Here lies the remains of

Sarah. This frail record of indelible affection to a beloved husband …
'Indelible affection'; I hope someone remembers me like that.'
Sylvia started, and gave a little cry of fright. A man stood beside
her, tallish, in a handsome coat, a foppish air about him, smiling now in enjoyment of her discomfort. He seemed to have
appeared from nowhere. Sylvia hadn't heard the gate opening
or registered the sound of his boots on the gravel.

'Jack Darcy?' She felt foolish the moment she said his name.
What if it wasn't him but some government agent who was
following Darcy and had somehow got wind of this meeting?

The man bowed, a little too much for Sylvia's taste. 'The
very same. And you're the young woman Molly told me
about. She tells me young James Brown is in trouble.'

'James Brown?'

'That's what he went by when he was with us, though I
knew he was lying. One of my men got wind of the fact that
he was in fact Lord Jim.'

'Lord Bluecoat they call him in my neighbourhood, because
of his blue school tunic.'

'Very nice, I'm sure. And how is all this of interest to me?'

'I think James admired you,' Sylvia said. She may as well
flatter him.

Darcy merely looked at her with eyebrows raised. She saw
that she should be careful: the man, whatever else he might
be, was no fool.

'And I think you liked him.' This at least might be true.

'I'd have liked him better if he hadn't killed one of my men.'
Darcy didn't seem particularly aggrieved by the loss.

'I'm sure he did what he had to do. The man attacked him. Very likely he was in the pay of the man who now has him.'

'Very likely. But I'm still not sure what my role in this is.'

Sylvia took a deep breath. 'His uncle pretends he has no idea where James is. He won't listen to the likes of me or my father. He has no fear of us. But if someone were to strike fear into him …'

Darcy smiled. 'Someone like me,' he said.

'Yes,' Sylvia said. 'He might listen to you; he might tell you where James is.'

'With my sword at his throat, you mean. And what might my reward be for this information?'

'Reward?' Sylvia said. 'I hadn't thought …'

'It's an expensive business, you know. It won't be a case of calling to his door. There will be preparations to be made, colleagues to be enlisted. I can see you've done little robbing or kidnapping.'

Sylvia was about to reply indignantly when she realised he was toying with her.

'He's bound to have money, and his house is probably full of valuables. I thought you might combine robbing and information getting.'

Sylvia hadn't thought any such thing, and she was shocked at how naturally the idea had presented itself to her.

Darcy was smiling again. 'You've thought of everything, haven't you? Does your father know what a little criminal you are?' he asked. 'Do you know what would happen if anyone were to hear us now?'

'The dead have no ears to listen to us,' Sylvia said.

'I hope not,' Darcy said. 'Some of them might well have something to say to me. Look, I liked the boy, as you said, so I'll undertake this. And since the dead are so obliging, I'll meet you here one week hence at the same hour. By the same indelible affection.' He pointed to the headstone, and then turned and was gone.

Sylvia didn't have to wait a week to find out that Darcy had indeed undertaken the enterprise. From Harry she learned that the city was buzzing with news of Jack Darcy's latest exploit. It had even made it to the pages of *The Journal*. An outrageous assault. The carriage of Lord Dunmain attacked. His lordship accosted, his watch, clothes and money taken.

'You'd better be careful,' Harry said. 'The sheriff will feel the heat of this; he'll have to look like he's doing something about it.'

'They'll hardly be looking for a young girl,' Sylvia said.

'Just make sure no one sees you with Jack Darcy. They hang girls too, remember.'

A week after her first meeting, Sylvia made her way across the city again, this time more nervous than the last, with Harry's words ringing in her ears. To comfort her, he said he'd wait for her by the Cornmarket House. This time when she entered the graveyard she was horrified to see that she wasn't alone. A man of middle years stood before a headstone looking intently at the inscription. Sylvia panicked and turned on her heel to go, but then thought better of it. To leave now would look more suspicious than staying put and doing the same thing the man was doing. She stood before a headstone at the far end of the graveyard and immersed herself in its inscription. After a while, the man left and she breathed easily again. Some time after the appointed hour Darcy appeared beside her.

'Did you find out where James is?'

'What happened to "Good day, sir, how are you"? That was quite a job, you know.'

'So I hear. But not unprofitable, I think.'

'A man has to live.'

Sylvia's face must have betrayed her impatience, for he quickly continued.

'It was difficult to find anything out at first. He needed a lot of persuasion, I'm afraid.' Darcy touched the hilt of his sword.

'Where is he?' Sylvia said, unable to restrain herself.

'It's not that simple,' Darcy said. 'Dunmain had the boy sent away, that much I did find out. But even if you are disposing of your own nephew, with people like that there's always someone else to do the work for you. You wave your hand and say let this be done or that be done and lo, it's done, but don't let anyone bother you for the detail of it.'

'But where was he sent, and who *does* know?' Sylvia was close to despair. It seemed the nearer she got the farther she was slipping away.

'The idea was to send him off to the American colonies as an indentured servant, which is a fancy term for slave if you ask Jack Darcy.'

Sylvia looked at him incredulously.

'But can you do that? Can you just abduct someone like that and send them off to the other end of the world?'

Darcy looked at her pityingly. 'You can do what you want if you have the money to pay for it,' he said.

'Did he say who arranged it?'

'A man called Grady. But I didn't see him.'

'It's his thug. He was in my house. You can't mistake him, a big, ugly brute.'

Darcy shook his head.

'It's no small thing to do what I did,' he said. 'The gentry take particular exception to being attacked. They own the place, after all, so they take it personally. So, begging your pardon, I have to lie low for a while. I'd like to live a bit longer. I'm not ready for the rope just yet.'

'But what am I to do?'

'Ships have captains and like most men they like to drink and talk. Try the port taverns, someone might have heard something ...' And he was gone, as quickly as he came.

Sylvia walked back to the Cornmarket House. In her mind was the picture of Lord Dunmain's leering thug. She had no chance of getting anything other than a hiding from him. She met Harry and told him about the encounter in the church-yard. He listened carefully.

'It's a common enough thing,' he said. 'There are many who sell themselves into servitude in the hope that a new life will open up for them. My own cousin did it. I was with him in the tavern when the agent persuaded him to try his luck overseas. I told him to be careful, but he'd have none of it. I even went with him to the Tholsel to see him sign on ...' He stopped as he said this, his eyes widening.

'Maybe ...' he said.

'What?' Sylvia said.

'They have to sign a register in the Tholsel when they get their papers.' He looked at Sylvia. 'Can you read?'

'Yes,' Sylvia said.

'Then let's go. But don't let on that we're looking for him. I'll say it's for my cousin, that I need to get in touch with him.'

They walked the narrow lane by Newgate and down the length of High Street until they came to a big stone building squatting at the corner with two massive pillars holding up the ornamental portico. There was a flow of traffic in and out, and knots of merchants stood conversing on the steps that led to the entrance. Sylvia paused on the pavement. She had never been inside such an important place and the look of this building filled her with dread. It was the kind of place, that once you went in, it might not be so easy to leave again.

'Come on,' Harry whispered. 'We'll draw more attention to ourselves standing outside than marching in.'

Sylvia gathered her courage and walked in as if she had every right to be there. When she entered the hall, she looked around to find the most sympathetic man. She spied one a bit less forbidding than the others and approached him, and asked if she might see the register for indentured servants as this poor boy's family needed to send an urgent letter to him.

'Do you think we have nothing better to do than run

around in the service of every ragamuffin in the city?' the man said, looking down his nose at Harry.

But Sylvia smiled her sweetest smile and he led them reluctantly to a room off the main hall where he pulled down a large bound ledger.

'What name?' the official demanded.

Sylvia looked quickly at Harry. She had to risk it.

'Lever,' she said. 'Jonathan Lever.'

The official bent over the book, running his finger down a long list of names. 'No,' he said. 'No Lever here. You must be mistaken.'

'Please sir, might I look, just so I can say that I have done my duty by the boy.'

The official twitched with irritation, but again Sylvia flashed a charming smile, and he turned the register around on the table. She scanned quickly down the page. There it was, near the end, a barely legible scrawl that was certainly not James's: James Lovett, indentured for seven years, in charge of Captain Thomas McCarthy of the vessel *George*, bound for Philadelphia.

'You're right,' she said. 'It's not there. He must have the wrong name. I'm very sorry to have bothered you.'

TWENTY-SEVEN

Flight

The carriage pulled up outside the stable. James, who had been inside cleaning, came outside to look as Amelia greeted the visitor and led him in. The man spotted James and called him over. A kindly-seeming face peered at him. He was a man of about thirty years and his clothes, though simple, were of good quality. A gentleman farmer, James guessed.

'I haven't seen you before. What's your name?'

'James, sir. James Lovett.'

'And nicely spoken too. You don't have the brogue on you, which must be a relief to Mr Mackenzie. Well, I mustn't keep you from your work.'

James felt the desire to blurt out the story that would explain his lack of a brogue, but bit his lip. The man turned and went into the house. From Amelia he learned that the visitor was an acquaintance of Mackenzie's, and that he had a farm about half a day's ride from here.

'But he is not like Mackenzie,' she said. 'He is not a man of anger, and no one runs away from his farm. And no one goes hungry there either.'

James went back to his work but he kept turning over Amelia's words in his mind. Visitors came rarely to Mackenzie's; it might be six months or more before another came. He thought of his letter to McAllister in its hiding place in his pallet. The man had a kind face – surely it was worth the risk. He knew that the longer he thought about it the less likely he'd be to do anything, so he quickly slipped away from the stable to the sleeping quarters and retrieved his letter and then went back to the stable. About two hours later the man emerged from the house. James was waiting with the door of the carriage open. The man nodded to him and was about to close the door when James reached for the letter and thrust it awkwardly into his hand. He was so anxious to get the letter to him that he hadn't stopped to think how exactly he would manage the transfer.

'Please sir, forgive me,' he began. 'I know it is a terrible impertinence, but I would be very grateful if you could send this letter on my behalf. It's for an old friend who knows me, who knows I shouldn't be here ...' James knew he'd said too much and cursed his stupidity.

The look on the man's face told him he'd been foolish to give in to his impulse.

'You see I'm not who I seem to be,' James pressed on. He didn't seem able to stop himself.

'What's this?' the farmer said. 'Do you think you can prevail on me to conspire against your master, whose hospitality I've just enjoyed? I thought you looked like a hard-working lad. Now I find you another Irish idle-bones who wants a free ride in the colonies.'

'No, it's not true,' James said. 'I was forced here against my will by a trick of my uncle. My father was–'

There was no chance to continue the story, for Mackenzie had appeared on the verandah and was calling down to his friend. 'What's going on, William?' he asked as he strode from the verandah to the carriage.

'I'm sorry,' James said quickly, 'I didn't mean anything by it.' He reached to take the note, but just as the man handed it over Mackenzie came alongside the carriage and snatched the letter from his hand.

'What's this?' His eyes were bright with a quickening anger.

'It's nothing,' James said. 'It's just a private letter ...' James was at a loss to say anything more. Nothing he said now would make things any better.

Mackenzie broke the seal and scanned the page, his face growing redder with every line. 'Just as I thought,' he said. 'The knave is plotting to run away.'

'I was kidnapped,' James began, but before he could say anything else he felt Mackenzie's fist connect with his jaw and then the man, the carriage, the day itself vanished in a glare of blinding white light.

When he woke, his face was still numb from the blow. It was dark and when he touched his jaw he found his right hand shackled with a heavy chain. The chain was attached to the wall, and as his eyes got used to the dark he saw that he was in a corner of the same stable he had been cleaning out today or yesterday or whenever it was before Mackenzie had knocked him out. He heard the horses in their stall and the stench of their urine filled his nostrils. He was hungry and thirsty and poked around in the straw in case there might be a crust or a bowl of water, but there was nothing. Maybe Mackenzie meant to starve him – he wouldn't put it past him.

A sudden shaft of light almost blinded him. Someone had opened the stable door and slipped in. He braced himself for another attack, but none came. Instead, a familiar voice spoke softly to him. Amelia. Thank God for that, he sighed in relief. He drank the water and gulped the bread she had brought.

'How long does he mean to keep me here?' he asked her.

'I don't know. He was very angry. He wanted to tie you to the apple tree.'

James pictured Connolly's back lacerated by the cowhide whip and groaned.

'I told him you mightn't survive it, and he'd be left with a dead servant on his hands, which would be a poor return on his investment.'

'Not much of an investment,' James said. 'He got me at a knock-down price since I had no trade and no muscle.'

'Any investment is a consideration for him,' Amelia said. 'And there would be the embarrassment. It's not considered good practice to kill the indentured servants. Slaves are another matter.'

Amelia looked anxiously at the door. 'I can't stay,' she said. 'He may come here any minute.'

She touched his forehead. 'Don't give up, James. This will pass soon enough.'

Amelia slipped out of the stable and he closed his eyes. How often had he heard words like these? That he mustn't give up, must be brave, must be careful and do his utmost to survive? Why? Wouldn't it be better just to accept that his life was hopeless and sink into it like a dumb animal? What was to be gained by endless striving when his situation was so hopeless? He looked into the future and all he could see was years of labouring in heat and cold with no respite. This stable was exactly the right place for him to be, he thought bitterly. He was a beast among beasts, nothing more.

But Amelia's gentle touch came back to him. She had taken a big risk to come and see him. The thought made him feel a little ashamed of his despair. And then Sylvia's image came into his mind. He had tried not to think of her because it was too painful and only made his imprisonment worse. But maybe that was wrong – maybe, instead of trying to forget, he needed to think of her; he needed to keep her alive in his heart to remind him of who he was and what might yet be possible. He let his mind drift back to Dublin and imagined he was walking with Sylvia from the Haymarket to Phoenix Street. He saw the traders, the beggars, smelled the meat and fish, heard the gulls screeching and the din of carriages and the shouts on the streets. He began to name all the names of the streets he could remember: Dame Street, High Street, Thomas Street ...

In his wanderings through the city he didn't notice Mackenzie come in, but when he opened his eyes, he saw the farmer standing above him. He sat up and looked at Mackenzie.

'If you ever try anything again, I'll string you up on the apple tree and flay you alive. Do you understand that?'

James nodded.

'Answer me, if you don't want to feel my foot!'

'I understand,' James said. He made his voice as flat as possible, with no edge of resentment or rebellion that Mackenzie might pick up on.

'Well, you can stew in your juices a while yet,' Mackenzie said, and turned on his heel and left.

Three more days James spent chained in the stable. By the time Connolly was sent to release him he was weak from hunger and still badly bruised. He accompanied Connolly to the boundary of the land, where they worked on repairing fences. Connolly did most of the work, letting James sit and watch.

'I'll give you the nod if himself shows up,' he said.

James was grateful. He hardly had the strength to lift his arm. He stared out at the land beyond Mackenzie's, a broad, sloping expanse that gave way to thick woods at the brow. Somewhere beyond the woods was the river, and on its banks the town where Amelia went for household supplies. James had never been there, but he knew it was a sizeable enough place, and that it was well connected with other towns across the land.

Connolly handed him a hammer and a couple of nails. 'Better at least look like you're doing something,' he said.

As the days passed, slowly James's body got itself back into the groove of labour and he set his mind to it with grim determination. He wouldn't give Mackenzie any reason to find him wanting. He wanted to disappear from Mackenzie's mind, to be an unnoticed and unremarkable labourer on the farm.

For he had made his mind up. There was only one way out of this miserable prison, and that was escape. But if he was to succeed, he first of all had to make himself invisible. He wanted to quiz Connolly on his escape, to find out as much as he could about the terrain, the neighbouring farms and towns, to find out the best direction in which to strike out and the obvious pitfalls to avoid. But the risk was too great. Connolly might say something, or might be forced to reveal whatever James told him. Nor could he afford to implicate Amelia in his plan; it could place her in danger and he didn't want anyone to suffer on his behalf.

So James decided that he would have to plan and act alone. From now on, he wouldn't work blindly, but would force himself to watch and listen to everything that happened on the farm. He would be the most alert creature there – not a thing that occurred would pass him by. Every broken twig, every skein of news or gossip would be gathered up, stored and added to the map of the district he must make in his mind; only when he knew everything he could, when he was ready, would he make his move.

The new, quieter James didn't go entirely unnoticed.

Amelia saw that something in him had changed. 'What's going on with you these days, James? You're not thinking of anything foolish, are you?'

She was concerned, and she looked at him with such clear eyes it was hard not to blurt out everything in a rush.

'No,' he said. 'The truth is, I'm not thinking of anything at all these days.'

Amelia gave him a hard look as if she didn't believe him, but she didn't say anything.

The trees had lost their leaves and the weather had turned cold. Runaways tended to favour the warmer months, so the cold suited James. It meant that fewer people would regard him suspiciously. Escape, he thought, was not a matter of how far you might run, but how you behaved, how you spoke, how you acted. He was determined that he would escape with his brain and not become one of those runaways who are caught within a few days and dragged back for a whipping and a life ten times more miserable than before.

As the days passed, he was careful to reveal no sign of preparation, and to show every outward sign of accepting his lot on the farm. He forced himself to smile a little more often than was his habit, and generally to give the impression that he had settled into his servitude in a spirit of submission and good cheer.

Mackenzie was not a very social man. He didn't throw parties. He rarely received visitors, but he did, every so often, go to Philadelphia on business, and when he went he was often gone for several days. James learned from Amelia that he would be gone the following week and that the farm would be run by an overseer hired for the purpose. As soon as he heard this, James began making his plans. He began by putting aside what bread and corn he could do without, concealing it in the small box where he kept his scant supply of clothes. From the tool shed he managed to acquire a knife. Then he waited anxiously for the day of Mackenzie's departure. When the morning came, he rose well before dawn and went to work in the woods, waking Connolly to tell him where he would be if he was wanted.

When Connolly joined him later that morning, he looked at James in some puzzlement. 'What's the idea, getting here so early? Who are you trying to impress?'

'No reason,' James said. 'I couldn't sleep, that's all. I had to be up and out in the air.'

Connolly didn't look convinced, but didn't say anything. The real reason for James's early start was his desire to avoid the attention of the overseer. The less he saw of James, the less he would be disturbed by his absence. He managed to get through the rest of the day without encountering the man, who, as Amelia reported, was happy enough to spend most of the time in the house sitting by the fire and reading Mackenzie's newspapers.

James took this as a sign that the gods were on his side. After they had eaten their meal, James quietly gathered his few supplies and walked out into the night. He desperately wanted to take his leave of Amelia but didn't want to put her in the position of knowing what he was about, and he knew too that she would do her best to talk him out of his plans. She would say he was foolish and headstrong, that he should serve his time and then walk out a free man.

'You only have to wait,' she'd often said to him, the knowledge of her own endless servitude in her eyes.

But James couldn't wait. He had only one thought, to get as far away as possible from Mackenzie's farm and on a ship back to Dublin.

He had to content himself with a last look back at the sleeping quarters before walking towards the boundary where he had been working all day. It took him a lot longer than it had that morning, and his heart beat wildly as he clambered through the dark, torn between the need to pick his way carefully through the undergrowth and the desire to run as fast as his body would allow him. He forced himself to be calm. It would be madness to give in to panic now. Eventually he reached the fence. He heard nothing behind him to indicate that he was missed. Ahead of him lay a vast expanse of alien land. He shivered in the cold night air. Then he climbed over the fence.

TWENTY-EIGHT

'We have to bring him back'

Her father was telling a long story about some incident in the market. Sylvia heard the words but didn't take anything in. She speared a little meat with her fork and lifted it half-heartedly. She seemed to be doing everything half-heartedly these days. It was hard to concentrate on anything. The world that had been so familiar to her was now a strange and cold place, and her position in it very uncertain. Her sleep was filled with images of ships tossing and turning on wild seas, as if her own bed was a frail boat caught in a storm. Who knows if James had even survived his terrible journey? And if he had, what had happened to him then? She knew he had strength, but he was not a big, brawny lad, and his life on the streets hadn't left much meat on his bones.

She felt a rush of tenderness as she thought of him. Her parents didn't know about her dealings with Jack Darcy. They would have been shocked to find out she'd been consorting with a criminal like him and horrified if they knew she'd put Darcy up to committing an attack on Lord Dunmain. But she'd have to tell them what had happened to James because she couldn't bring him back herself. She didn't intend to sit on her knowledge — the information she'd extracted from the ledger in the Tholsel was only the beginning, and she wouldn't rest until she'd put it to some use.

Her father was still talking. Her mother was listening in a kind of dreamy, abstracted way. She didn't talk about James much any more, but Sylvia knew she missed him.

'I know where he is,' Sylvia said suddenly.

Her father stopped his story. 'What do you mean?' he said.

'I know where James is.'

There was a startled pause. Nancy's look of dreamy abstraction had vanished and she looked hard at Sylvia. 'Where is he?'

That was a good start, Sylvia thought, not *how do you know* but *where is he*?

'He is on a ship on his way to the New World. Given into servitude by his uncle.'

Her father's eyes narrowed. 'You didn't find that out by reading a newspaper. Who told you?'

Sylvia shrugged. 'I found someone who knew.' She pressed ahead. 'We can't leave him. We have to go there. We have to bring him back.'

She didn't mean it to come out so nakedly. Her parents looked at each other.

'Sylvia,' John Purcell said, 'you know how much we care for James, ever since that day I carried him back from Smithfield.

But if what you say is true, I don't think we can save him.'

Sylvia's eyes flashed angrily. 'How can you say that?' she said. 'We can't abandon him now that he needs us most. We have to do something.'

'But what?' her father said. 'We're simple people, Sylvia. What can we do? We can't just jump on a boat and rescue the lad. It's not that easy. It's the most dangerous crossing in the world. We'd be lucky to get to the other side alive.'

'It may not be easy, Father, but we still have to do it. He's one of us now,' Sylvia said.

She meant much more than that, but she couldn't say it out. She looked at her mother for support. Her mother's face was creased with worry.

'I don't know, love,' she said. 'It's such a long way. To lose James is terrible. But I couldn't bear to lose you and John as well. I couldn't bear it.'

Sylvia reached across and took her mother's hand.

'You won't lose us,' she said. 'Many people make that journey and live to tell the tale. Isn't that right, Father?'

John Purcell was no more convinced than his wife, but he tried to look as if they talking about an undertaking no more perilous than a trip across a river ferry.

'She's right,' he said. 'After all, there'd be no New World if people couldn't get there.'

But Nancy wasn't to be fobbed off. 'I know you want my blessing, child, but no matter how much I love James, I can't bring myself to give it.' And she left the room without another word.

They sat in silence a while. But Sylvia couldn't keep quiet for long.

'We have to try, don't we? We have to at least try?'

There was such force in her voice that John Purcell gripped the edge of the table.

'Alright,' he said. 'What do you want to do?'

'Thank you,' she said, 'I knew you'd help. For the moment all we can do is wait until the captain of the ship returns to Dublin. Then we can find out what happened to James.'

'Don't tell me any more,' her father said, 'I can guess the rest. It will take some doing to get your mother used to the idea. And we're going to need money, lots of it. Did you happen to think about that?'

Sylvia was relieved that his objections had crumbled and they had progressed to practical matters.

'I have some ideas about that,' she said. 'There are many here who know James, who might be persuaded to give a little for his release. Maybe the school might help.'

She had other ideas too, but these she kept to herself.

'You really want him back, don't you?' her father said.

There was no hesitation in Sylvia's voice. 'Yes,' she said. 'I do.'

She didn't waste any time putting her plan of action into effect. She let it be known throughout the neighbourhood that a fund was being created to rescue James.

'Is it Lord Bluecoat you mean?' she was asked more than once, and she discovered that the name was widespread in the area. As she travelled further, she found that James's nickname and his story had spread there too. When she crossed the river to tell Harry her plans, she was surprised that Lord Bluecoat's fame was even well known in the southern districts.

'Many knew about him before,' Harry said, 'but the name Lord Bluecoat seems to have stuck. It's a good thing, too – it keeps his name alive. The more famous his story, the less his uncle will like it.'

Harry looked directly at Sylvia. 'There's one other thing,' he said.

'What?'

Harry shifted on his feet. 'I know I don't have any means,' he said. 'And a shoeblack isn't worth much in the world, but I want to help …'

'Of course, Harry, that's very kind. And all help is very welcome.'

'No,' Harry said, 'I mean I want to come with you. I want to help you find him.' He grinned. 'I'm not the tallest,' he added, 'but I'm handy with my fists. You never know when that might come in handy.'

Sylvia was taken by surprise, but of course it made sense. And it would be good to have Harry along.

'You'll need sea legs as well as fists,' she smiled, and Harry saluted.

'Aye, aye, Cap'n.'

Contributions to the fund flowed in through the weeks that followed. Even the habitués of Red Molly's were persuaded to part with some of the fruits of their trade and, though she knew it was wrong, Sylvia accepted the money for the greater good that might come out of it. And Darcy even funded Harry's passage. 'You can thank a drunk old lord for his generosity,' he grinned, and Sylvia thought it prudent not to inquire further.

It was late summer when the captain returned. It was a friend of Harry's who spotted him drinking in a tavern. As soon as he heard, Harry ran to Phoenix Street with the news. Sylvia ran to Ormond Market and found her father in his stall.

'Alright,' he said, removing his bloody apron. 'We'll go there now and see what we can find out.'

The captain was still at the tavern when they arrived, sitting at a table in the corner tucking into a large dish of mutton. John Purcell and Sylvia walked straight over and sat down. The captain looked up, none too pleased.

'There's plenty of other tables,' he said. 'Why crowd me?'

'We want some information from you,' John Purcell said.

The captain grew uncomfortable as Purcell explained what he wanted.

'How can you expect me to remember every passenger on the ship? Do you know how many we carry?'

'You'd remember this one,' Sylvia said. 'Because he shouldn't have been on it.'

The captain looked at Sylvia properly for the first time. He wasn't used to a girl's voice addressing him, and this one seemed unusually forthright. Something about her compelled attention.

'Someone paid you to take him,' Sylvia followed up. 'We know who was behind it. We just want to know what happened to the boy.'

The captain looked around the tavern. It was crowded; there were many folk who knew him.

'You know how to spoil a man's grub, I'll give you that,' he said to Sylvia.

He pushed his dish away and took a good slug from his glass before standing up.

'A bit of fresh air, I think,' he announced and began pushing through the crowd.

John Purcell and Sylvia followed him out to the quay. The shriek of gulls filled the air.

The captain considered the Purcells. 'Why should I tell you anything?' he said evenly.

John Purcell replied in the same even tone, 'Because if you don't, you'll find yourself dealing with the Ormond Boys, and that'll be just the start of it.'

'I thought you'd say something like that,' the captain said. And then he told them what they wanted to know.

'Do you trust him?' Sylvia asked her father as they walked back along the quay.

'Not much,' her father replied. 'But it sounded convincing enough.'

'There's only one way to find out,' Sylvia said.

'Are you sure about this, Sylvia?' her father said. 'It's a great undertaking. And dangerous. Do you know that?'

'I know it,' Sylvia said. 'But if what the captain said is true, then James needs us desperately.'

Her father made no reply.

They walked in silence along the river and got on a ferry. As they crossed the water, her father suddenly spoke. 'I've heard tell the ships from the north are safer,' he said. 'We could get a passage from Newry.'

Sylvia's heart leapt. She knew she could trust her father. And for the first time since James had vanished, she felt sure that she would see him again. Yet now that the journey seemed real, she also felt a twinge of anxiety, and the thought of leaving her mother behind filled her with dread.

At last the day came for the journey to begin. Sylvia hardly slept at all the night before and when she rose it was a long time before the first light penetrated the small window of her room. Even so, when she came downstairs Nancy was already bustling about the kitchen, boiling oatmeal for breakfast. Sylvia couldn't bear the thought of food.

'Your stomach will thank you later,' Nancy said. 'You'll need all your strength for the journey.'

Sylvia knew her mother didn't want her to go – she thought the plan was foolish and dangerous. But she had stopped protesting now: she knew how set her daughter was on it, and she knew better than to argue with her when her mind was made up.

John Purcell came into the kitchen with a heavy tread. He took his wife's hands in his and looked her in the eye. 'Nancy,' he said, and for what seemed like an age he said nothing more. 'You know you'll see me again, woman, don't you?'

'Oh John, I only wish I did!' There were tears in Nancy's eyes but she blinked them back fiercely.

Sylvia looked away and tried to force the oatmeal down.

There was a soft rapping on the door and when she opened it Harry stepped in, shyly saluting the family. His few belongings were wrapped in a small cloth bag, as if he might be travelling from one part of the city to another instead of halfway across the world.

'I'll look after your family, Missus, don't you worry,' Harry said, and, in spite of herself, Nancy laughed. 'You'd better, at that,' she said.

Soon, even at that early hour, the little house was filled with well-wishers who'd come to see them off to the coach that would take them north on the greatest journey of their lives.

• • • • • •

TWENTY-NINE

Taste of Freedom

Dizzy with hunger, his body numb with cold, James stumbled out of the forest into a clearing. It was three days since he had run from Mackenzie's farm. That first night he had run straight towards the trees at the brow of the hill beyond Mackenzie's boundary. Once he'd entered the cover of the trees he had kept running as fast as the darkness would let him, trying to block out from his mind the terrifying noises that filled the forest. It seemed every creature on the earth must be creeping and flitting and running through the trees that night. Clammy leaves brushed his face, and several times he tripped on a tangle of undergrowth.

He tried to keep his body on a straight path and not double back on himself. His idea was to head northward until he met the Delaware river. He didn't have a clear idea beyond that, except that he might somehow find passage on a boat, or find his way towards the relative safety of a big city like Philadelphia, where he might lie low and recover himself. But as he ploughed through the trees, he lost his sense of direction and when the first light began to break through the trees he realised that he had no clear idea of where he was. He ate a little of the bread he'd brought and rested a little. He pushed on until he came to a small clearing. The day was clear, with good sunlight, so James took a twig and placed it in the ground, then moved it towards the sun until the shadow disappeared. Then he waited a while until the shadow grew from the stick on the other side. He reckoned that shadow gave him an east-west line and he bisected it with another twig to find north. Had he remembered it right? It was a trick Connolly had shown him one day in the woods when there was no sign of Mackenzie.

James followed that line through the trees again and kept going as long as he could. As the afternoon wore on, he felt the chill in his body and knew he couldn't spend another night without shelter. They wouldn't try to look for him once darkness fell, he thought. He stopped and considered his surroundings. In the distance he saw a tree that had been torn from the ground and lay propped precariously against the trunk of another, its roots exposed. He made for it without delay. It was perfect: the root system protruded out of the ground to form a natural roof, with a deep and comfortable-looking space underneath, which James began to fill quickly with fallen leaves and clumps of earth and grass. Then he stepped down into the bed-shaped space and covered himself with some of the leaves. He thought about lighting a fire, but

wouldn't allow himself to take the chance. He remembered
Connolly brought back with his tail between his legs after
two days and tied to the apple tree. It was better to be a little
chilly than suffer that.

James was woken by barking, faint but distinct. He leapt
from his shelter and hastily disassembled it, scattering the
branches and debris in all directions even though he knew if
the dogs came this far they would surely know where he had
slept. He felt his stomach tighten with fear as he thought of
them. But they were not near yet. He must be calm. He leant
his forehead against a tree and forced his exhausted mind to
clear itself and think. James had known he would be pursued
of course; there was no surprise in that. And he was still a good
way ahead, to judge by the sound of the barking. He resisted
the urge to flee and forced himself to stay still for a moment.
He cocked his ear to the sound of the barking and listened
intently. It did not seem to be getting any nearer. James tried
to put himself in the shoes of the pursuers. They would expect
him to go northward towards the Delaware; this had, in fact,
been his intention. But maybe he had strayed, and maybe if he
kept on straying he would avoid his trackers.

He began now to move through the trees away from the barking, in what might be a westward direction. He kept on going
at a slow-running pace, wishing the endless avenues of trees
were streets that he might easily navigate. James never thought
nature could be so endless, that you could pass through it for
days and days without encountering a human habitation or
any sign of human life. The day wore on, and still he kept

moving. By now he had exhausted his meagre rations, but he knew he couldn't afford to think about food. He remembered Amelia telling him that somewhere to the west the peoples of the Five Nations lived. He hoped he had not strayed into their territory. His brain filled with all kinds of dark imaginings of what he might suffer if captured by Iroquois warriors. He felt sure he saw faces flitting between the trees. He stopped suddenly, plagued by hunger and thirst. An Iroquois brave would know how to fend for himself in a forest, James thought, but all I have is street craft. When evening came, he drew some moisture from leaves and imagined he was sitting down to a great dish of mutton in Red Molly's. Darkness fell quickly and he had neglected to make a shelter. He gathered leaves and brushwood and piled them at the foot of a tree and huddled as best he could.

* * *

And here he was now, on the third day. He came out into the clearing and saw that he had reached the end of the forest. The land sloped down to a track and, beyond it, a great river. He looked around cautiously and, seeing nobody, ran to the river and leaned over the bank to scoop his fill of water. What river was this? It surely couldn't be the Delaware, or he'd hear the barking of dogs and the shouts of men. There was only a great silence all around. As he looked into the distance, he could make out the blurry outlines of ships, and the sight filled him with hope. If he followed the course of the river he might be able to get himself onto a vessel to the north or even to a port where he might embark for Europe. He sat down under a tree a little way from the bank and fell into a deep sleep. Several hours later, he was woken by loud voices. He opened his eyes and saw two men on horseback, one of whom had a woman behind him. The second man carried a large portmanteau and several bundles. Not recognising any of them, James sighed with relief. He stood up, pressed himself against the trunk and peered out through the lower branches.

'We'll stop here,' the man who had the woman with him said. 'It's as good a place as any to rest.'

He dismounted and helped the woman down, then both men tied their horses to a tree very near James. The second man, who seemed to be a servant, untied one of the bundles and spread a cloth on the grass, on which he placed wine and food.

James eyed the scene greedily; it was all he could do to keep still and not race to the table napkin at once. He didn't keep still enough, though, and managed to brush against a branch so that the leaves rustled. The place was so quiet it might as well have been a gunshot, and the servant turned immediately in his direction, his cutlass drawn. James came out from the cover of the tree and raised his hands.

'Who is it?' the other man shouted, immediately moving to shield the woman.

The servant ran at James as if he meant to decapitate him.

'Please, I mean no harm,' James said in a clear voice. 'I've been travelling for days and I'm hungry and thirsty. You need have no fear of me.'

They all looked relieved, and the man invited him to join them and share their meal. As they ate, James learned that they were fugitives like him, though the cause was different. The man, who introduced himself as Tom Black, and the woman, Charlotte, had eloped and they feared they would be pursued by her husband, who was a powerful man in the local town. They were planning to take ship in a little town on the Delaware and make their way to Holland. Because of the danger they were in, they were travelling by night. As it was now almost dusk, they would be leaving soon. This sounded like an excellent plan to James, and when he asked if he might join them they agreed willingly enough. They quickly finished their meal and packed up. James noticed how tender the couple were towards each other and felt a pang as he wondered if he would ever see Sylvia again. There was little time to brood, however, and soon they were all mounted and riding through the woods, which, even though their progress would be slower, they felt would offer the most protection.

The night was dark and, after a couple of hours of slow passage through the forest, Tom Black called out to his servant. 'Let's rejoin the road, or we'll be too long delayed. It should be safe enough now.'

The servant murmured his assent and they faced their horses towards the edge of the forest and soon gained the track that would take them to the little town near Newcastle. James was glad they were travelling by night as he realised that he was heading back in the direction of Mackenzie's farm and, if it had been light, he could well be seen by someone who knew him. The night air was cold, but he didn't care; he could taste freedom in the chill. Every furlong was a stage nearer the end of the terrible prison of his recent life.

They were not more than two or three miles out of the forest when they heard the noise they most dreaded: the fierce clatter of hooves on the ground that signalled the approach of many horses at full tilt. James looked around and saw the flicker of lights in the distance. There could be no doubt that it was a party of pursuers.

'No!' the woman cried, and James thought he'd never heard a more desperate sound.

'Head back to the forest,' Black cried and, at once, they turned the horses away from the track and up the sloping ground towards the cover of the trees. But the noise of the hooves was unrelenting and louder by the second. Their change of course seemed to make no difference. The torches were clear now, clear enough to be counted. Not less than a dozen, James reckoned, as he held on to the servant urging their horse up the slope until the trees came into view. They still had a chance, if they could get in to the forest.

'Come on!' James said. 'We can still do it!'

It was too late. They had barely reached the edge of the forest when their pursuers caught up with them. The servant leaped from the horse and drew his cutlass, and Black seized his lover and held her close to him as he brandished his sword.

'It's no use, Charlotte,' a voice said from one of the horses.

James, who had slipped off the horse and was now standing beside the couple, ready to defend his friends with his bare hands, stared at the owner of the voice, an older man with the air of someone used to being obeyed. Several of the party had dismounted and drawn their weapons. One had a pistol aimed at Tom Black, while two others quickly overpowered the servant and another seized James roughly, knocked him down and pinioned him with a knee on his chest. James could hardly believe he'd come so close to freedom only to be caught so simply.

'I can finish him here,' the man with the pistol said of Tom Black.

'No,' said the leader, who had remained mounted. 'He'll die in the manner prescribed by the law. There's no need to anticipate that now.'

'Do what you like with me, but let Charlotte go,' Black pleaded.

'It's too late for that' came the reply. 'There'll be no bargaining. You shall all suffer the consequences of your actions.'

'Run, Charlotte,' Black said, pushing her to one side, and lunging suddenly at the man with the pistol.

The pistol fired, but Black had managed to tip the barrel upwards with his sword, and a nearby tree bore the impact of the ball. It was all Black managed to do, for, within seconds, he was attacked from all directions, and his sword fell uselessly to the ground.

'Bind them' came the order from above. Black and Charlotte were bound and set on their own horses. James and the servant were tied to the horses' tails and had to run smartly to avoid being dragged on the ground. They travelled like that for many hours until they came to a sleeping town. Their procession through the silent streets was noisy and unusual enough to cause a few window frames to be raised and heads to peer down. One or two observers called down to know what the news was, and were met with answers from some of the riders, but the commotion was quickly stopped by the wronged husband. When they came to the town gaol one of the horsemen opened up the doors. James later discovered he was the gaoler. They were all bundled into different cells and shut up for the night.

* * *

'My God,' Harry said, holding onto a barrel on the deck. 'No one told me the sea moved so much. Do you think we'll ever see land again?'

Sylvia tried to steady him, but she had barely found her own sea legs. The churning waves splashed over the side and soaked the deck.

'I'm sure she will,' she said, though her voice had to work hard to reach Harry's ears through the din of the waves and the wind.

'I wish I had learned to swim!' Harry shouted.

Swimming would be no use in these waters, Sylvia thought. If you didn't perish of the cold, some awful watery beast would be sure to devour you, but she said nothing. Her father was below, heaving with sea sickness. Many had warned her of the terrors of the journey, but she had pushed the warnings aside. She knew now she would need every bit of her courage if she was to make it to the other side of this great ocean. And if her sufferings were bad, what must James's be like? What terrors must he be enduring now? And yet, even if the thoughts were full of fears, just thinking about him gave her strength.

'Come on.' She grabbed the shivering Harry by the sleeve of his coat and they made their way below.

* * *

The morning after his capture, James found himself before the court with the three haggard conspirators. The business proceeded swiftly, since Black, Charlotte and the servant readily admitted the charges. All three swore that James had nothing to do with the affair, being merely an accidental travelling companion. When he was questioned, James maintained that he had never been in the town, or anywhere near it before, and had been making his way, by slow degrees, to Philadelphia, where he sought to be apprenticed to a printer. James wouldn't have believed himself and didn't expect the judge to be taken in, but whereas in the case of the other three all the particulars were known and admitted, in his case there no evidence of any kind. They could hardly have been in the building three quarters of an hour before the judge came to the sentencing.

James was shocked to hear the sentence of death pronounced on his three companions. Surely the judge could not mean it? Charlotte gave a little cry; Tom Black and his servant stared blankly. When it came to James's turn, the judge said that although his story wasn't convincing, there was nothing, for the moment, to connect him to the other miscreants.

'It is therefore my decision that you remain in the town gaol until further notice, and that each day you be exposed in the marketplace at noon. If any should recognise you, or possess any information that connects you to this town or to Thomas Black, you shall suffer the same fate. Take them away.'

Back in his cell James lamented the fate of the others. He could not understand the cruel vindictiveness of Charlotte's husband or the judge. The husband was clearly a potent force in the town, for James couldn't imagine any unbiased judge pronouncing a sentence as harsh as that. The crime after all was driven by love, but even if it was a mighty force in the affairs of men, love was a small power in the law. The powerful always got their way, James knew that much. If ever he had power, he thought, he wouldn't use it so vindictively.

Every day, at ten minutes before noon, the gaoler came to take him out to the marketplace. There he was shackled to a post and around his neck a sign was placed, 'If anyone knows this boy, let it be known at once to Judge Williams.'

The first day, many came to inspect him curiously, and some of the town boys jeered him and threw fruit at him until they were shooed away by the traders. Once the novelty passed, no one paid much attention to him and he seemed to be as much a part of the market as the fruit stalls or the haberdashery. He even began to look forward to his sessions in the square, since it was his only break from the monotony of the gaol. In its peculiar way it was a kind of freedom, and the town, even though he was a prisoner in it, was at least preferable to hacking down trees on a dreary plantation. And the day would surely come when they got tired of exposing him in the marketplace and would let him continue on his journey to real freedom.

THIRTY

Lost Property

So this is Philadephia, Sylvia thought as she, Harry and her father walked through the crowded streets near the wharf. It was big, like Dublin, but it seemed to have been designed by a professor of mathematicks, someone very particular and precise who loves straight lines and right angles. She thought of the twisting lanes and alleys of her own city, a labyrinth that had to be learned by its citizens, as if the city wanted to hide itself from those who would know her too well. This, on the other hand, was like a toy town, though its people were vivid and real enough. She heard English, though not like any she had heard before, and another harsh-sounding language that her father said was German. The shock of this new place filled Sylvia with panic and made her yearn for her mother. She closed her eyes now and thought of her, as if she could send a signal to her mother from this strange new world, to let her know that they had made the crossing and were still strong. Then she opened her eyes again to fix them on her surroundings.

From the mayor's office they had been able to obtain the address of the planter who had hired James, but right now they needed somewhere to rest and prepare themselves for the journey. After much searching, they found a place they could afford and settled themselves there. As Sylvia tossed and turned in bed that night, she felt through her exhaustion a strange absence she couldn't explain until it came to her: the eerie silence of the night, where not a single steeple rang the hour. The bells of Dublin were so familiar to her that she hardly even registered them, but she wished she could hear them now, in the hush of this city whose stillness failed to provide much comfort.

She was not sorry to leave Philadephia the next day. They set out on one of the roads that led out of the city. It took many days to reach the district where James's master lived. This country was vast, and much of their way was through thick woods, which greatly frightened Sylvia. John Purcell did his best to calm her, but it wasn't easy. They managed to get a lift from a German family on the back of their small cart a small part of the way and eventually they reached a small town not far from Mackenzie's plantation. Since, by then, they were thoroughly exhausted, they found an inn where they could recover themselves.

'Pretend to be my son,' John Purcell said to Harry. 'It will avoid awkward questions.'

Harry nodded, trying to take in his surroundings as if he

was used to staying in inns. I'm a raggy sort of son, he thought to himself, but I'll prove what I can do when the time comes.

Early the next morning, having inquired the way from the innkeeper, they set out for the plantation.

'I don't know how anyone can find anywhere in this country,' Sylvia said as field and woods blended into each other with barely a sign of human habitation. 'Why don't they put their houses where a person could see them?'

'Probably because they need water,' her father said with his usual practicality. 'I know I would. It's not like a city, where everything is near at hand.'

'It's a wilderness,' Sylvia said. 'How can anyone want to be here?'

John Purcell thought of the determined settlers he had encountered on the ship. They were men of God, determined to worship and cultivate their land without hindrance, and he didn't think they would be put off by a few trees. He was not so attached to his own life in Dublin that he couldn't imagine the possibilities this colony seemed to offer. For now, though, he had other business to attend to.

Eventually, some time after noon, they came to the farm, which was entered by a long twisty path that brought them to the farmstead, a very ordinary building which had no smell of great wealth about it. It looked like the kind of place a man would sweat hard in, Purcell thought as he looked around. He heard the sounds of labour before he saw anyone. A man was splitting logs in the yard, and as they approached the house a servant, who had spied them from within, came out.

Amelia looked closely at the strangers. They didn't seem to be vagrants, but they had neither horses nor carriage. She had never seen visitors arrive on foot before and wondered if they had been robbed.

'Is everything alright?' she asked as she came down the steps.

'We're looking for Master Mackenzie,' John Purcell said. 'Are we at the right place?'

Amelia immediately recognised from his accent that he was not from these parts.

'This is the place,' she said. 'I'll tell him you're here.'

'Please, miss, can you tell me if James is here?' Sylvia couldn't wait any longer.

Amelia looked at her in amazement.

'James? He is, or was here—' She was prevented from going into any more detail by the appearance of Mackenzie at the top of the steps.

'Who are these people, Amelia?' he asked gruffly, assuming, as she had when she'd first seen them, that they must be vagrants looking for work or alms.

John Purcell didn't much like the look of the man regarding him coolly from the steps. There was a roughness about him, the arrogance of one used to getting his own way with very little opposition.

'We are friends of James Lovett, whom I believe is an indentured servant here,' Purcell began.

'Wrongly indentured,' Sylvia added, but Purcell held her arm.

'What's this?' Mackenzie shouted. 'You're here to see the

boy? By what authority?'

'No authority, sir, but friendship. The boy was taken from his native city and sold into servitude by his uncle—'

'That old story,' Mackenzie interrupted. 'What makes you think I want to hear a lot of cock-and-bull stories?'

'But it's true!' Sylvia was not to be held back. 'It's no story but the plain truth. He's not a servant but a born lord.'

Mackenzie brushed her interruption aside.

'I'll tell you what he is,' he said. 'He's mine, bought and paid for with good money. If you found me, you know that.'

'We don't dispute that,' Purcell said. 'We know you acted in good faith—'

'Do you now?' Mackenzie said. He spat the words out. He was still at the top of the steps, looming over his visitors. 'Well, I'll tell you something, I mean to get my value out of him no matter who he is, and no pair of Irish tramps will persuade me otherwise.'

John Purcell had to restrain himself. If someone spoke like that to him in Dublin, it would be last thing he did. But he held his tongue.

'May we speak to him?' Sylvia said. Seeing this man made her fear for James's safety.

Her request was met with a grim smile.

'Well, you may at that,' Mackenzie said, 'but you'll have to find him first.'

'What do you mean?' Purcell said.

'I mean that the worthless slave has run away,' Mackenzie replied. 'A temporary inconvenience, let me assure you. And when he comes back, when I bring him back, then he shall learn the real meaning of servitude.'

John Purcell and Sylvia received this news in silence. Harry stood back a little, scanning the land as closely as he could, as if James might sense their presence and make a sign that would allow them to find him. Sylvia didn't know whether to be horrified or relieved. She was bitterly disappointed that she couldn't see James, but if this was his master then his escape was a cause for relief. However, her heart sank at the thought that he might fall into this man's hands again. If only they could find him before that happened. They had come all this way; maybe it might still be possible to find him and bring him back safely to Dublin. She lurched between hope and despair. The land was so vast and so full of danger: how could she possibly think they might find him? Mackenzie, on the other hand, had the force of law on his side and a knowledge of the territory. The country was teeming with those who would be only too glad to return his property to him. And then – she shut her mind to what might happen then.

She felt her father's hand on her shoulder.

'There's no use continuing here,' her father said. 'We'll go back to the town and see what we must do.'

As they walked down the long drive, Amelia darted out from a little stand of trees.

'Quick,' she said. 'Over here.'

Once they were all safely hidden in the trees she spoke. 'James is in great danger,' she said. 'If he is caught, it will go hard with him.'

'Is this the first time he has escaped?' Sylvia said.

'Yes. He tried to send a letter before to his friend from Ireland, but he was caught and beaten?'

'What friend?' John Purcell said.

'I do not remember any name,' Amelia said. 'He lived with him in a big college once. That is all I know.'

'The Liberty Boy!' John Purcell said.

'James told me about him,' Sylvia said. 'James saved his life. He went to live in America. Maybe he could help us.'

'If we can find him,' John said, without much hope in his voice. 'This is a big country.'

'You must try to save the boy,' Amelia said. 'He will die here otherwise.' And she slipped through the trees and was gone.

* * *

The gaoler led James to his accustomed post. James felt like a circus animal being led out to perform its turn.

'How much longer will this go on?' he asked the gaoler.

'Till we get sick of the sight of you,' the man replied. 'Maybe when they've hanged the other three, they'll turn their attention to you.'

This was not a comforting thought to James; nor was it intended to be. He felt it would take the death of all four of them to satisfy the gaoler's sense of completion. James took up his usual position and gazed out over the stalls. It was quiet enough at this hour, but as the morning wore on the place began to fill up. This was a market day, when the small town swelled with the influx of farmers and trusted servants from the outlying districts. In spite of the added attention they brought, these were the days James liked best, when he could survey the great bustle and let his eyes wander among the crowd, picking out those he thought looked kindly, and those whose faces were cruel, whose hands he could easily imagine applying a rawhide. He looked, too, at the young girls in the excitement of their day out, imagining Sylvia might be among them. Occasionally, one or two of them looked at him curiously, and he managed a weak smile before they quickly turned away.

Today the town was the most crowded he had seen, which puzzled James until he saw the construction on the far side of the square. A platform had been built, on which stood two upright beams and a cross bar – the unmistakable form of a gallows. Then they meant to go through with it, and this was the day chosen for the purpose. He looked at the miserable spectacle and at the crowds slowly gathering round it. A festive excitement began to charge the air as food hawkers shouted their produce, and knots of townspeople and visitors stood around. It reminded James of execution days in Dublin, although here the atmosphere was more restrained, with none of the baying bloodlust of the Dublin crowd.

James was glancing idly from group to group when suddenly he froze and the blood drained from his face. There was Mackenzie, on the other side of the square, deep in conversation with another farmer. James quickly averted his eyes and prayed that Mackenzie – for it was indeed him – wouldn't look across. He might as well have prayed for the sun to disappear from the sky. Even on a day like this, eyes would still be drawn to the stranger shackled in the marketplace, and it was only a moment before James felt the gaze of his master turn on him. Mackenzie was at the post in seconds, looking his property up and down and laughing softly.

'So this is where you got to, this is your lordship's new demesne?'

James didn't reply; there was no point in it, Mackenzie would have his pleasure. Mackenzie indeed looked like a man bursting with barely contained pleasure. He announced his find to all who could hear him. Even in his distress, James was pleased to note that at least some of the stallholders did not look entirely happy at the discovery. Mackenzie went to find an officer of the law to claim his property but found that no one would be available until after the execution. So James was obliged to stay in his position and watch the town gaoler hang first Tom Black and then Charlotte. Many in the crowd wept, though many others were greatly amused. James retched violently at the scene, and Mackenzie whispered into his ear.

'You'll have plenty more cause to retch when I get you home.' He didn't show any outward cruelty but, when anyone came near, was instead the model of mildness and civility. The gaoler, who was also the executioner, released James after the day's main business was done and was so impressed by Mackenzie's demeanour that he saluted him cordially.

'Many wouldn't be as charitable as you with a runaway, sir. You're to be commended indeed.'

Mackenzie drank in the compliment as he led his charge off, and even let James sit behind him on his horse as they made their way through the town. Once they were out of view of the townspeople, the real Mackenzie reappeared. He pushed James off the horse with an oath and tied him to the horse's tail in just the way James had been led into the town, and, in that fashion, he had to run as fast as he could behind the horse, often stumbling on the rough ground and falling flat on his face until the force of the horse pulled him upright again. When they eventually reached the farm James was bruised and filthy, his face cut from the many falls, his hair bedraggled and wild. The servants stood silently observing his progress as Mackenzie led him into the yard. James saw the distress on Amelia's face as she stood outside the house. He felt a sudden surge of defiance as his eyes met hers. James didn't care what Mackenzie did to him; he would never break his spirit or stop him from trying to gain his freedom. He was damned if he'd let this brute of a man determine the future course of his life.

Mackenzie barked at Amelia to gather all the servants. Meanwhile, he untied James from the horse's tail and led him to the apple tree.

'You know what's coming. Make yourself ready for it.'

James removed his coat, waistcoat and shirt. He fought the urge to shiver in the cold and stood as straight as he could as Mackenzie came towards him with the rope and bound his hands, then threw the other end over a thick branch, hoisting James up until he stood on the tips of his toes before he made the rope fast. By the time he was finished, his audience was assembled. Mackenzie ordered Amelia to bring him his rawhide from the house. James caught Connolly's eye and its flash of sympathy. He remembered the day he saw Connolly whipped at the same spot and Mackenzie's little speech beforehand. Mackenzie had taken off his coat and rolled up the sleeves of his shirt. James waited to hear the speech on the folly of escape and the just desserts that were the reward of capture, but none came. What came instead was burning pain, lash after lash of it till he thought he couldn't bear it any more, and, try as he might to suppress them, the screams came tearing out of his body.

• • • • • •

THIRTY-ONE

An Encounter

'Come on then,' Harry said. 'One city is much like another in the end. Let's see what we can find out.'

Sylvia wasn't so sure. This seemed like a frightening enough place. They said its name meant brotherly love, but she didn't see much sign of that, just milling crowds fretting and hurrying. But she knew Harry was right. It was no good sitting in the inn or pacing the narrow street outside; they had to do something. She wondered if all the men here were like Mackenzie, uncouth and cruel, bent on hurt. She kept seeing his scornful face as he loomed above them on his verandah. Was this the end of their journey, after all they had endured to get here? If only James had stayed where he was a little longer, she was sure they'd have found a way to spirit him away. She tried to think her way into his mind. If she had been him, where would she have gone? Not the country, that was sure. She had a horror of fields and woods and couldn't imagine James was any fonder of them. And small towns were dangerous, full of prying eyes and ears. No, if she had been him, she would have tried to find her way to a city like this, where it was easy to conceal yourself in the crowds. He could be here now, wandering the very same streets as her; he could be around the next corner.

Harry led her from street to street. He stopped and talked to hawkers, beggars, and shoeshine boys with an ease Sylvia envied. Some joshed with him because of his accent, but he was quick to joke back. He had many animated conversations, and Sylvia could see that a lot of information flowed his way.

'It seems it is a common thing for slaves or servants to run away,' Harry said. 'And many come here and try to melt into the city. Some find jobs with kinder masters and mistresses, some try to smuggle themselves onto ships, some are caught and returned to their owners. But there's no word of James.'

'Then we need a new plan,' Sylvia said, although she had no idea yet what that might be.

* * *

James aimed his axe at Mackenzie's head and struck. Shattered bark flew from the tree and landed harmlessly in the undergrowth.

'You look like you meant that,' Connolly said, but James didn't reply.

He had barely spoken a word since his return to the farm. Mackenzie's beating would have silenced anyone, but though his recovery from the fury of the rawhide had been slow and painful, his silence had a deeper cause. Not long after the beating, he had been cleaning out the stable when Amelia came to him. Amelia was his main comfort in those bleak days. If it hadn't been for her whispers of encouragement and constant small attentions, James was sure he wouldn't have survived. But that day her face was downcast as she approached him and James knew instantly whatever news she brought could not be good. When she had finished telling him about the two visitors from Ireland and Mackenzie's treatment of them, he fell into a deep silence. It was too much to take in that Sylvia and John could have come all the way from Dublin to this place and have arrived exactly at the time he wasn't here. It was like a glimpse of salvation cruelly snatched away before it had time to register. Amelia's admiring description of Sylvia only made the pain worse. James had thanked Amelia for telling him and then returned to the silence that had been his home since. So he had no reply to make to Connolly as he hacked at the tree that he had converted in his mind into the body of his hated master.

'At least you got away for longer than I did,' Connolly said. 'It could be a lot worse.'

James merely swung his axe again. That could do his talking for him.

* * *

John Purcell might have resigned himself to abandoning

the search for James and fixed his sights on the perils of the homeward journey, but Sylvia was far from finished.

'I won't even think about home yet,' she said to her father as he broached the subject the next morning.

'How long must we look?' he asked. 'Our resources are finite, Sylvia. And we have to think of your mother. These are lonely days for her.'

The mention of her mother hit Sylvia hard. She missed her badly and would have loved nothing more than to see her again at this very moment, but she wasn't about to admit as much to her father.

'There must be someone in this great city who can help us,' she said, although she didn't really think that was likely.

'I might have an idea,' Harry said.

'What?' John and Sylvia said at once.

'It's something one of the shoeboys I spoke to said. It seems that when a slave escapes, their masters put out an advertisement in the papers, giving all the particulars and offering a reward to whoever finds him.'

'We can hardly do that,' John said. 'It could lead to James being recaptured again. Mackenzie would be bound to recognise the description, or you can be sure someone would tell him.'

'No,' Harry said. 'Not James. I was thinking of his friend, the one Amelia mentioned.'

'That's a great idea!' Sylvia said, excited now. Then she frowned. 'But we don't know his name, and even if we did, he might be using another.'

'Leave that to me,' John said. 'I might have the answer for that.'

And so, when the next edition of the *Weekly Mercury* came out Harry rushed off to buy it and bring it back to the inn. He handed it shyly to John Purcell.

'Not much of a hand at the reading,' he said.

John took the paper and scoured it for his advertisement.

'Here it is,' he said finally. '*Ormond Butcher, newly arrived from Dublin, seeks Trinity Liberty Boy to impart news of dear friend*. And then the address of the inn.'

'Do you think he'll see it?' Sylvia said.

'I don't know,' John said. 'All we can do is wait awhile. If we don't hear anything, then we'll have to take ship back to Ireland.'

'No!' Sylvia said, despairing.

'Don't worry,' Harry said. 'It seems to me that gentlemen never stop reading newspapers. And how many Liberty Boys can be here?'

For days they waited. Too impatient to sit still, Harry hung around the streets, doing the rounds of shoeboys and street sellers, loitering outside coffee shops where gentlemen went to read their newspapers. But nothing came of it. John took out his leather purse and began counting out the remaining coins.

'We can't stay here much longer,' he said.

'I could find work,' Harry said. 'There's always gentlemen who need their shoes shined.'

'You're a good lad,' John said. 'But it would take more than that. We've done our best. All we can do is pray James finds a good life for himself if he isn't taken again.'

'But what if that horrible man finds him?' Sylvia said.

Her father had no answer for her.

In spite of Sylvia's pleadings, John Purcell began to make preparations for the voyage home. He had found passage on a ship bound for London in a couple of days. John was paying the landlord the reckoning for their stay when there was a rap on the door and the landlord excused himself. A well-dressed young man crossed the threshold and examined the little group closely.

'Forgive my intruding,' he began, 'but I wonder if you have relations in Dublin. You resemble to an extraordinary degree a butcher I once met in the Ormond Market.'

It was John Purcell's turn to stare. Sylvia saw the surprise on his face slowly resolve itself into recognition.

'The young gentleman from Trinity College, isn't it? Still a Liberty Boy then? I'll warrant there aren't many here.'

The man smiled. 'It is you, then! I was never much of a Liberty Boy, to tell the truth,' he said. 'Just that one foolish jape, which, but for you, could have cost me my life. The name is Hammond, by the way, John Hammond. I saw the adver-tisement in the *Mercury* only an hour ago. But what are you doing here? And this must be ... ' He indicated Sylvia, bowing elegantly to her.

'My daughter,' Purcell said. 'Do you remember the boy who was with you that day?'

Again the man smiled, this man who called himself

Hammond but whose real name was McAllister.

'Why of course I do,' he said.

'James Lovett, or rather Lord Dunmain,' Sylvia said. 'Abandoned by his father and usurped by his uncle.'

'Quite,' McAllister said. 'But I still don't understand what brings you here. Have you come to seek your fortune in the New World?'

'No fortune,' Sylvia said, 'but James. His uncle had him shipped here as an indentured servant.'

'What?' McAllister said, adding, 'We mustn't talk here. Do you take coffee? There's a place near here I favour.'

He led them to the coffee house and there the Purcells told him the whole story. McAllister, as they now knew him, listened carefully, stopping them occasionally to extract further details. He questioned them closely on their dealings with Mackenzie and the exact location of the farm. He didn't seem surprised that James had run away.

'The indentured servants are very often abused,' he said, 'and particularly those from Ireland. And it must have gone very hard for James. We can only imagine what he must have had to put up with.'

'Where would he have gone, do you think?' Sylvia asked impatiently.

McAllister looked at her, sensing her urgency. 'You're very fond of him, aren't you?'

Sylvia coloured, and McAllister immediately regretted his question. One clear look at her would have told him she loved James. Every movement of her features, the coiled tension of her voice: all were unmistakable evidence of her feelings.

'Forgive me,' he said. 'But as to where he might have gone, the truth is many don't get very far at all. The territory is unfamiliar, travel is slow and difficult. Most are caught pretty soon—'

'What happens them when they're caught?' Sylvia asked.

'I suppose that depends on the master. From what you tell me of Mackenzie, I imagine he would deal as harshly with James as the law allows him. And the law allows a great deal, I'm afraid. And the term of servitude would be increased, of course.'

'He may not be caught,' John Purcell said. 'He could be right here under our noses for all we know.'

'I'll make inquiries,' McAllister said. 'I know a good many people in the city. Someone might have seen something. But we need to be sure he hasn't been found. I'll tell you what, I'll go to Mackenzie's farm myself and see what I can find out.'

Sylvia's eyes shone. 'Would you really?' she said.

She looked at her father. 'Why don't we join him, Father?'

'No,' McAllister said. 'I can move quicker alone. Besides, Mackenzie has seen you already, so you'd just arouse his suspicions.'

John Purcell looked relieved at this news. He was in no hurry to leave the city again. Sylvia wasn't entirely convinced, but she made no objection. Until an hour or so ago she had been in despair, and the possibility that she might ever see James again had been utterly remote. Now she was sitting in a coffee house with someone who had known him in Dublin and was more than willing to help. Maybe it wasn't too foolish to allow herself to imagine that they might be able to return to Dublin with James. Her father seemed to sense her excitement and rested a hand on her shoulder.

'It's only a small chance,' he said. 'We shouldn't hope too much.'

Sylvia smiled. 'I know, Father. But I'll take a little hope over none at all.'

Then she looked at McAllister. 'I've no doubt you might move quicker on your own, but you won't know I'm there—'

'No,' McAllister said, 'it's out of the question—'

'If you knew what we've endured so far, you wouldn't be so quick to fob me off. I'll be no hindrance to you, but don't ask me to sit still in this city waiting anxiously for news of your adventure. I won't do it.'

McAllister looked to John Purcell for support. 'Won't you convince her?' he said.

'I've never been able to convince her of anything she didn't want to be convinced about, and I'm not about to start now,' John said. 'It looks like we're all going.'

* * *

Day succeeded day, an endless grey monotony. Toil and sleep, sleep and toil. And sleep a restless tossing and turning, full of useless dreams that broke over him in waves of sadness when he woke. He knew he was no worse off than any of the others here; he had no special right to feel sorry for himself.

He was alive, after all. His body still functioned.

If he was a beast, he would have no complaint. But he wasn't a beast, and though it might be much diluted, he still had enough of his old self in him to know that this life was no life. But how often had he said that to himself over the years? What life was the real one? Maybe there was no real life, just a series of random scenes thrown together. Why should he expect it to make sense? Once a little, angry, persistent flicker inside him had somehow forced him from his bed, somehow assured him that the world would right itself and his place in it be properly acknowledged. But now the flicker was nearly dead. Every day his tools felt heavier and more useless in his hand, as if the world was a weight he wasn't able to bear any more, as if everything in it was meant for someone else.

He was a long way from home now, and a longer way from himself.

* * *

McAllister rode up the dirt track to Mackenzie's farmstead. He had left Sylvia, Harry and John Purcell in an inn in the local town with strict instructions not to move until he returned, no matter how long that might take. Sylvia had insisted he leave them one of the brace of pistols he had with him for protection. He'd thought it unnecessary but he had given up arguing with Sylvia. She was feisty enough when he met her first, but it was as if she had grown another cubit in the time that had passed since then. There seemed to be nothing she couldn't learn. She wanted to know all about the countryside they were passing through; she pored over the maps of the territory and of Mackenzie's farm that McAllister had brought. The girl from Phoenix Street had grown to be a match for many a man, and McAllister envied James her attachment to him. If only he could meet someone half so spirited.

He had an idea of the reception he could expect from James's master and steeled himself for a rough ride. Mackenzie didn't disappoint him. McAllister's clothes and bearing at least got him farther than Purcell and Sylvia, and he didn't have to stand in the yard and be dressed down from the verandah, but the man sitting on the other side of the table presented the same sullen face and rough manners. McAllister had got to the end of a slightly rambling speech, in which he presented himself as a lawyer with a communication for one of his indentured servants, a certain James Lovett. He had concocted the letter himself and had it ready in the pocket of his coat, but it didn't look like it was going to be necessary to produce it.

'Do I have the look of a messenger boy, do ye think?' Mackenzie was saying, working himself into a temper.

'But surely you can't object to the boy receiving a letter?' McAllister's voice was calm and reasonable. All he really wanted was knowledge that James was there.

'I can object to whatever I like. And especially to a runaway who would cheat me of my money.'

'A runaway? You mean he's not here?'

'Oh he's here alright, and well versed in what happens to runaways,' Mackenzie said with satisfaction.

So he's here, McAllister thought. That's all I need. There was a second letter in his pocket, and his mind now moved to the tricky problem of getting it to James. The slave who had showed him in, with her proud bearing – Sylvia was sure she could be trusted. It was a great risk, but McAllister could think of no alternative. Mackenzie had tired of the conversation. Most men in this backwoods country would have welcomed company, but not Mackenzie, it seemed. His own grim company suited him best. Well, McAllister would leave him to it now, before the man threw him out.

'You know,' he said, as he stood up and took his hat, 'there is no law that requires a man to abandon his humanity as soon as he gets a little land and some hands to help him work it.'

Mackenzie laughed. 'When I need the advice of a city gentleman in how to conduct affairs of which he knows nothing, you'll be first on my list,' he added.

The slave who had shown McAllister in accompanied him back to the yard. As his horse was brought to him, he quickly pressed the second letter into her palm, without even glancing at her. Nor did he risk speaking to her in case Mackenzie should be watching from the house. Amelia's palm closed on the carefully folded paper and she made no comment. The fact that she accepted it without question gave McAllister some hope that the message would find its way to James. He mounted his horse and rode back down the track. There was nothing more he could do before darkness.

• • • • • •

THIRTY-TWO

A Lantern in the Woods

J ames read the letter once, twice, three times. He couldn't believe what it was saying.

'Tell me again what he looked like,' he said to Amelia, though she had already described the stranger in great detail.

'Same as last time, James, tall enough, and thin and quite intense, with a sharp nose. And carried himself like a gentleman.'

'But how did he find this place? How does he know I'm here?'

'I don't know, James. I know nothing about him, only what I have told you. But I did tell your friends about him, so maybe they found him,' Amelia said. Even talking about him now made her nervous. 'Be careful, James,' she said. 'There are ears everywhere.'

James lowered his voice. 'He has come for me,' he said. 'He means to take me away from here.'

James read her the letter. She looked at him, her eyes anxious and fearful.

'James, this is dangerous. If Mackenzie catches you again, he'll surely kill you. Your back has barely healed; you're still weak. This isn't very wise, I think.' Still, she knew he must go.

'Oh Amelia,' James said, 'is this not death here? How long do you think I can survive in this place? And if this is true, how can I refuse it? I might never get another chance like it.'

There wasn't much Amelia could say in response that she hadn't said before, but she reached her hand out and touched James's arm. 'I don't want to see you go, James, that's my problem. No, that's not right. I *do* want to see you go. It's just that I will miss you.'

She looked away. 'You must go, but you must be careful. He'll kill you if he catches you again.'

The two were silent awhile before Amelia spoke again, her voice full of ache and loneliness, 'God speed you, James. I'll say goodbye now because there will be no time later. And you mustn't give anyone the impression you intend to go. No one, you understand?'

James nodded. He understood too well. 'I only wish you were coming with me, Amelia.'

Amelia shook her head sadly. 'It will be hard enough for you to get away. If I were to go with you, they would stop at nothing to hunt us both down.' She gripped his hand. 'Just remember me,' she said. 'Remembering would be enough.'

* * *

This time James packed nothing, not even as much as a hunk of bread. He didn't care about food or clothes; his only thought was to follow the instructions in McAllister's letter. His old friend must have got hold of a map, for his directions gave evidence of a good knowledge of the layout of the farm. The spot McAllister had chosen for their rendezvous was the same place James had made his first escape from, in the wood at the northern extent of Mckenzie's land. Feeling that it might be cursed with bad luck, James wished McAllister had selected somewhere else, but there was nothing he could do about it now.

He did everything just as he did every night, checking on the horses in the stable, bringing in a stack of logs from the pile in the yard, eating his usual meal with Amelia, Connolly and the others. He made the same small talk and shuffled off to his usual hard bed, but he did not fall asleep. He listened intently to the sounds of the hut and the others sleeping, and at about fifteen minutes to midnight he lifted his blanket, raised himself carefully from his pallet and pulled on his clothes. He carried his boots outside and pulled them on in the grass, keeping his eyes peeled in case his absence had been registered. There was no sound, and no sign that anyone had heard. He crept away from the hut and the house and made his way slowly through the undergrowth to the edge of the woods where he had been working earlier that day. It was as if he was re-enacting the night when he had first escaped from the farm, and he tried to put all the crowding thoughts of the misadventures that had followed that flight out of his mind. It wasn't easy, and his eyes darted nervously from tree to tree, half-expecting someone to leap out and attack him. He was much more afraid than he had been the first time, not least because he knew exactly what he could expect if he was caught.

Someone did step from behind a tree so close to him he had no time to turn and bolt. He cursed his stupidity, but the hand that reached out didn't strike a blow; it simply rested on his shoulder, and a soft voice whispered his name.

'It's alright, James. It's me, McAllister, you got the message then.'

'Is it really you, Mr McAllister?' James fell into his old way of addressing him, as if they were still in Trinity College.

'No need to "mister" me any more, James.'

McAllister looked closely at the boy. 'I'd hardly recognise you, James. You look worn out.'

James shrugged. 'I can't say I'll be sorry to leave.'

McAllister started suddenly. 'Did you tell anyone you were coming here?' he whispered urgently.

'Not a soul,' James said. 'Why?'

'There's a light over there; it looks like a lantern.'

McAllister pointed back in the direction James had come from. James saw it too, a swaying light like a lantern held on a horse. He remembered very clearly the last time he saw a light like that. He had been so careful. Who could possibly have seen him?

'Quickly,' McAllister said. 'The sooner we get out of here the better.'

He untied his horse and mounted, and then reached his

hand down to James. 'Hold tight,' McAllister said as they galloped through the trees.

Soon they'd leaped across the boundary of Mackenzie's land and were moving swiftly up the slope of the adjoining meadow to the thick woods on the crest. James chanced a quick look around and saw to his horror that the light was now near enough for him to make out the clear outline of a horse and rider.

'He's close behind,' he shouted in McAllister's ears.

'Damnation!' McAllister swore, and urged his horse on.

They reached the shelter of the trees and pressed on. McAllister had committed the map to memory, but a forest at night isn't friendly to maps or map readers. He rode blindly, his one objective now to put as much darkness between him and the following horseman as he could. But the rider with his lantern seemed surer of his territory, and the sound of the hooves was clearer with every passing second. Then came the loud, unmistakable voice. 'Stop there! Stop or I'll fire!'

'Mackenzie!' James shouted. 'How in God's name is he here?'

So he didn't believe my story after all, McAllister thought. He must have guessed I would try something. Unless someone told him. Unless Amelia, but no, he couldn't imagine Amelia would have given them away. He didn't have time to think about that now. He wheeled his horse around to the right and plunged into the thick of the forest, but it was as if that was exactly what Mackenzie expected him to do, for his own horse wheeled round too, and, in a second,

McAllister fell from his horse as James heard the deafening report of Mackenzie's pistol. Before James had time to steady his horse, Mackenzie was upon him, his second pistol levelled right between his eyes. James could hardly believe what was happening. It didn't seem possible that his escape could be over before it had even begun. He glanced down to where McAllister lay groaning on the ground. He was still alive then.

'You must think me an utter fool,' Mackenzie said. 'Do you think I'm that easily taken in? It was clear as day from the minute your fancy friend showed up that something was afoot. Well, the law can take care of him, but by God I'll take care of you.'

James fell from the horse as if the sheer force of Mackenzie's words had struck him, but his fall was calculated, and he landed on his feet and ran like a demon into the darkness. Mackenzie followed hard, and no matter how fast or what way James ran, the horseman was right behind him, pounding through the undergrowth. If only some great hole would appear to swallow me up, James thought, his breath coming in gasps, his body weakened by fright and exhaustion. He was no match for Mackenzie, who leapt from his horse and pinned him against a tree.

'Our appointment won't wait,' he snarled at James and struck him on the head with the butt of his pistol.

When James came to, he was tied to the tree and Mackenzie was standing in front of him, his coat thrown on the ground and the sleeves of his shirt rolled up for action. James closed his eyes and tried to force his mind to picture any scene

other than the one he was confronted with. He fell back into
Phoenix Street and found himself walking slowly with Sylvia
on a bright, clear day. He could hear the gulls screech above
the streets and the heavy smell of the river filled his nostrils.
Sylvia's voice came to him as if she was standing right in front
of him. The first blow crashed into his cheek and loosened a
few teeth. James felt the blood seep into his throat.

'If you hit him again, I'll kill you' came the voice, and as James
slowly opened an eye he thought he must have died already.
There, astride a horse neither of them had heard approach, was
a figure in a cloak brandishing a pistol. But that voice …

Mackenzie spun around and, as he took in the figure, he
drew his sword and rushed. The horse shied and the figure
fell to the ground. The pistol ended up inches from Mackenzie's boots. He laughed and bent to retrieve it. He aimed at
the cloaked figure and cocked the pistol. But a second figure
now stepped from behind a tree, a figure James recognised
with a shock. Could it be? The slim figure held a pistol and,
for the second time that night, James was deafened by a shot.
Mackenzie fell in a heap on the ground and was utterly still.
The hooded figure who had been hurled to the ground now
clambered up. She undid her hood and James gasped. Now he
knew for sure that he had entered the land of the dead.

The girl spoke to him in Sylvia's voice. 'James, are you
alright? It's me, Sylvia?'

She cut the rope with a knife and released him. He looked
around. It seemed to be the same dark world he had left
behind him. But what was Sylvia doing in it, surely she

wasn't …? His straying thoughts were quickly gathered by the pressure of her arms around him.

'James,' she kept saying. 'My own James, is it really you?'

'I should be saying that,' James said. He still didn't trust his senses. 'Is it really you? And how do you come to be here?'

'It's a long story,' Sylvia said, 'but we don't have time for it here.'

The figure with the pistol now spoke. 'Need your shoes shined, old friend? They look a bit mucky to me.'

James gasped. 'Harry? Is it you?'

'It's me alright. Couldn't leave you to your own devices.'

James could hardly believe it. He still wasn't sure he was not dreaming, but as he stepped forward he almost tripped over the unmoving form of Mackenzie. When he looked up, Harry and Sylvia were still there — it must be real, then.

'Do you think he's dead?' he said.

He pulled Mckenzie's head to one side and saw the wound in the middle of his forehead.

'I don't think we have anything more to fear from him,' Sylvia said.

'I'm not sure that's true,' a voice announced in the darkness.

Sylvia wheeled round. 'Jeremy!'

McAllister came limping towards them. He was clutching his arm where the ball had hit him. James and Sylvia both ran over and embraced him.

'You're hurt,' James said.

'It went straight through,' he said, 'but I hit my head when I fell and just came to.'

Sylvia examined his arm. She made him take off his coat and rip a sleeve from his shirt, and with that she fashioned a tourniquet to staunch the bleeding. His head didn't seem to be cut.

'What did you mean, about Mackenzie?' James said.

'Dead men talk,' McAllister said. 'They can tell who killed them and where they might be. We need to conceal his body.'

They set about digging in the hard ground with their hands, but the work was slow.

'There's no time for this,' James said. 'What if he should be missed, and someone comes after him?'

'I can't think who would miss him,' McAllister said, 'but you're right, we need to go.'

They dragged Mackenzie's body into the shallow dent they'd made and heaped leaves and brush on top. It wasn't much of a concealment, but it would have to do.

Harry helped Sylvia onto the horse she'd fallen from.

'I'll try and keep her on it this time,' he grinned. 'You go with Mr McAllister here,' he said to James.

'We can't all go back to the inn,' McAllister said. 'It would arouse too much suspicion. When we reach the outskirts of the town, you can go back to your father and James will ride with me back to Philadelphia.'

'But that will take days. Are you sure you're alright?' Sylvia said.

'We'll take the most circuitous route we can,' McAllister said, 'in case anyone should think to follow. But we'll be alright. When you return to the city, go to the inn you first stayed in, and we will look for you there.'

They rode through the night without further adventure and separated when the town came into view. James hugged Sylvia so tightly she could hardly breathe. Then he shook Harry's hands and held his shoulders as if he still couldn't quite believe he was a real creature.

'I wanted to make sure you're really here.'

'Don't worry, James,' she said. 'We're here, all of us, flesh and blood. But you're not all here.' She looked at him with concern. 'You look like you've left a good half of yourself on that farm. You look like a ghost, James Lovett.'

'Well,' James said, 'I'll try not to haunt you too much. But you're a sight for ghostly eyes, Sylvia.'

Sylvia laughed. 'So the haunting begins. I hope there's plenty more where that came from.'

• • • • • • •

THIRTY-THREE

Reunion

Richard Lovett was pacing his drawing room. His informer stood near the door, intimidated by the gusts of anger his news had raised.

'Back, you say? How can that be?'

'I don't know, my lord. I only know that he came ashore from the *Princess* with the butcher and his daughter and some ragamuffin. He looks a bit different from the scrappy boy he was. Taller, stronger, something more ...' He searched for the right word, which was slow in coming. 'More *definite* about him, if you see what I mean.'

'I have no idea what you mean,' Richard Lovett responded. He had no interest in what the boy looked like. It was beyond comprehension that he should have returned; it was scarcely to be believed that he was still alive. A perilous journey on a disease-ridden ship followed by punitive labour in desolate, sun-baked fields should, one or other of them, have done for the boy. It should have been as good as a knife through his heart. Yet here he was in the streets of Dublin with his damnable butcher. It was a devilish provocation. He threw a coin at the skinny, hard-faced little man who brought him the news and called for his thug.

'We should have settled this business long ago,' he shouted at Grady once he had arrived and heard his master's news.

The thug nodded his long head in agreement. 'It's not too late,' he offered.

Lovett bristled. 'I don't want you anywhere near him,' he said.

Grady struggled to hide his disappointment.

'Find me a good pistol man,' Lovett said. 'I'll put an end to this once and for all.'

* * *

Some things you never forget. The sight of the city in the distance as the ship approached the twin arms of the bay. A new life seemed to call out to James and, even though his memories of this place were dark enough, the bells pealing in the distance made the hair stand up on the back of his neck. Sylvia held his hand as if she read his thoughts.

'It will be different now, James, you'll see.'

And those early days had been all he could have wanted. Phoenix Street was a miraculous place, and a flood of well-wishers filled the house from morning till night. Nancy was beside herself with happiness to see everyone back under her roof again. She'd grown thin from worry.

'Where's the rest of you?' John had asked as he hugged her.

'Out hunting for her lost family,' Nancy said. 'But who knows, maybe she'll come back now that I can put my feet up and be waited on by all my prodigals.'

It was only when she saw her mother that Sylvia realised what a perilous journey it was that they had undertaken. In her mother's eyes, and in the eyes of everyone who greeted her, she read the pure surprise that she was alive, that the three of them had made it back. Most people had given them up, she realised. And James found out that he had become something of a legend in his absence. People constantly stopped him in the street.

'Is it Lord Bluecoat himself, returned from the dead?'

'You're not the Lord Bluecoat that was kidnapped by his uncle and sold for a slave?'

'Will ye look who it is! The blessin's of God on yer honour.'

There didn't seem to be anyone in the city who hadn't heard of him and what the man who called himself Lord Dunmain had done to him. Of his uncle he heard little enough, except that he still paraded in public, usually accompanied by his thugs, and was fond of strolling in Stephen's Green on Sunday morning. James filed away that piece of information. When the ship had approached the landing place James's first instinct had been to rush ashore and take a carriage to his uncle's house and confront him immediately. But the instinct was soon governed by the understanding that that would be the very worst course of action and would play right into his uncle's hands. He was not, after all, the same raw boy who had been bundled out of the city like a rag doll. He knew a little of how the world worked, and how men like his uncle worked. No, he would wait a little before confronting him, and he would enlist the protection of the law, even if he was by no means confident the law could be trusted to do right by him.

Several days later, he walked down Capel Street and crossed the river. Exactly as before, ships crowded the water near the Custom House dock, and the bridge was loud with the clatter of horses and carriages. The beggars, the hawkers, the men and women about their business, the ragged children – it was all just as he had remembered it; nothing had changed. The city, like the river, went on as it always did; it didn't notice if you stepped out of it and it didn't register your return.

He stepped into Essex Street. For a moment, his heart sank when he saw the blank space where Harry plied his trade. Harry had wasted no time in returning to his work. Once the ship had docked, he was off before James could speak to him.

'You know where to find me,' he'd said, and hurried away with his small bag.

In spite of the crowds, the street had a strange emptiness to it. Then a familiar figure emerged from under the arch and took up a position by the wall. James watched him for a few moments. It was strange to watch him here again, almost as if nothing had happened and he had been here all the time. A gent came up and Harry set to work with spudd and wig. The wig at least looked unchanged, still the same filthy skein of ancient hair, but it did the work as proficiently as ever. When

Harry had finished, James went to him and touched him on his shoulder.

'Need a shine?' Harry said.

'No more shining, Harry,' James said. 'We're friends now, equals. I should shine *your* shoes.'

'The world's not like that,' Harry said. 'And you shouldn't try to make it so.'

'Just you try and stop me,' James said.

They went under the arch to their old spot by the river.

'I used to love to gaze at these ships,' James said. 'Imagining where they might go, imagining a new life in faraway places. Now, I don't much care if I never see another ship again, and if I never go to sea again it will be too soon.'

'I'm glad to hear it,' Harry said, as they walked back to his spot. 'But what about your uncle? Aren't you still in danger? How do you know he won't try it again? Or worse?'

James might have been able to answer that question accurately if he had looked along the street and seen the tall slim figure who hugged the corner of the narrow alley that cut into Essex Street opposite the piazzas. The figure was observing the two boys very acutely and his hand was thrust deep into his coat pocket, where it lay snug around the smooth wood of a pistol butt. The figure turned full into Essex Street and began striding purposefully in the direction of James and the shoeboy.

'If I am in danger,' James said in answer to his friend's question, 'it won't be for long. I intend to meet the danger head on, and have it out with my uncle by whatever means necessary.'

Suddenly, Harry had a customer in a hurry and had to attend to his business. James turned away from his friend just in time to see the tall figure in the dark coat striding towards him. Something about the pinched intentness of the figure's face held James's attention, but he was still not quick enough to see the glint of the metal barrel of the pistol.

'James!' He heard Harry shout behind him and felt himself stumbling under the weight of his friend's body at exactly the moment that he heard a deafening report and felt a searing pain rip through his body. The ghostly figure with the pistol vanished in the crowd. James was briefly aware of a great commotion thundering above him and the anxious face of Harry peering down at him and calling out his name before the world disappeared from his senses.

When he came to, it was to find himself in the familiar surroundings of Phoenix Street, barely able to move from the pain in his shoulder. A small army of well-wishers was crammed into the room: Sylvia hovering over him with damp cloth to cool his forehead, Nancy's anxiously smiling face and John Purcell's grim one, good old Harry, who gave his friend a wink and a wave, and a man he hadn't seen in a long time, nor expected to see again.

'Doctor Bob,' James said. 'How do you come to be here?'

Doctor Bob – for it was indeed the doctor who had saved James's life once before – held up a dull metal ball about half the size of his thumb.

'This little fellow required my specialist services,' he said. 'You may thank your quick-thinking Sylvia for fetching me in good time. And your good friend for knocking you down when you did. Otherwise, you'd have more than a flesh wound and we'd be waking you in this house tonight.'

'This has gone on long enough,' James managed to say in spite of the pain in his shoulder.

And so, some weeks later, when his wound had healed, James found himself back in the graveyard off York Street, where he'd lain in hiding so long ago, waiting to take part in his first robbery. And now here he was again waiting for Jack Darcy to appear, except this time there was no cloak of darkness to cover him. How strange life is, James thought, how like a dream that you have over and over again, with the same scenes repeating themselves. Doctor Bob had got the word to Jack Darcy – to tell the truth James was surprised to hear he was still alive, he had always seemed destined for an early death at the end of a rope in Stephen's Green – and Darcy had agreed to meet James. James stood in front of a gravestone and pretended to be very interested in the inscription. *The above named died of a malignant fever. Universally regretted …*

'This is getting to be a habit.' The voice seemed to leap from out of the grave.

James started in terror, but when he looked up he saw the grinning features of Jack Darcy on the other side of the headstone. He didn't look much different from the last time James had seen him that night in Red Molly's which seemed like a lifetime ago. A little skinnier, his face gaunter than James remembered, but still the same dapper cheerfulness. His coat was elegant, if somewhat worn, and his velvet hat was trimmed with gold as if to show the world that Jack Darcy wasn't to be trumped for fashion.

'A habit?' James smiled, glad to see him, even if his memories of the period he'd spent with the gang were not exactly untroubled. 'How so?'

'I mean meeting you or your lady friend in the land of the dead to hatch plans for your advancement.'

Darcy doffed his cap and performed an elaborate bow. 'My lord, I should have said. Or at least as soon will be, if I have anything to do with it. So how can I help?'

'I'd like to take a stroll with my uncle,' James said.

* * *

The following Sunday, Lord and Lady Dunmain were taking the air in Stephen's Green, as was their custom. All fashionable Dublin turned out to parade up and down The Beaux Walk, nodding and bowing to each other, stopping to talk and exchange the latest news and gossip. James saw his uncle immediately. He was walking from the opposite direction with his usual swagger, as if he owned the walk and the park it was set in. He was a man who reached out and grabbed the world, James thought as he looked at him now, and it didn't much matter to him who might be the true owner of whatever he fancied. It was the most natural thing imaginable that he should step, without a thought, into his brother's expectations and send his nephew across the ocean into slavery or death. A quick glance was enough to establish that the cruel features James remembered so well hadn't softened. It took him a couple of seconds to recognise the woman with him. She was plumper than he remembered, her face more thickly powdered and her body covered in finer silk, but it was her alright, Miss Deakin. James gave a little shiver of revulsion at the sight. His uncle stopped to talk to a party of strollers, men like himself, full of puff and swagger, and the sound of their laughter and loud braying voices filled the park. A little back from the group stood a man James had not forgotten, the thug Grady with his long face and huge hands. A little older, a little heavier, but just as pig-ignorant, James had no doubt. He would soon be upon his uncle's group. Well, there was no point keeping him waiting. James strode right up.

'Good morning, Uncle,' he said. The men in the group looked at him in astonishment.

'Uncle?' a red-faced man said. 'Did he say uncle?'

'You'll forgive me if I don't call you aunt,' he said to Miss Deakin.

Her face quivered behind its white powder and she reached a hand out to Dunmain.

'Sirrah, you had better explain yourself,' a portly man said.

Dunmain remained silent, staring at his nephew, looking him up and down as if to assess what danger, if any, he might be in. He looked past James to see if anyone was with him, but Darcy was too well hidden.

'How can a man with no nephew be an uncle?' he asked mildly. By now Grady had joined the group and was staring open-mouthed at James, but James saw his uncle's hand almost imperceptibly reach out to restrain his thug, and Grady, though he looked like a bulldog straining on the leash, was forced to remain still and say nothing.

'My, Uncle, can you have forgotten me so quickly?' James responded with the same mild manner his uncle used. 'Don't you remember how you kidnapped me and sent me away to the colonies as a servant? I think I'd remember something of that nature.'

Dunmain's friends looked even more astonished than before. Could there be any truth in this? The young man was well enough dressed, and sounded the part. Was there perhaps a slight resemblance in the shape of his forehead or the lustre of his eyes?

'This man is no relative of mine,' James's uncle said, as if he read their thoughts. 'Though it is not the first time he has tried this trick.'

'He is an insolent trickster' came Miss Deakin's high voice.

'Did I not live in Dunmain House with my father, Lord Dunmain, your brother? Did I not come with him to Dublin and live with him in his house in Dublin after he abandoned my mother and married the woman who is now your wife? And am I not James Lovett, the rightful Lord Dunmain?'

Other strollers now stopped to hear what seemed a most interesting conversation.

Grady looked fit to burst. 'Shall I pulverise him?' he said to his master in what might have intended as a whisper but was clearly audible to everyone.

The small crowd bristled with excitement.

'What name is this you take upon you?' His uncle had dropped the civil tone and was now plainly hostile.

'I take none upon me, sir, but that which I brought into the world with me and was always called by. Nobody can deny that I am the son of Lord Dunmain.'

'By whom?'

'By his wife, the Lady Dunmain.'

'Then you are a bastard, for your mother was a whore.'

Now it was James's turn to be astonished. He knew his uncle was a cold and ruthless man, but this was beyond effrontery. He couldn't bear to hear his mother insulted. Instinctively, he drew his sword, but as he did so he felt the hands of Grady circle his throat until he could hardly breathe. There were gasps all round, with men and women scattering out of the way. James struggled for air; he could feel himself slipping away. He should have known his uncle would try to provoke him. Why had he been so rash? This was a man that could only be defeated by cunning. And he had been stupid. He heard a woman screaming. And then there was silence, and out of the silence another voice rang out, clear and confident.

'Let him go if you want to live, cur.'

James opened his eyes. The tip of Darcy's blade grazed Grady's neck, a little dribble of blood already oozing down the coarse skin. Grady's hands were occupied in throttling James so he could do nothing about it. James felt the grip around his throat slacken and gulped some air into his lungs.

A woman came forward to help him. 'Are you alright, young man?' she asked him.

From her attention James sensed that the crowd's attitude to him might be changing. The three original men who had stopped to talk to his uncle had slipped off discreetly, and the crowd that now observed the scene was not rushing to Dunmain's aid. James retrieved his blade from the ground and replaced it in his scabbard. This situation required more than a blade.

'You are a blackguard and a thief, sir,' James said calmly.

'Let's run them both through,' Darcy offered. 'That would be two boils lanced at once, and the city would be a better place.'

'The city will be a better place when you're dangling from a gallows in this green,' Dunmain said, though his voice wasn't as confident now.

'Kill him,' Darcy said.

'No,' James said, 'there will be no killing today.' He looked his uncle in the eye. 'I will defeat you, uncle, but I'll do it properly, I'll let the law speak for me. Let the courts decide which of us is true.'

THIRTY-FOUR

Epilogue

Red Molly's was jumping. Every corner, every alcove, every nook and crevice was packed. It seemed as if the whole city had poured in the doors. Drink flowed, spilled, tumbled and was knocked back in large quantities. Steaming food floated high over the revellers' heads, making its way on seemingly invisible arms through the throng. James's back ached from the endless series of slaps it received from well-wishers.

The trial was a sensation, the longest the city had ever seen. People had travelled from all over to observe it. As it dragged on, James had begun to doubt his wisdom in trusting to the law. His uncle looked richer and more powerful than James had ever seen him, for he had now come into all the estates that James's father had hoped for and had borrowed on the strength of, and the finery he wore to the court was a clear ement of his intent to win this battle. He smiled e crowded room at James, a smile so full of malice, cunning and confidence that it chilled James. It was, he knew, an unequal battle. But the city was full of it. James's case had electrified Dublin. He found himself suddenly famous, mobbed wherever he went, acclaimed like a king.

'Make way for Lord Bluecoat!'

'Good luck to you, young sir, and bad cess to your uncle!'

So unequal was the contest that even after witness after witness appeared to testify that he was indeed his father's son, even as he managed to puncture every elaborate counter-claim his uncle brought forward, James couldn't bring himself to believe the judge when he found in his favour. He was the rightful heir to the Dunmain title and estates. He, and not his uncle, was Lord Dunmain. Through it all his uncle continued smiling and patting his elaborate robes. But James wouldn't be skulking through the streets again. There would be no more hiding.

Still they kept coming up to slap him on the back.

'A great day, Jim, great to see arrogance beaten down!'

'You know it doesn't matter, James?' Doctor Bob said as he drained his wine glass.

'Why is that?'

'Because the law isn't designed for you. Today was a good day, enough to convince a neutral man that the law has a purpose after all. But your uncle will appeal it immediately, and if that doesn't work, he will appeal the appeal. The case could keep the courts busy for another decade. In the meantime you won't be able to get at your inheritance. And you'll still be a wanted man. You could be dead before you gain the title.'

James smiled. 'Oh I know that,' he said. 'I think I've always known my cause was hopeless.'

'I told you we should have killed him,' Darcy said. 'I could still do it. It's not too late. Anything to oblige an old friend.'

'No,' James said. 'But thank you for your offer. I don't want anyone else to die, not even him. It isn't worth that much to me.'

James looked round at the company. He felt as if he were seeing them for the first time. He realised that all his life, no place had ever seemed real to him, just a temporary state to be hurried through, or escaped from, until he could get to a better place. Was this victory the better place? Or would that be the day he finally came into his estate? He looked at Sylvia. He thought of everything the Purcells had done for him. He looked at the vivid, alert faces of everyone around him. Maybe this was the place, he thought. Maybe ... Doctor Bob's voice broke in.

'It's a lot of money,' he was saying. 'A lot of land. Your uncle will never give up the fight for it.'

'And I won't either,' James said. 'Even if it takes the rest of my life.'

'In the meantime it's back to school for you,' Sylvia said with a laugh. 'I don't think your old blue coat will fit, though.'

'I think we can rise to a new coat,' Doctor Bob said, to the cheer of the company.

'You'll be Lord Bluecoat again,' Darcy said. The company cheered again.

'To Lord Bluecoat!'

think of a finer title,' James said. 'Lord Bluecoat it

* * *

'It's not the end, is it?' Jack Darcy said.

They were back in the graveyard where they had met before.

'No,' James said. 'Not just yet.'

'You could have killed him that day in the Green.'

'And been hanged in the same Green for my trouble.'

'So what about the law then? Have you lost your faith in that?'

James was silent awhile. 'I've had a lot of law in my life,' he said finally. 'It was the law that kept me a slave, and keeps others as slaves even as we speak.'

He thought of Amelia. What had become of her? Most likely sold on to another Mackenzie. That was the law. But there were ways round it. He wouldn't rest until he discovered a way of finding Amelia again. McAllister would have to help him again. It would take money and cunning, but he wouldn't give up.

'Bob is right. The law is for those who can best afford it. I needed to show the world who I am, and what my uncle is, and I've done that. But the law won't stop him, the law will keep him rich, and keep me from what should be mine. I want something more than the law.'

Darcy smiled. 'What do you have in mind?'

'I'd like to send my uncle a gift,' James said.

* * *

Lord and Lady Dunmain were getting ready for bed when they heard a noise. Lady Dunmain, or plain Miss Deakin as James would have called her, was at her dressing table taking off a pair of heavily jewelled earrings. The noise caused an earring to fall to the floor.

'What on earth is that?' she said as she bent in irritation to rummage for the earring.

It sounded like loud hammering. Richard Lovett strode to the door.

'Grady!' he roared. 'What is that racket?'

The hammering continued.

'It's the door,' Richard Lovett shouted. 'Someone is hammering on the door!'

Grady appeared from the depths of the house, rubbing his eyes. He had fallen asleep in the kitchen over a pitcher of grog. He undid the bolts and opened the heavy front door, swaying dagger at the ready. The hammering had stopped. He stepped out and looked around, but there was no one to be seen.

'I can't see anyone,' he shouted.

Richard Lovett pounded down the stairs and out into the night air.

'Who would dare hammer on my door like that?' he said. And then he saw it, nailed to the door: a large black wreath, the kind you see at a funeral, or that might be hung on a front door to indicate the death of someone inside.

'What does it mean?' his wife asked him when he had settled down enough to return to his bedroom.

'It means war,' he said. 'It means I didn't do the job properly when I had the chance.'

'The boy should have been killed a long time ago,' his wife said. 'I urged it on his father, but he wouldn't listen. He was too soft.'

'Well, I'm not soft,' Lovett said. 'And it's time he found out.'

'What are you going to do?'

'It's done. I've sent Grady to find a good knife man. There'll be no more mistakes.'

* * *

When someone tries to kill you once, you do everything you can to make sure it doesn't happen again. So James left Phoenix Street and went back to an old haunt, the Phoenix Park, not as a robber this time, but as a guest of Jack Darcy. It was a strange feeling, as if he had gone backwards in his life, but he knew his uncle's men wouldn't find him here. There would be time to think, and plan.

'We'll have to go to him,' Jack said.

'I know,' James said. You can only hide for so long, he thought.

* * *

Richard Lovett and his wife came back from their evening in the theatre. It had been a good show, and there had been drinks and diverting company afterwards. Now it was time to retire for the night.

'Go upstairs,' Lovett said. 'I'll join you shortly.'

He went to the library for a night-cap and so didn't hear anything untoward. Even if he had been directly behind her, he still would not have heard anything, because although Miss Deakin's mouth opened and her eyes widened in fright no sound escaped her throat. In the end, gripping the banister tight, she stumbled down the stairs and into the library, mouthing silently at her husband and pointing with her finger in the direction of the bedroom.

Lovett bounded up the stairs and into the room. There, on the bed, was a large black wreath. He wheeled around and shouted for his man.

'Grady! Get up here now!'

At that moment, two figures stepped from behind the heavy curtains.

'Grady is otherwise engaged, you'll find,' the first figure said. 'Along with the rest of your men.'

'Hello, Uncle,' the second figure said.

'You!' Lovett said. 'Do you know the penalty for breaking and entering?'

'The same as the penalty for murder, isn't it?' James said evenly.

'You mean to murder me? Is that what the wreath means?'

'And don't you think I would be justified? How many times have you tried to kill me?'

Richard Lovett snarled.

'I'm not like you,' James said. 'I don't like killing people. I don't believe in murder.'

His uncle looked relieved.

'A black wreath was hung on the door of my father's house when he was pretending I was dead. So I like to think of it as a calling card, to remind you I'm still alive.' James fished in his pocket for a document. 'There is something else,' he said, handing the document to his uncle.

'What's this?' Richard Lovett said.

'Read it,' James said.

'... *one Richard Lever, together with his wife Constance, indentured for seven years, in charge of Captain Thomas McCarthy, of the vessel* George *bound for Philadelphia* ...'

Lovett looked up. 'What's this?' he said. 'Who are these people?'

'Those are your new names. Richard and Constance Lever. Richard is a labourer and Constance ...' James looked over at Miss Deakin, an angry red flaring though her powder. 'Constance doesn't do much really. But with training she might make an excellent scullery maid.'

'How dare you?' Miss Deakin spluttered.

'You can't be serious,' Richard Lovett said.

'I'm very serious,' James said. 'You need to learn a little of the world, and so this is my gift to you. When you return to Dublin, we can meet again in the courts and settle the issue of my inheritance – if it is still at issue. Of course I can't guarantee that you will return – it's a tricky business. I couldn't have done it without the help of great friends.'

'I hope you don't suffer from sea sickness,' Jack Darcy said. 'I hear it can be a terror.'

'The captain might help you,' James said. 'You know him, after all. He's the same captain you gave me to. His orders are different now, though, and he knows better than to disobey them.'

'You'll never get away with this,' his uncle shouted. 'As soon as we arrive, we will make ourselves known. You only have to look at us to know what we are.'

'Indeed,' said James said. 'That brings us nicely to the next part.'

Darcy went to the curtain and emerged with a large sack which he now emptied onto the floor. A jumble of shoddy looking clothes spilled out.

'What's this?' his uncle said.

'Clothes fit for a labourer and a maid. You're right about people judging you by what you wear. You'll find it's probably best not to insist on your nobility. Not everyone will think it's funny, and it takes very little to cause offence. Believe me, Uncle, I know what I'm talking about.'

'I will not be seen dead in this outfit,' Miss Deakin said. She was shaking with indignation.

'Would you like to be seen dead in what you're wearing?' Jack asked mildly, stretching his sword to her throat. 'I can easily arrange it.'

And so, a little later, a labourer and a scullery maid left the house of Lord and Lady Dunmain in the company of several strong men, to set off for a life they would never have imagined, let alone chosen.

'Are you sure about this?' Jack Darcy said as they took their leave of the captain and stepped onto the quay. 'He could come back sooner than you expect. It's not too late to run him through.' Darcy fingered the hilt of his sword. 'No one would object.'

'No,' James said. 'I'll give him the same chance he gave me. Whatever happens next, the gods can decide.'

* * *

'Now we can all begin,' James said, surveying his friends. He, Harry and Sylvia were standing on the quay near the Custom House watching ships take on supplies.

'I used to love standing here,' James said. 'I thought the world began here.' He waved at the ships. 'Adventure, exotic places, *real* life.'

'And now?' Sylvia said.

'Now I see that this is real life, to be here with you and Harry.'

The gangplank of one of the ships had been raised. There were shouts and whistles, and the ropes that secured the vessel to the quay were cast off and hauled back on board. The name *George* was inscribed on the wood.

'I don't think I'll ever go to sea again,' James said as he watched the *George* move slowly downriver.

The further the boat got from the quay the more he felt his lungs swell with new life. They all watched it, and no one spoke again until it had gone out of sight on its way to sea.

'Now we can begin,' Sylvia said finally.

'Amen to that,' Harry said.

Author's Note

I came across the story behind *Black Wreath* by accident. I was looking for information about eighteenth-century Dublin for an article I was writing and one of the books I read was Maurice Craig's *Dublin 1660–1860*, which told the real-life story of James Annesley. I found I couldn't get the story of my head and so I sat down one day and wrote the opening chapters of what became *Black Wreath*. Something about a boy abandoned in the dangerous Dublin of the 1700s, fighting for his life, struck a chord and I soon found myself immersed in his world, reading everything I could on the subject. James Annesley, who became James Lovett in the novel, was born in 1715 in County Wexford, the son of the fourth Lord Altham, who was every bit as nasty a piece of work as Lord Dunmain in the novel. He concealed his son's existence so that he could sell his inheritance, just as in the novel, and his uncle Richard, who assumed the title after his father's death, really did sell James into indentured servitude. He was shipped to Philadelphia and spent thirteen years effectively as a slave on harsh plantations. The real James managed to escape to Jamaica where he enlisted as a sailor on a British ship and made himself known. He finally made his way back to Dublin, where he sued his uncle in what became one of the most famous legal cases of the time. Although he won his case, his uncle put every possible legal obstacle in his way for seventeen years. When the real James died, in 1760, his uncle still held on to both the title and estates. My James is a bit luckier.

Some writers of historical fiction stay very close to the events they're writing about, but I found as I wrote that other characters and actions jumped into my head and demanded attention: Jack Darcy and his gang, Harry Taaffe the shoeboy, Sylvia Purcell, Doctor Bob, Red Molly. Harry was inspired by a drawing of a shoeboy in eighteenth-century Dublin by an artist of the time, Hugh Douglas Hamilton, which I pinned above my desk. The city of Dublin is one of the most important characters in the book and another great source of inspiration was John Rocque's 1756 map of Dublin, which I taped to my wall and gazed at, following James's progress through its twisting streets and alleys with names like Cutpurse Row, Murdering Lane and Gallows Road, wondering what would happen to him next.